Where You'll Land

Where You'll Land

Jacqueline Simon Gunn

Copyright © 2018 by Jacqueline Simon Gunn

All rights reserved. No part of this book may be reproduced or transmitted in any form or by any means, electronic or mechanical, including photocopying, recording, or by any information storage and retrieval system, except in the case of brief quotations embodied in critical articles and reviews, without prior written permission of the publisher.

This book is a work of fiction. All names, characters and events are from the author's imagination. Locations are used fictitiously. Any similarity to actual persons, living or dead, is purely coincidental and not intended by the author.

ISBN: 9781730787294

Printed in the United States of America

Interior design: Creative Publishing

In loving memory of my aunt, Evelyn Storch.

You should only fall in love with someone whose arms are open and strong enough to catch you.

Section I
Alex's Story

*"I wonder if this is how people always get close:
They heal each other's wounds; they repair the broken skin."*
—Lauren Oliver

Chapter 1

Alex

I rolled my window all the way down, letting the summer air blow into my car. I was headed south on the New Jersey Turnpike. Things had been falling apart for one year, five months and six days. OK. OK. OK. It wasn't things. My mother would call that externalizing: blaming my own internal chaos and distress on the outside environment. Both of my parents are psychologists, so I can't get away with anything.

I had been falling apart for the past year, five months and six days. *I* had been crumbling to pieces. I'm ashamed to admit that it was over a boy, Zach Clayton, my first and only boyfriend. We had been together for six years, when one day he wasn't sure what he wanted, but he strung me along nonetheless. For a whole year, he had me on this string of hope, this torturous string of hope.

Maybe you've been there. He wasn't sure if he wanted to be with me long-term anymore, but he couldn't leave me alone either. It was the worst kind of limbo, the kind where a tiny strand of hope dangles in front of you. You run after it like a kitten runs after a string, and he keeps pulling it back. You keep going after it, because he leaves it close enough to touch but far enough away that you can only grasp the loose ends yet can't quite hold onto the string — or to him.

Funny thing about the hope-string: As much as you want it, it's also your ultimate demise. It's only when your hope is gone and there's nothing to run after that you're finally free. Hope can have sharp edges as it leaves you. I learned this the hard way. The same way I have learned most things in my life.

That lesson arrived five months and six days ago, on a Friday evening. My friend Addy came over. She and her boyfriend had just broken up, and she was a wreck. "Alex, pleeeaaazzze. Put that aside just for tonight. I need to go out," she begged me.

I was busy going through old clothing, trying to organize my external life in hope that it would help me organize my internal life and figure out what I wanted to do. I had just been accepted to two different graduate programs; one in New York and one in Miami. I wasn't sure if I wanted to leave Zach or not. "OK. OK." I threw a long sweater over my T-shirt and jeans, swiped some mascara on and we were out the door.

Timing is everything. We walked into The Battered Drum, a bar along the Hudson River in Weehawken, and there was my hope-dangling-ex-not-yet-ex-boyfriend, Zach, sitting side-by-side at a bar table. His arm rested on the leg of a girl with hair so blonde it looked yellow. I'm brunette. Her blondeness seemed to matter. I gasped.

Addy squeezed my arm and said, "WHAT A DICK! Let's go before he sees us. I hate men."

I shook my head. I was speechless. It took a full minute for the pool of tears to dam up in my throat. Addy pulling on me felt like a distant sensation, which I disregarded as I made my way over to the table without thinking. My hands shook as I rolled them into fists. *How could he?*

Zach must have felt me before he saw me, because before we even met eyes, he quickly took his arm off the yellow-haired girl's leg and moved his chair back.

"Hello." I stood before them, trying to keep my lips from quivering.

"Alex." Zach jumped up from his chair and came toward me. I stared at him. I wasn't sure if I wanted to slap him or cry. Maybe both. As he reached for my hand, I looked at the yellow-haired girl, who wore a look of confusion. Who knew what he had been telling her. That mix of emotion quickly turned into solid fury. I tightened my fists.

Addy pulled my arm. "Let's go."

I glared at him and spewed, "This is your version of taking some space to figure out what you want."

He grabbed my hand. "I'll call you tomorrow."

"Are you kidding me?" I took my hand back. I had given him enough of me. "I'm done you bastard. Do not touch me. You have put me through hell this year, saying you needed some time before we got engaged. And *this* is what you've been doing? Tell me the truth. I want to hear it. We were never going to be engaged, were we?" I glanced over at the girl he was with, wondering if she heard. I wanted to scream at him. I wanted her to hear, but I was too self-conscious, suddenly aware of everyone else in the bar who was potentially witnessing this humiliation I was enduring.

"Alex," he murmured, then bowed his head.

"*Say it*. After six years of a serious relationship and another year of this limbo while you figure out your life, the least you can do is tell me the truth."

He shook his head, then looked up at me with annoyance and said flatly, "We were never getting engaged."

The fury in me rose to a fever pitch, yet I somehow found the strength to contain it. I spoke calmly through gritted teeth. "Don't ever contact me again. Ever. I hate you."

"Alex," I heard him calling after me as Addy and I rushed out before I burst into tears.

I had been gradually crumbling for the entire last year. Finally, seeing him with someone else and having him say we would never be engaged, released me from that hope-string.

§

Like a never-ending nightmare, Zach continued to call. God forbid he considered my feelings for once. The more I asked him not to, the more he called. Every time I felt like I was putting my pieces back together, he would call or I would run into him. It would set me back weeks. I could not wait to move away from my lifelong Northeastern New

Jersey home and eliminate any possibility of running into Zach. Six days before I loaded my car and headed south on The Turnpike toward Miami, Zach left a voicemail that said: "Alex Daily, you are *the one*, the only one. Please forgive me. I don't know what I was thinking."

The saddest part of the whole thing. By the time I received that phone call and heard the words I had wanted to hear so desperately only a year and five months earlier, I felt nothing for Zach. The pain he had caused me usurped even the good memories. I hated him for that. I hated him for taking away my only chance to have fond memories of my first love. Or maybe I hated myself for not seeing who he was for over half a decade of my life. I had been in love with an illusion, not with who he was.

Now I headed south to Miami with all my possessions, an empty heart and hope for a new beginning.

Chapter 2

Alex

I sat with my elbows resting on the bar, staring at the back of the bartender's head, exhausted from my long drive. What was he doing back there anyway, fermenting the alcohol himself? "Excuse me," I said, mildly, even though I really wanted to shout. My mother had scarred me for life with her emphasis on proper decorum. No matter how much I wanted to scream across the bar to get what I needed, I felt too self-conscious to do it.

Finally, he turned toward me. "What can I get you?"

"I'll have a margarita on the rocks, with salt."

"You got it." As he mixed the drink, he asked, "Are you here from New York or New Jersey?"

"Jersey. What gave it away?"

"C'mon, I'm a psychic. Can't you tell?" As he placed the drink in front of me, I noticed the laughter in his eyes when he said, "Your accent."

I put my hand on my cheek. "Of course. I always forget about my accent. You know, because I'm used to it, and

I don't hear it." *What a stupid thing to say,* I thought to myself. I took a long sip of my drink to quell a bit of my social anxiety. "Where are you from?"

"Nothing as exotic as Joisey." He placed an elbow on the bar and rested his head in his hand, clearly making himself comfortable. "I'm a born and bred Miamian. Soo, what's your name?"

"Alex. What's yours?"

"Michael."

"Not Mike? Michael?"

"You can call me whatever you want, but usually I go by Michael. And you look like you could use a shot. It's on the house."

"Are my nerves that obvious?"

"Maybe a little." He shrugged his shoulders. "But it's Saturday night, and I see you're here alone. So, I figured you might need something stronger, in case you were trying to forget what brought you in here in the first place."

"Thank you. I'll take a shot. I don't care of what. Surprise me."

I had walked into Estella's, a hotel bar not far from my apartment building, for a drink. I had arrived on South Beach the night before, after two long days of driving. I felt lonely. I didn't know anyone besides my new roommate, Carter, who I had connected with through a friend of a friend. I felt like a forlorn lover walking the foreign streets of South Beach, longing for the familiarity of home.

"Here." He handed me a shot glass, clicked his glass with mine and we threw them back.

"Straight tequila," I said, puckering my lips from the pungent taste.

"You're less likely to be hung over if you don't mix. Here." He gave me a glass of water. "So, what brings you to South Beach?" he asked, placing both elbows on the bar with his head resting on his hands. He had dark hair and brown eyes that crinkled in the corners when he smiled. And although I had promised myself no emotional entanglements for at least a year, since I was, after all, still in breakup rehab, I couldn't help but notice how attractive Michael was and how easy our interaction seemed. *Sex*, I thought to myself. It would be nice to feel a warm body.

His warm body.

"I moved here for graduate school."

"Oh, I'm a graduate student too. Where are you going, and for what?"

"North Miami University."

He raised his brow. "Me too."

"I'm going for my doctorate in psychology."

"Me too, again. How cool is that?"

No sex, I admonished myself. You shall remain celibate, or at the very least *no one from school*.

§

But after his shift, I found myself back at his place, which just happened to be an apartment complex a few blocks from mine. As soon as he kicked the door closed with his foot, he placed his hands around my face and we began kissing. He ran his fingers along my neck and through my hair and I pressed my breasts against him. The kissing intensified. We moved onto the bed.

He raised my shirt slowly, while kissing my stomach. My back arched into him right as I began to feel the effects of the three margaritas and the three shots I had had. "The room's spinning."

"You want some water?"

"Please," I said, hoping the whirling would stop and I wouldn't vomit.

The next thing I remember was waking up next to him in his bed. I looked under the sheet and was relieved to find that I was fully clothed. I touched his back gently to see if he was awake.

"Hey," he said, softly, as he turned around and faced me, propping his head up on a bent arm.

"Hey." I searched his face. "Um… nothing hap— "

He released a small laugh, "Don't worry. Nothing happened."

"Oh, good." I sighed. "I mean, no offense. I— just— "

"None taken." Michael's eyes crinkled at the sides as he smiled, just as they had the night before. He exuded a warmth I hadn't quite registered earlier, because I had been so preoccupied with unsuccessfully trying to control my drunken desire for him. I realized then, as I lay facing him in his bed, that the desire was purely sexual and alcohol-induced, *thankfully*. I did not want or need any emotional preoccupations.

"I'm starving. Breakfast?"

"Sure. I'll take you for the morning-after obligatory breakfast." He chuckled, and I noticed that laughter in his eyes again.

Sitting across from him at a café, I said, "You know, you're attractive and all, but I'm still reeling from my last breakup and since we're in the same program…"

He placed his hand over mine across the table. "You don't have to let me down easy. It was something that almost happened that felt right in the moment. That's all. You take yourself way too seriously, don't you?"

"Maybe. Don't you? We're going into a serious business."

"I do, and I am. But I think there has to be some balance. Some lightness. Some humor. I'm taking some of your pancake. Hope you don't mind." He stuck his fork in my plate while giving me a playful smile.

"What's mine is yours. And I'll take some of your eggs then." My arm lightly brushed his as I reached across the table. "Are you free today? I'd love to see more of Miami than just the inside of South Beach bars."

"I would love to be your tour guide, but I have errands to get done, and then I actually have a date tonight."

"You were gonna sleep with me before a date with another woman? Are you a cheater?"

"If we had had sex and it had been good, I would have cancelled." He saw the sour look on my face. "I'm joking. C'mon, it's a first date. Shit, he really messed you up, huh?"

"Who?"

"Your ex. He really hurt you." There was genuine compassion in his voice.

"He did." I crossed my arms. I didn't want to get into it and he had that tell-me-more therapist face on. "I don't wanna talk about him."

"OK. Just know that no matter how hard it is right now, you'll get over it."

"I know."

"Raincheck on the tour."

"For sure. I probably should go home and rest anyway. I'm still feeling the effects from all the tequila."

"Definitely don't want to see you puke."

"C'mon, I'm from Jersey. It takes a lot more than a few tequilas to make me puke."

"Ah, I've heard that about Jersey girls." We both laughed.

When we walked out together, he put his arm around my shoulder and squeezed. "So, next week I'll show you around."

"Sounds good. Text me."

"I will."

§

I decided to go for a swim that night, finally having recovered from all the tequila. A magnificent breeze glided through the palm trees, making them dance as I ambled my way toward the swimming pool behind my building. The crashing waves of the ocean only a short distance away echoed in the evening air. I fitted my goggles firmly on my face, jumped into the water and began my warm-up, letting my arms ease into their natural cadence as my body buoyed back and forth along the top of the water.

As I hit my zone and felt myself moving faster, a mild ripple sprinkled across the pool, and I felt the tug of the water. *Someone else is in here*, I thought. I stopped at the edge after my lap to see who had joined me. A man waded in the pool. His hair was wet. The moonlight and stars shined, making a dim light, which shimmered off his face, revealing his chiseled cheekbones.

"What's up?" He smiled, awkwardly.

"Oh, hey," I said, feeling distracted. I didn't want to be rude, but I didn't want to interrupt my swim either.

"You're a fast swimmer."

"Oh." I chuckled, feeling a little embarrassed that he had watched me. "Thanks."

"You push yourself, don't you?"

"Yeah. I do."

"Why?"

"I want to be the best I can be. Don't we all?"

"Maybe." He contemplated. "Sometimes I think when we push ourselves, we don't enjoy what we are doing because we always have a goal in mind. I'm Will."

"Alex." I took his outstretched hand and shook it. I eyed him curiously, fully taking in his face. Although it was dark, I could see his pensive expression in the way his brow creased and his eyes squinted.

Honestly, the guy was gorgeous, but again, I was not in Miami to date. In fact, it was the last thing I had thought I wanted when I laid eyes on Will that first night, but sometimes we think we want what we have, that it's enough, until someone comes along and makes us reevaluate.

As I let my eyes wander across Will's face and then along his shoulders, I couldn't help but admire his physique. I was firmly committed to not being in a relationship. *Sex*, though.

No, I admonished myself. I had already had one near one-night stand the night before. What the hell was wrong with me? Here I was, thirty years old, and it was like someone had slipped me an aphrodisiac when I arrived in Miami. I turned to get back to my swim when Will continued the conversation by asking, "How long have you lived here?" He leaned against the wall of the pool.

"In Miami?"

"Yeah?"

"Only a couple days. I just moved from New Jersey for graduate school."

"Oh." He chuckled. "I thought your accent was from New York."

"I get that a lot. I grew up close to Manhattan. What about you? You from here?"

"No. Mauston. It's a town in Wisconsin. I moved here two weeks ago."

"Cool. For what?"

"Graduate school."

"What are you studying?"

"Psychology."

"Me too. Where?"

"North Miami University."

"Me too," I said. "What a crazy coincidence. Us living in the same building."

"It is interesting, but it's not a coincidence. It's synchronicity."

"Ah, a Jungian."

"You don't have to be a Jungian to believe in synchronicity. It's the only thing that makes sense. There has to be some order to the world beyond what we know."

"I agree. There is some order beyond human comprehension, and I despise limitations."

"Yeah. I saw that while I watched you swim."

I felt my face flush.

Something about the way he spoke and what he said disarmed me, which was very hard to do. But there was something about his manner that made me feel like he saw something about me that I hadn't revealed to him. I felt this weird, premature intimacy standing beside him, sharing the same body of water in my bathing suit. I crossed my arms over my chest.

I noticed him eyeing my crossed arms. He didn't exactly frown, but I could swear I sensed a hint of judgment.

We spoke for a few more minutes about his move, nothing too personal, a few casual exchanges. I couldn't quite read him. He had a quiet way. His words were sparse, but thoughtful. And they seemed to curl in the air, before they settled into my ears, touching me like fingertips.

Feeling vulnerable, I sank my body into the water, leaving only my head exposed. "Nice to meet you, Will. I should get back to my workout."

"Of course." He glided his body into the water and swam the crawl stroke. I watched his large, smooth strokes slice through the water. He looked like he barely came up for air.

I swam next to him, matching his stroke. I couldn't help but be competitive when it came to sports, especially when challenged by a man's strength. He hadn't mentioned that he was an avid swimmer, but from the look and speed of his stroke, he clearly was. Impressive.

When I got out a half hour later, he stopped briefly and said, "See ya."

"Yeah. Only a week 'til classes start. I'm sure I'll see you around."

"You will." He waved.

As I walked away, I thought it was a stupid thing to say. We live in the same building and will be attending the same graduate program. Of course, I'll see him around.

Chapter 3

Alex

I ran into Will at the pool a few times during the first few weeks of the semester. On occasion we swam together, talked, and even enjoyed the hot tub. It seemed so casual. But there was something about our conversations that felt more familiar, almost like we saw the world the same way. Our intellectual sensibilities were so similar. I tried my best not to think too much about our exchanges, but I noticed that I thought about him sometimes. OK, I thought about him a lot of the time. Too much, actually. Then one afternoon, I was parking my car and I heard him say, "Hey," to me through my rolled down window as he was walking past.

"Hey." I waved, as I put the car in park. He stood waiting for me.

"I can't believe how hot it is." I pulled my hair up into a ponytail, as we walked toward our building entrance. "Even with the air on in the car, I'm still sweating. It's been a month since I've moved here. I thought I'd be used to it by now."

Will's face looked flushed from the heat. "At least there's a nice breeze, and the ocean. And pools everywhere."

"True. It is really beautiful here."

"Nice car."

"Oh, thanks. My parents bought it for me a few years ago. As a starving graduate student, I wouldn't be able to afford it."

"Starving?"

"Yeah. Starving student."

"You live in a luxury condo on South Beach overlooking the ocean and drive a BMW. That doesn't look hungry to me." He challenged me with a lilt in his tone.

"My parents are nice enough to help me."

"I see." He paused. He appeared to have his pensive expression on, the one where his brows creased and eyes squinted. I had come to know that this was his deep thought look. Whenever he made that face, I knew he was going to come out with an idea that challenged me. I crossed my arms over my chest. He continued, "Sometimes starving and hungry are used to describe deep yearnings for something intangible."

"Spoken like a philosopher," I teased. "Or a shrink."

"Lots of people who have everything they need are the hungriest."

I instantly felt my face flush. Will had the uncanny ability to unnerve me. I changed the subject. "What kind of music do you like?"

"All kinds. When it comes to music, anything goes. I think music can be soothing and even healing, don't you?"

"Absolutely." I smiled.

"Before deciding on the clinical psychology program, I had been looking into my master's in music therapy, since I play the piano. But then a counselor, I'm in touch with from college, encouraged me to pursue my doctorate. I'm interested in research as well as clinical work."

"Interesting. I play the piano too. And I write music sometimes, just for fun. My stuff's not really any good, but it's therapeutic for me to write lyrics. So, I agree with that."

He moved closer to me. I felt the brush of his body as we walked and I wondered what it would feel like to have his arms around me. I shook off that thought. "Do you have any specific research interests? I'm interested in research too."

He smiled. "I'm interested in the effects of poverty on mental health. I believe that psychotherapy needs to be changed for lower income patients. The major models of psychotherapy, like everything else in the skewed world we live in, is biased toward the middle and upper middle class. It's one of the reasons I came down here for school. Dr. Ravens' research specialty is in exploring how to apply traditional models of psychotherapy with inner city dwellers."

"Interesting. I worked in Newark, New Jersey as a case manager right after college. The inner city is definitely a different culture. People outside of that world don't realize the obstacles there. But the expectation is that they follow the same rules as everyone else, and yet, they aren't afforded the same opportunities for success. I want to make a difference in the world. I want the world to be a better place because of me. Idealistic, huh?"

That's what Zach had always said to me. "You're an idealist," he'd add a *babe* at the end, "You're an idealist, *babe*," to make the comment seem light, even magnanimous, but his tone was condescending. I realized that now looking back.

"Of course not," Will said. "If we aren't going to make a difference, then why are we spending all of this time and money in a helping profession." He opened the front door to our building and let me walk in first. "We really have a lot in common." His eyes wandered across my face and along my shoulders, giving me chills.

"We do," I said, trying to shake the sensation. As we waited for the elevator, I felt something inarticulate dangling between us. I looked up at him. Our eyes connected. I quickly glanced away, but the feeling stayed in the space between us. Then, I heard myself ask him, as if I had no control over my own tongue, "So you wanna go for a swim later?"

We are friends, I reassured myself. *Nothing wrong with asking a friend to go for a swim.*

"Sure," He responded.

"Cool. I'll meet you down at the pool at 5."

"OK."

§

The summer sun in Miami still blazed at 5:00. Will was wading in the pool when I got downstairs. I noticed a bronze hue covered his arms, shoulders and chest. I couldn't help but appreciate his athletic physique. I wasn't tanned. Carter, my roommate and a native Floridian, had warned me about the Miami sun by telling me, "Wear sunscreen even when you don't think you need it. This sun will toast you. Even as a black man, I wear sunscreen all the time."

I walked toward Will, gingerly put my bag down and took the towel off from around my waist. The intensity of his gaze as he watched me made me feel bare. I quickly slipped into the pool. The water was mild from boiling in the sun all summer, but still it felt refreshing. "You ready?"

I was about to slide my upper body into the water when Will said, "Wait."

I raised my eyebrows.

"Let's hang out for a bit. Doesn't the water feel great? Standing here in the water with the sun's rays beating down on us feels great. Doesn't it? And if you listen, you can even hear the waves crashing. I mean, this is the life."

"It is." I inhaled the fresh, moist air, and leaned back against the pool wall. Will stood beside me, close enough that if I bent my elbow even a little it would touch his arm. I was careful to keep it straight. South Beach was a tropical nirvana. And being next to Will felt pretty good too.

I felt something stir in the pit of my stomach, standing there with him in silence. His arm soon grazed mine, sending a shiver down my back and when I looked up at him, he gazed down at me. Something passed between us, some sort of recognition of something. It made me uncomfortable; uncomfortable, because I already liked him too much and I thought he could read it all over me; uncomfortable, because I didn't want to like him or anyone for that matter. I pretended I had an itch on my arm, so I had an excuse to move away from his. I broke the quiet moment with, "So what's it like in Mauston?"

"Small, rural, kinda boring. It's nothing like here."

"Neither is New Jersey. Although we do have the ocean. But the Atlantic isn't the same up north as it is here. Have you ever been to New Jersey or New York?"

"No, but I'd like to go sometime. Truth is, I haven't traveled much at all."

"How old are you? I never asked you."

"Twenty-five. You?"

"Thirty," I said, "and you have plenty of time to travel."

"Coming down here for school was a big step toward making the life I want. Mauston is too small. In small towns you live like a celebrity in the small radius that is your home. Everyone knows everyone. Everyone knows everyone's business. I couldn't stand living like that anymore. I knew there was a big world out there, and I didn't want to settle or become complacent. I couldn't wait to leave."

He said it as a general statement, but his tone and the heavy look in his eyes made me think it was personal. "I've heard that about small towns. No, I'd imagine not having privacy isn't fun. But that's still home, right?"

"Home isn't a place, it's a state of mind."

"Hmm...?"

"I mean, home isn't necessarily where you're from. It has more to do with where you feel safe. Where you go to feel peace, a sense of belonging. But that's not what you meant. Is it?"

"Not exactly. But your point is both well-taken and valid. I guess what I meant to ask is if your family is there?"

"Yes. My family is there," he said quickly, then asked, "Do you have siblings?"

"No. I'm an only child."

"Are you close with your parents?"

"Yeah. We get on each other's nerves, but we are close."

Will, who had been standing close, moved slightly away from me. It was subtle and hard to pinpoint, but I felt him become distant. He said something, but his voice had developed a faraway sound, almost like his words were only echoes that blurred together.

"Are you OK?"

He put on a broad, easy smile. "Fine. You ready to swim?"

I questioned him with my eyes.

He splashed me and laughed. "Come on." He glided his body in and began swimming.

I followed.

§

We swam together a couple more times after that and sat together in the two classes we shared. Sometimes at night, when I swam alone, I hoped that Will would come down and join me. We seemed to be developing a nice rapport, but I thought about him more than I wanted to. I tried to shake the feeling whenever it came.

Then one night while sipping a beer outside by the pool with Carter, Will walked by, basketball in hand, with a tall, dark-haired guy that I recognized from school. I whispered to Carter, "That's Will, the guy I've been swimming with."

"Mm-mmm. And who's the other guy? From here he looks strapping."

"I don't know his name. He's from school too. And, I'm guessing he's straight."

"You always say that."

"And you always think they're gay."

"It *is* South Beach."

"True." I smiled.

"Alex, hey." Will stood in front of me, smiling, glowing and looking gorgeous. I immediately felt self-conscious.

"Hi," I said, twirling a piece of my hair, trying to quell my nerves. "Um…" I felt tongue-tied. "Uh… this is Carter, my roommate. This is Will and, sorry, I don't know your name."

"Jude Booker. We're in the same program."

"I know. Nice to meet you." I shook his hand, which felt warm. He had clear blue eyes and sharp features. His body was lean and chiseled.

Carter shook his hand, and I swear I heard *mm-mmm* deep in his throat.

"You guys want a beer?" I pointed to the six pack of Heineken on the small table.

"Thanks." Jude went to grab one, when Will said, "Let's play first." He looked at me. "Will you be out here for a while?"

I shrugged my shoulders. "I dunno. Maybe another half hour or so."

"We'll come back."

"OK."

As soon as they were out of earshot, Carter said, "You're right, he's straight. He's hot, though."

"Yeah. Not my type."

"What's not to like?'

"Liking someone and thinking they're hot are not always the same. I mean, he looks like a model or a soap opera star. He's too perfect, too polished. I like a more rugged guy."

"Like *Will*?" He raised an eyebrow.

"Will's a friend."

"Uh, huh. Is that why a little drool is dripping from the corner of your mouth? Because he's your *friend?*"

"It's the beer."

"Riiight."

I looked out toward the basketball court. "I made a commitment to myself not to get involved with anyone while I'm down here, especially while I'm in school. Besides, I only go out with men who show interest in me. And Will is a friend. A classmate."

"It looks to me like he's attracted to you. He has that look in his eyes that men get. Trust me. I know men. Gay men. Straight men. And the ones who are straight until they get a couple cocktails in them."

I laughed. "I dunno. I sort of see what you're saying, but it seems to me that he treats me more like a friend.

Anyway, I really don't want him. Like I said, I'm not looking for any sort of romantic relationship."

"Riiight." He looked at me and rolled his eyes. "You can lie to yourself, but not to me."

"I'm not lying."

"Girl, please," he smirked. "Besides, you can't always play it safe."

"I'm not. Just stop and hand me another beer," I said with a small bite in my tone. I didn't want to go on with it.

He squinted his eyes, but let it go. Lounging back in my chair, I contemplated the exchange. The knots in my stomach made it hard to ignore the truth. Carter was right. I was totally infatuated with Will.

I swung my eyes over at the basketball court and watched Will and Jude running around and slapping the ball back-and-forth. "Let's go back upstairs," I said to Carter.

"Yeah?"

"I need to go to sleep early."

"You like him."

"No. I don't." I heard the protestation in my tone.

The smirk and the side-eye Carter shot my way spoke volumes about his opinion on the matter.

Chapter 4

Alex

Will and I started spending more time together. Swims and sitting together in class turned into hanging out at night, walking along the beach together, having casual dinners and sitting at the pool listening to music. The more time I spent with him, the more pulled I felt toward him.

The way his eyes wandered across my face, taking in every nuance in my expression, may have been the deepest intimacy I had ever felt with a man. I had always thought sex was the most intimate act, but it's not true. Gazing deeply into someone's eyes is the most intimate, because there's an honesty that can't be disguised.

I knew I had been guarded with men ever since the beginning of the breakup with Zach, a year and a half ago. What I hadn't realized was that I had been numb. The way he continued to call after I had asked him to leave me alone made it impossible to move on. I suppose my only psychological defense against feeling the pain was to not let myself feel anything at all.

It had started when, after six years together, Zach blindsided me. From out of nowhere, he had said, "We're twenty-eight. After six years together, we should either get married or break up. And I'm not sure which one I want. I need time."

"What?" My eyes had welled. "You want to break up?"

"No." He had taken my hands in his, but I felt his distance. "I just need a little space to figure myself out. Can we take a step back, see each other a little less often?"

I had looked at him through the pain I felt in my heart. "OK. OK."

I had said OK, because I loved him, and I had only known myself as a woman through him. I had to give him a chance to sort his head out. Had I known that he was seeing other women behind my back and just dragging me along on that damn hope-string, I would have ended it right then, when it should have ended.

Zach still called occasionally, trying to use my hope as a weapon. But I never picked up. I hated him or maybe I hated myself for holding onto someone who would do to me what he had done.

Will was different than other guys, including Zach, who always seemed to come on to me physically before anything had developed emotionally. With Will, we talked about things that mattered, and he seemed to understand me so intimately, but he never made a move. He would walk close to me, letting his arm brush against mine, and sometimes he would touch my hand with his fingers when I said something he agreed with. "Yes, me too," he would say, letting his fingers linger on my hand. The emotional intimacy without a move toward something more physical was strange. Even Carter had mentioned it after seeing us together a number of times. "That guy's crazy about you."

"I'd thought so, but he seems to only want to be friends."

"Absolutely not, but I guess you can wait and see, right?"

"Yeah," I had said, offhandedly, not wanting to show Carter how preoccupied I felt by it.

Friendship sounded good on paper, but the more time I spent with him, the more I wanted to be closer with him. So, in a way, when Jude Booker started hanging out with us, it made it easier.

Jude was charismatic, intelligent and kind of famous. I had thought he looked familiar. He was Books, the guitarist from a relatively well-known Los Angeles rock band, *The Black Outs*.

OK, he was hot. And I found him intimidating. It was hard to trust someone who appeared to have everything going for him. Jude was tall, lean and muscular with chiseled cheek bones, a magnanimous smile, crisp blue eyes, and a confidence that radiated off him. On top of his stellar physical appearance, he was smart, well-read, an athlete and a musician. He had left his band to come to Miami for graduate school. The guy was flawless.

"Why did you leave? Your music was going somewhere. You were living the dream," I had asked him one night while the three of us were drinking beer on the beach.

"It wasn't anything like I thought it was going to be. Life's like that, you know." Jude looked up at the sky. The waves crashed along the shore in a grand and rhythmic beat all around us.

"Like what? What do you mean?" I asked before taking a sip of my beer.

The moonlight cast a glow on Jude's face. I couldn't help but admire his handsome features. He was wearing a white T-shirt that hugged his arms and chest in all the right places.

"Sometimes we don't know where we are going until we get there. I thought I was pursing an image of a life, to play the music, record songs, tour with my band. In the beginning, it was what I wanted. But the more famous we became, the more pressure there was to perform a certain way. Our manager developed a militant fixation on our public image, particularly with social media. One night, I staggered home from a buddy's bachelor party drunk off my ass, and the next day it was plastered all over social media. My manager called me careless. Even more, I felt humiliated. I mean, getting drunk one night isn't a big deal, but people embellish to make the story juicier. When there was public speculation that I needed rehab, I started questioning the path I was on. Sometimes you have to recognize that what you have isn't what you want, then change it."

"Man, I get it," Will piped in, animated by the direction in which the conversation had gone. "I've had my privacy intruded upon being from a small town where everyone knows everyone. I hated it. When things went wrong…" he trailed off, then continued in a softer voice, "everyone knows when something goes wrong."

"Don't you miss the music, though?" I asked Jude. "I don't know what I would do if I had to stop swimming, and I've never even made a career out of it."

"I still play. And yes, I miss things about it. But I wanted a more settled life, now that I'm forty." Whoa, *Jude was forty! He looked more like he was in his late-twenties!* "I lost my girlfriend after a rumor traveled around in the LA music circles that I had been with another woman. It wasn't true. But they had pictures of me with this other woman, another musician, that at some point I had mistakenly hung my arm around because she was crying over her ex-boyfriend. People see what they want to. So, the story spread that it was a romance, and my girlfriend believed it. After that, I realized no one would ever know the truth about who I was if I stayed. They would know the version of me that the media decided to portray. I have a master's in psychology, and it's been a passion of mine since I was a kid. Coming here made the most sense. No regrets." He pierced me with his eyes and raised his beer.

I looked into his eyes and swallowed, falling into his gaze.

"No regrets," Will and I said in synchrony, raising our beers to click together.

"Alex and I both play the piano." Will looked at me. "We should all play sometime."

"Let's do it." Jude smiled with cavalier confidence. He seemed so self-assured, he could make anyone believe anything he said. I had to admit, I found his magnetism enchanting.

Later that night, alone in my bedroom, I looked at my reflection in the mirror, remembering the way Jude's eyes had penetrated me. He had said, "People see what they want to." I agreed with that.

When standing to the side of someone else and looking at them in the mirror, they look different than when looking at them face-to-face, not only because you're looking at a reflection, but because the angle is different. So, nothing that anyone sees is really the way it is. It's only the person's interpretation skewed by the angle of their perception, or their mood, or their experiences, or even their beliefs in what the world is like. The mirror distorts reality.

What did Jude see when he looked at me? I stared straight into my own eyes. I looked at my wide nose, my full lips. I opened my eyes wide so I could see the green in them. Sometimes my eyes looked brown, other times green. I looked at the beauty mark to the side of my nose. Other people often said it was *sexy*. I hated it.

I need to have it removed.

I thought about Jude that night. He seemed like someone I could learn from. And I couldn't deny (although, I would never admit this to another living soul), that I felt mildly star struck by him.

§

"You want to test each other?" Will called the next day, asking me to practice the Rorschach Inkblot Test on each other. We had a class in the administration, scoring and interpretation of the Rorschach, a projective test used to understand the way people interpreted their environment. The ten ink blots were abstract and open to many different interpretations. What people saw and how they processed the amorphous images gave information about the person's perception and personality. We had to give the test to ten different people, then score and interpret it.

"OK," I said. "You wanna come down? Carter's out on a date."

"Sure. I'll be down in a few. Did you eat?"

"No."

"You want to order in?"

"Sure. Let's do that."

Will came down about ten minutes later. As soon as I opened the door, his presence enveloped me. This kept happening with Will. I didn't only see him, I felt him.

He smiled, and his eyes lit up. Will's smile was different than Jude's, less confident with a boyish hesitation. Will's smile was trustworthy. I could tell because he didn't always give it. Jude, on the other hand, had one of those smiles that was hard not to feel spellbound by, but was given too generously.

I practically inhaled him as he came into my apartment. *Stop it*, I admonished myself. I loved that fresh scent he always had. I knew it was from his detergent, because we had done our laundry together a few times.

"Let's order now. Is that OK? I missed lunch because I spent my entire day in the library and lost track of time." He walked right in, sat on the sofa and made himself at home.

"Sure."

"Do you want to split that pizza from the place across the street?"

"Sounds great."

"The usual?"

I nodded. "Get a couple of Gatorades too. I'm out. And it's so hot."

"The red one, right?"

"Yeah."

Will took his sneakers off and put his feet on the ottoman. I watched him while he was on the phone placing the order. I ran my finger across my lips, imagining that it was his fingers running slowly over them. I knew he would touch me gently, lingering and relishing my body in the way every woman wishes a man would do. Not just sex but bringing my body to life through his touch.

Stop it, I admonished myself again. I shoved those images into a locked compartment and kneeled at the table beside him, plopping the box of Rorschach cards down on the wood. "You want to take it first, or should I?"

He released a small laugh. "You always want to 'dive' right in, pun intended. Let's hang out for a bit and eat first.

You have a hard time relaxing. I saw it in you last night at the beach. You seemed restless."

"I felt relaxed last night." I thought what he observed might have been my mixed emotions about my mild fascination with Jude combined with my growing affection for him.

"I'm not sure I believe you, but I'll let you off the hook. You definitely like getting down to business."

He was right about my ambitiousness, but I also thought the more we stuck to business the less confused I would be by my draw toward him.

He began to discuss a book he read, a commentary on the life and work of Henry David Thoreau. To my delight and chagrin, Thoreau had been one of my greatest literary inspirations starting in high school. Now Will spoke about him, as if he read my mind, sifting through and describing the value of his work. "He felt truth came from the absence of distraction," Will said.

"Yes," I exclaimed, feeling the excitement that happens when you connect with someone. "I find that exact space, like he found in Waldon, through my sw—"

"Swims," Will finished the sentence with me.

I looked into his eyes, almost embarrassed, like he could see my heart accelerating.

Our eyes locked and I felt a kiss coming, the pull was so strong. Then he broke the moment with, "Exactly. I've found nothing as peaceful as being immersed in the water and engaging with it, being one with the water while swimming."

It was the same way I had always felt in the water; few people I talked to understood this so personally.

I observed Will as he continued to speak about Thoreau and transcendentalism, a little about Emerson's work. His voice had an easy tempo. He could easily have been a DJ on the radio, or the narrator of an audio book. I tried to focus on what we were talking about, attempting to distract myself from an overwhelming desire for him to touch me. To kiss me. I wanted to know what it felt like to be underneath him, to be rolling around in a bed with him, to have him running his fingers through my hair.

"You wanna cocktail?" I felt hot. And bothered.

"Sure." He gave me a curious look. "It's not like you to drink when we're working."

"I'm feeling rebellious."

He raised his brow. "You are always rebellious."

"No, I'm not. You've said it yourself. I'm too structured and too scrupulous."

"True. You're very orderly with your work, but your whole way of being is subversive. You live the way you want. You're a self-sufficient woman, uncompromising in who you are. What is it that Camus said? 'Be so absolutely free that your existence is an act of rebellion.' Or something like that."

My jaw nearly hit the floor. That was one of my favorite quotes. "The only way to deal with an unfree world is to become so absolutely free that your very existence is an act of rebellion." I swallowed. "That's how you see me?"

"Exactly how I see you. I like it." He laughed.

"And is that how you see yourself?"

He looked up at the ceiling and rubbed his hand along his chin.

"What? You can tell me."

He looked deep into my eyes, and for the first time I saw great pain. Despite the rugged, masculine strength he exuded, I could tell he was sensitive. But right then, I saw layers of suffering.

I reached out and rubbed my hand along his thigh. "You look so sad. Something bad happened to you?"

"I—I," he put his hand on top of mine, "I did something bad. It's very hard for me to talk about. I'll tell you some time. But not now." I felt the intimacy swell between us. My hand on his leg, his hand on mine. He looked at me and I was sure I read desire in his eyes.

He searched my face. I felt him leaning in toward me. I closed my eyes and drew closer to him.

His lips reached mine, delicate and warm. And we kissed. A long, solid kiss on the lips. He tasted good. He put his hand on my cheek, softly, then pulled back, gazing into my eyes.

"I need to use the bathroom," he said in a whisper. "Too much afternoon coffee." He got up, a whiff of his fresh scent lingered in the empty space he left on the couch. I touched my lips, trying to quell the longing for more.

The pizza arrived just as Will came out of the bathroom. I mixed us both margaritas. He put music on. We ate the pizza and talked about swimming, music, a little about Jude's choice to leave his band. We administered the

Rorschach on each other. Nothing too intense or intimate came up for the rest of the night. But that kiss lingered in the air between us, an unspoken promise of something burgeoning.

Chapter 5

Alex

Mary Jane, my new friend from school, came over to work on a class assignment a couple of weeks after the kiss with Will. "Hi," she said with a wad of gum in her mouth when I opened the door. She sported a skintight blue dress. Fancy for working on a class assignment. But Mary Jane had spent her whole life in Miami. Tight-fitting clothing for a casual afternoon was typical in Miami, I had come to learn.

"Come in." I extended my hand toward the living room. "I thought we could work on the balcony. It's shady out there right now."

Mary Jane snapped her gum and said, "OK. I brought cookies." She handed me the box.

"Thank you." I took the box and walked toward the kitchen. Mary Jane followed.

This was only the second time I'd hung out with Mary Jane outside of school. She was thirty years old and very brazen. I enjoyed hearing her snap out opinions in class, especially when it went against the grain of the collective. She didn't believe in psychiatric diagnostics and was very vocal, almost to the point of verbal assaulting other classmates when she thought a label was slapped on someone too cavalierly.

"People use labels when they don't have a fucking clue what's really going on with the person. It's like a safety net for the intuitively impaired," she would say. It cracked me up. In a way, she reminded me of home. People where I grew up said what was on their mind without much of a filter.

I agreed with her too. I would write arguments against traditional models of psychotherapy and diagnoses, but I never would have had the courage to say it so boldly to the whole classroom, even challenging the professor in our psychopathology course. Even though my parents were psychologists, they still managed to leave me with some neuroses. I was a strong person trapped in a self-conscious body. Their rules to be gracious and soft-spoken went against my nature to be strong, bold and unconventional.

My mother fostered poise, because, as she explained beginning when I was about four years old, it was an emotional posture: the emotional equivalent of sitting up straight and not putting my elbows on the table. Sometimes I just wanted to slouch and let my back hunch, with elbows on the table — or the emotional equivalent.

In my teen years, I enjoyed teasing my mother with acts of rebellion. Sometimes I would sit at the dinner table just like that on purpose and watch my mother's proper decorum decompose while she raised her voice, pointing to me and telling me how to sit properly. My mother bared her teeth when she hollered. If she ever hollered while looking in the mirror, she would probably never do it again. After she yelled, my mother would give a small cough, to clear her throat, smooth the front of her dress or shirt and sit daintily as if nothing had happened.

Watching Mary Jane was cathartic, because she would say things I only dreamed of saying aloud. She was my first female friend in Miami. I spent all my free time with Will, Will and Jude, Michael or Carter.

Mary Jane didn't waste any time digging into my private life either. "What's the deal with you and Will Easton? He's like a stallion, if you don't mind me saying." She released a chuckle. "Or even if you do."

"Nothing. We're friends. Good friends."

"Alex Daily. My new friend. You aren't going to get off that easy. I see you two together all the time. And I see how close you are. Are you sleeping with him?" Mary Jane had big brown eyes and she opened them extra wide. "Do tell."

I contemplated telling her. It would actually be nice to have a woman's opinion about what exactly was going on between Will and me, because honestly, I didn't have a clue. After we kissed, I thought for sure something was blooming. Two weeks had passed, and we had spent a load of time together, but nothing more had happened. It was starting to consume me. The incongruence between how it felt when we were together — close — romantic and his lack of action toward anything more than friendship was confusing.

What if everything I thought I felt between us was only what I wanted to see or feel? What if it wasn't real? Like the mirror, what if my reality was skewed by the perception of what I felt inside, *my* desire, *my* romantic feelings projected onto him?

So, to get an objective opinion, I told Mary Jane about our friendship, my growing affection and desire to be romantically involved, the way he seemed to know me. "He just gets me. I've never had that with a guy before," I explained.

I told her about the kiss. "It really feels like he's interested. He sits so close to me, closer than a friend. I don't get it, honestly. As close as I feel to him as a friend, I can't figure the guy out."

Mary Jane listened, nodding as I relayed the story, with curiosity. "I thought for sure you guys at least had sex the way you are together. Hmm…"

"Yeah. I know. Exactly. I wish I was brave enough to ask him how he felt."

"No. Don't ask him. Just make the first move."

"Yeah?" I scrunched my face. The thought made me anxious.

"Haven't you ever made a move on a guy before? They love that."

"I haven't. I've always believed that the guy wants to be the one to make the move."

"There are no absolutes in relationships. Some guys are shy or afraid, and they love when the girl they are interested in makes the first move. I've done it with guys who loooved it. They wound up being my boyfriend."

"I dunno."

"What's up with you? You seem so maverick-like to me. Even the way you dress, you wear those ripped jeans and those V-neck T-shirts like a uniform. It's like wearing an overcoat down here. And you don't say too much in class, but when you do, I can tell you hate the textbook too. You're an independent thinker. You've got to speak up. Don't be afraid of who you are."

"Thanks. I know what you mean. I'm still fighting my childhood."

"Aren't we all. I tell ya, I'm never having kids. I don't want to be responsible for fucking someone's life up royally."

I laughed. "That's a very strong position. Like Winnicott said, 'good enough mothering' is good enough and not being perfect teaches us to tolerate frustrations that come up in life. There's no such thing as a perfect childhood. I'm grateful for my parents even if my mother can be a real pain in my ass."

"Mine too." Mary Jane's lips twisted into a sly smile. "So, what's the deal with Will's friend Jude? The man is a god. Did you see the muscle bursting out of his short-sleeve shirt yesterday? And his eyes are as clear as blue crystals. The guy makes me sweat."

"Don't you have a boyfriend?"

"Yeah. Fred. We're not serious though. At least not yet."

"You're dating, but not committed?"

"Something like that. As I've said, there are no absolutes in anything. Anyway, just because I'm curious about Jude doesn't mean I want him or anything."

"I don't know him that well. I've hung out with him with Will a couple of times. He's older, like forty."

"Reeeally. I thought so. He has a maturity to him. Older guys are better in bed. They have learned how women like to be touched. The young ones always go straight for the goods."

Mary Jane was clearly way more experienced than me. But I definitely thought Will, even though he was younger, would know exactly how to touch me. The other day, I had watched as he stroked a leaf through his fingers, then another time I watched as he smoothed out a fitted sheet on his bed. He had a slow, soft touch, like his fingertips had an intimate relationship with everything they rubbed. And I wanted it to be my skin.

"What else do you know about Jude?" Mary Jane asked with a demanding inquisitive look.

"He's from L.A. and used to play with a band. *The Black Outs*. You ever hear of them?"

"The name sounds vaguely familiar. I can't believe he's a musician. Oh, my God, could he be any hotter." She retrieved her phone. "Let's look for videos."

She found a string of videos posted on the internet by *The Black Outs*. "C'mere." She waved me over to her.

"Oh, my Jesus," Mary Jane squealed. Jude was playing guitar in his new age sounding rock band. He wore a skin-tight shirt, which showed his rippled abs and strong arms. His hair was slightly longer and messy. A tattoo on his shoulder peaked out of his shirt. He sang backup as the song went on. Jude was sexy, no doubt about that.

"My God," Mary Jane squealed again, fanning herself in a purposefully dramatic manner. "Maybe you should go for him instead of Will. I would need to know every detail."

"Ha. He's hot. But he's not my type at all."

Mary Jane gave me a bewildered look. "Alex Daily, you only live once as far as I know, and a guy like Jude should never be taken for granted." She started another video, a song called *Violent Words*. It was a rock ballad with lyrics that suggested a heart-wrenching breakup. "Mm-mmm. He is tasty."

"He is attractive," I said, mildly.

"Make sure to invite him and Will to my intimate gathering next week." Mary Jane had a condo on North Miami Beach, right on the ocean. She was a having party, which she called an 'intimate gathering' because it was going to be small (only around forty to fifty people). Intimate and fifty people seemed like an oxymoron, but Mary Jane enjoyed contradictions, saying, "It shakes up the status quo."

"I'll tell Will to bring him. Sounds fun."

"And puh-lease, wear something sexy. At least a skirt for God sakes. Will will enjoy that, I'm sure." She raised her eyebrows and smiled.

Chapter 6

Alex

I thought a lot about Mary Jane's suggestion to make the first move with Will. Every time I was with him in between that Saturday with Mary Jane and her party, I planned to do something. Maybe reach out and kiss him. Maybe wrap my arms around his neck. I thought of rubbing my chest up against his.

I couldn't get myself to do any of those things. At the same time, I felt my desire for him oozing out of my pores. I didn't know how much more I could take of it.

But nothing happened between us that week, despite the fact that a couple of times while we were hanging out, Will was so close to me I could feel his breath along my skin. I thought being suitably drunk would help. Liquid courage for the socially awkward. I would liquor up at Mary Jane's party and just get it over with.

§

The party started at nine on Saturday night. Will and Jude came by at eight, and we went to Estella's for a beer beforehand. Michael waved me over as soon as we walked in.

"Hey, you," I said, leaning my elbows on the bar. "I wish you didn't have to work and could come to the party."

"I tried to switch shifts, but no luck." He turned toward Will and Jude. "What's up?"

Jude shook his hand and said, "Hey."

I swear I felt Will tighten before he offered his hand and gave Michael a cool, "What's up?"

"What'll it be?"

"Three Heinekens?" Jude looked at Will and me. We both nodded. "Three Heinekens," he said to Michael, who said, "I only have it on tap."

"That's perfect," Jude said.

We slipped onto three stools, Jude and Will on either side of me. Michael came back with the drinks. "What time are you heading over?" he asked me.

"Party starts at nine. We're gonna grab an Uber after this beer."

"I heard about this place," Jude said, looking around. "It must get packed."

"Oh, yeah."

"You must see some wild shit."

"Yeah. I try not to pay too much mind and just serve the drinks, though. It'd be easy to get caught up in the drama."

"I hear that," Jude said.

Jude and Michael bullshitted about South Beach life, while Will and I talked to each other about a book we were reading on personality disorders for class. When we finished our beers, Will said, "You guys ready."

Jude asked, "You wanna get another beer first? I like this place."

Will said, "I don't want to be buzzed before we even get there." I felt him stiffen, when he turned to me and said, "Don't you want to go?"

"One more beer," Jude said, eyeing Will.

"Will's right," I said to Jude. "Besides, I told Mary Jane we'd be there on the earlier side."

"Alright. Let's order the Uber," Jude conceded.

"Talk to you soon," I said to Michael, who nodded and replied, "Have fun. I'll definitely make the next one."

When we walked out, Jude said to Will, "You don't like that place, or you don't like him?"

"Why would you say that?" Will shrugged his shoulders.

"You seemed like you couldn't get out of there fast enough."

"Man, don't analyze me," he said with a pinch in his tone. "I just wanted to get to the party. Sometimes a cigar is just a cigar."

Jude shot him a shrewd look.

Will was hard to read, but something made him tense. I thought it had to do with Michael too, which was interesting. They barely knew each other.

When we arrived, Mary Jane came to the door holding a huge cocktail glass with a little yellow umbrella floating on top. "Hellooo," she said, boisterously. She wore a two-piece outfit consisting of a tight sleeveless top, short shorts and platform shoes. All of it yellow.

In fact, the whole apartment was spotted with yellow decorations. Yellow plates and napkins and silverware. Yellow plastic cups. Yellow streamers hung around the walls. Yellow flowers in translucent vases with a yellow hue.

"This is Fred," Mary Jane introduced him. Fred wore a yellow button-down shirt.

"I didn't know you liked yellow so much."

"I don't. I mean I don't have a favorite color. Having a favorite color is a form of discrimination."

"Makes total sense," Jude said, jokingly.

"I'm serious." Mary Jane scrunched her lips up in the corner. "I choose a different color to celebrate every party. This time it's yellow."

"This is Will and Jude," Mary Jane continued her introduction of Fred, her boyfriend. He was tall and husky. His shirt was unbuttoned on top, exposing the hair at the top of his chest. A thick gold chain around his neck hung down in between a tuft of dark brown hair and bronzed skin.

"Hello. Nice to meet you." He shook all our hands. His voice matched his body, thick and brawny. "MJ told me about you. A Jersey girl." He smiled at me. "I have family in Jersey. Toms River. Do you live near there?"

"No, that's the Jersey shore," I said while giving Fred the once over. I thought he would fit right in on the Jersey shore. "I'm from Northeastern New Jersey. Right outside of Manhattan."

"Ah. I could see that. You have that artsy Brooklyn or downtown Manhattan look."

I did wear a skirt as per Mary Jane's request. Denim and to my knee. A halter on top, platform sneakers with a hole at the toes.

"I like the outfit," Mary Jane said, then added, "the skirt could be shorter, but we'll work on that." She laughed.

"I would have worn yellow. Had I known."

"It's all good. At least you're not wearing black."

Fred hung a thick arm around Mary Jane, and after a hearty laugh said to me, "Don't listen to her. You look great. MJ says she doesn't discriminate with her colors, but she has a minor antipathy toward black. That's what happens when your parents name you after black shoes."

I squinted one eye, giving Fred a curious look.

"Mary Janes. You know those shoes with the strap across the instep. They come in different colors now, but back when MJ was born, they were only in black. And according to her parents, her mother's favorite. Look." He grabbed a picture off a shelf and handed it to me. "See, look at their shoes." It was picture of a woman holding a toddler on her lap, both wearing Mary Jane shoes.

"You were so cute," I said to Mary Jane, then handed the picture back to Fred.

"Thanks." She smiled, then said to Fred, "Black is the absorption of all colors on the visible spectrum, hon." She elbowed him and continued with a teasing bite, "Therefore, if I choose not to wear black, it's not discrimination because I wear the colors that it absorbs." She looked at Jude, Will and me. "He likes to tease me about my beliefs." She wrapped her arm around him. She seemed so small next to Fred's large frame.

"Guilty." He kissed the top of her head. "I enjoy watching her when she goes off on one of her diatribes."

"Let me get you guys a drink. And there's some food inside. More outside," Fred said, guiding us into a large room packed with people and loud, reverberating music.

The condo was huge: two floors, a winding staircase leading upstairs to the bedrooms, a large kitchen with an oversized steel refrigerator, a dining room and living room, a generous-sized guest bedroom on the first floor with a bathroom. Outside there was a large deck, which had a large screen TV, three large couches, a few tables, a hot tub and barbecue. It sat right on the ocean.

Mary Jane had inherited money from her grandmother a few years earlier and used the money to buy the condo. Fred and she did not officially cohabitate. "He is a frequent guest. A regular, if you will," she had said with a humorous, almost snarky tone. The subtext I had heard: Fred lived with her but hadn't given up his own place. Looking around the apartment, I felt certain that I had been right. His belongings could be seen everywhere, including framed photos of his parents and him on the wall.

Will and Jude each got a beer. Fred made me a daiquiri, then stuck a yellow umbrella in the liquid. The three of us decided to sit outside on a big cushy sofa, along the water.

Dance music pumped out of speakers that sat on shelves. A couple of boats dallied in front of the deck. The occupants briefly stopped by the party but didn't get off their boats. "We don't know them," Mary Jane said when she joined us outside and I asked about them. "Or at least I don't. Maybe Fred does."

I sat between Will and Jude. Mary Jane sat on a chair cattycorner from Jude. We talked about classes and some of the other students, gossiped about professors and created stories about their personal lives: "I bet Dr. Ravens is like this. I bet Dr. Dominico cheats on his wife. He has that look."

Mary Jane laughed wildly when Jude said something that could be construed as funny. Will and I would smile, but Mary Jane would let out a long laugh, folding her body in half, torso over legs, generous cleavage on display. It egged Jude on. The harder Mary Jane laughed, the more Jude talked, telling stories from his life in L.A. and of the scandals of being in the L.A. spotlight.

I surmised, even though I didn't know Jude that well, that this was his big-party persona. A façade he must have learned while living the life of a celebrity. Underneath, I felt he had a well of depth and complexity, maybe a side of himself he had become disconnected from over the years having to cover it from others. Or maybe a side he only exposed after he knew someone really well. Either way, I enjoyed him.

But I also thought Jude was a little too magnanimous. I felt some sort of vague emotional danger, like he would be able to pull almost anyone close and would eventually tear them apart. Or maybe I feared that he would eat me alive. Which would never happen, since I wasn't into him.

Will's knee skimmed against mine. Although it wasn't a solid touch, more of a delicate whisper, it still gave me butterflies. The four of us talked. Mary Jane laughed and laughed, and Will's and my knees danced like an intimate conversation. It almost felt like a date. *Almost* being the operative word.

"You want another?" I stood to get another drink to stop the knee dance. Besides, I had planned to get suitably liquored up and initiate some sort of physical intimacy with Will.

"I'll come with you." Will got up. I felt the brush of his body next to mine.

I don't know how much longer I can take this, I thought.

"Let's do a shot," I said, once near the table that held the hard liquor.

His eyes glistened. "I've never seen you do a shot."

I blushed. "It's a party."

"What'll it be?"

"Surprise me."

He poured two shots of tequila, put some salt on his hand, then offered it to me. "Here lick," he said, smiling.

I looked at the salt on his hand. *My God, is he teasing?* I licked the salt and his hand, my eyes gazing upward into his. I swear I saw desire in his eyes when he looked back into mine.

Two more licks, two more shots. I felt buzzed, partially the shots, partially from being around Will. He grabbed a couple of beers and asked, "You want another daiquiri?"

"No. I should switch to beer."

He grabbed another for me and gestured for us to go back outside.

When we got back to Jude, Mary Jane was not sitting there anymore. Instead, Jude now spoke to an attractive woman, who I had noticed in the hallways at school, with dark hair, dark, haunting eyes, pale skin and a short, curvy body. She sat in a short skirt, one leg crossed over the other, looking entranced by Jude's conversation. It was almost the same gaze Mary Jane had bestowed upon Jude.

"Guys. This is Kendra Willows. She's in our program," Jude introduced the woman to Will and me.

As I got a closer look, I saw how beautiful Kendra was. She looked older, maybe late thirties, early forties. Later, I found out that she was forty-nine. She looked amazing. "What's your secret?" Mary Jane and I had asked her once.

"Genetics. And avoid the sun. Never go out without protection." No wonder she was pale as a ghost. Pale, but with radiant skin — and not one pore.

Jude and Kendra talked as if they had known each other for years. Will and I sat with our knees doing that dance again, listening. I kept fantasizing of a kiss with Will. A few times I shot him a shy smile, wondering if he felt the same.

Kendra talked about her husband, George, "He's running for mayor." I was surprised to hear she was married. She wasn't wearing a ring and seemed very interested in Jude. But after listening to them talk, I understood their easy rapport. Like Jude, Kendra knew the frustration and intricacies of having her life on display. "I wish he wasn't running. He has been involved in politics for years, but we were never really in the spotlight. Mayor has increased his public profile, dramatically, and with that our whole family is now in the public eye."

Jude put his hand on her knee in a gesture of warmth. "I get it," he said, looking directly in her eyes. "If you ever want to vent your frustration, I am here to listen." He retracted his hand from her knee.

"One benefit of being in graduate school with a bunch of psychologists-to-be is we should never be short of an empathetic ear," I said, thinking of how my parents had always encouraged me to talk through my feelings, even when I didn't feel like talking. They'd say, "If you hold things in or try to avoid truths about yourself, they will come back to haunt you. Remember, the unconscious always wins. Always." It could have been branded into my skin, they said it so often.

The night went on with more drinks, another lick and shot with Will. Although I felt good and tipsy, I just could not get myself to make that leap into a kiss or any gesture that was obviously romantic. The party was a bad setting because I'd have to get him to a private corner, which would be awkward. As this went around in my intoxicated mind, his leg rested firmly against mine. I looked at it sitting there, inspecting the blue of his jeans, thinking about his bare leg underneath and how his skin would feel.

I downed the rest of my beer and got up to use the bathroom.

I needed a minute away from Will.

"Excuse me. Restroom calls."

Mary Jane was coming out of the condo as I was walking in. She grabbed my face and kissed my cheek. "You are adorable." Mary Jane was drunk and very happy.

"You too." I laughed. "I'll be back, going to the bathroom."

"OK. Have fun in there. Jude's hot as fuck," she said too loudly in my ear.

"Is fuck hot?" I teased.

She made her lips pouty. "I know. I know. Using fuck as an adjective isn't the most eloquent use of language, but only using proper words and language is pigeonholing other words, such as fuck, which, in my opinion, shouldn't be considered a curse. I didn't make the grammar laws up, so I don't have to agree with them."

I laughed. "I agree. Creative arguments require going outside the lines of convention. Jude *is* hot as fuck." And he was. "OK. Gotta pee."

"Go for it, sister." She pinched my cheek, gently.

There wasn't a line for the bathroom, which was surprising given the number of people at the party. Drunk people. I was washing my hands and looking at myself in the mirror when there was a knock on the door. "One minute."

When I came out, Jude waited by the door. "Hey." He smiled. There was something I noticed in his eyes, something different, a sparkle. Maybe he was attracted to me. No. I was drunk. A guy like Jude would never be attracted to me. I was too skinny; my nose, too wide; my eyes, not deep-set enough; my personality, too awkward.

Jude would go for one of those exotic model types that were all over South Beach. Not that I cared. I didn't. I would never go for him either. He *was* hot as fuck, but hot didn't mean I liked him; it was an objective observation of someone's physicality and persona. Interested in someone, liking someone romantically, went deeper. And I liked Will.

But in my drunkenness, cloaked in his stare, I felt good, sexy, older. That was the thing with a guy like Jude, and right there in front of the bathroom I realized why Mary Jane and Kendra hung on his words: He made people feel like they were the most fabulous person he had ever laid eyes on. The momentary undivided attention and admiration he showered on me made me feel like I'd grown three inches.

So when he said, "Come here," and gestured toward the closed door to the guest bedroom, I followed without question. Jude made it so that there were no questions. You did what he asked, because he made you think you wanted to.

"I want to show you something."

I followed him into the room. Before I could even think about what we were doing in there, he pulled me close and said, "I have been dying to do this all night," and kissed me.

He kissed my lips hard and then opened his mouth, circling his tongue with mine. It took me a moment to register what was happening. *I'm kissing, Jude!* Chills ran up my back. He pulled his arms around my thin frame. Feeling his body close made me hot all over. He rubbed my back, then ran his fingers through my hair.

This kiss was *hot*.

My lips felt glued to his.

As he guided me toward the bed, I felt lost in the kiss. He tasted good. He felt good. But...

No.

"Wait," I whispered. I couldn't hook up with Jude. I liked Will. And we were all friends. If he was some random hot guy, I probably would just let myself go and enjoy the evening, but he wasn't.

"What is it?" His expression seemed so genuine, so concerned.

"I – I." I felt the truth about Will on the edge of my tongue but swallowed the words. "Let's go back out with the others. You're very attractive, but I don't want to do this. It's not personal." Part of me admonished my own tendency to be too controlled over my decisions regarding intimacy. I sweated as he still stared at me. "I hope you understand."

He kissed my lips, softly. "I like you."

"I like you too, but we are friends, OK?"

"I can't promise that I won't try again." He gave me that generous and charming smile, and my stomach jumped. The guy was hot and sexy and magnetic. And part of me thought: *Please don't try again. If you do, I may give in.*

"Come on let's go back outside."

He followed me as I walked out, leaving behind the unfinished kiss in the bedroom.

Chapter 7

Alex

A week later, Will still hadn't made a move. Growing more frustrated, I decided to call Michael for advice. I needed a man's opinion, and I knew he'd be honest.

"Hey, what's up?" was how he answered the phone.

"Whadaya mean, 'what's up'? I can't call just to say hi?" I teased him.

"You can do whatever you want. You always do." His smile could clearly be heard on my end. "Wanna grab a drink?"

"I can't."

"Big date?"

"Not exactly." I sighed.

"What's up? *Really.*" His voice turned warm and serious.

"I need your opinion, without judgement."

"Course."

"It's about Will."

"Ah, he's still acting ambivalent?"

"I don't know if it's ambivalence. Maybe I'm misreading his overtures, because I want to believe that he's interested."

"He kissed you."

"Like you did."

"Oh, stop. You can't compare it. We were wasted. Besides, we're totally open with each other. Me and you, we're really friends. I told you, just kiss him first."

"Mary Jane said the same thing. It's just – it's not so easy with him. You know I got crushed by my last boyfriend. I keep thinking if he wanted me after that first kiss, *he* would make the move. If I make the next move, I feel like I could be setting myself up for disaster."

"I hear what you're sayin'. He seems to like you. I saw the way he was with you the night you guys came by the bar."

"And how was that?"

"He sat close to you. And he seemed more interested in you than anything else."

"But the fact that he hasn't made another move would suggest otherwise. This is the problem."

"Maybe he's not the right guy to take a chance on, ever think of that?"

"Yeah." I sighed. "I tried not to be interested, but I can't fight it. He's the first guy who I've felt anything for since Zach. I feel like I have to explore what that means."

"If you don't take a chance you may never know."

"Do you like when girls make the first move?"

"Hell, yeah. It's sexy when a woman knows what she wants. Just kiss him tonight and get it over with. At least then you'll know if he's interested or not. Either way, bet you'll feel better."

"Yeah." I leaned back into my couch, letting what he said settle in. I knew he was right. I just didn't know if I could actually do it. I felt some kind of barrier around Will, which was making it even harder. "You're probably right."

"Come to the bar tomorrow if you're around. I'm on a double. Or call me and let me know what happens."

"'Kay. Thanks, Michael."

I never mentioned the kiss with Jude to Michael, because I was trying to pretend it never happened. But when I hung up the phone, I thought to myself that school had only started a couple of months ago, and already I had kissed three guys in the program after I promised myself I would avoid romantic entanglements with anyone I went to school with.

I shook my head, disappointed with myself and went to get ready to go out.

An hour later, Will and Jude came by, and the three of us went to a local dive bar, Thelma's, right off Ocean Drive. A local hang out, no tourists, which wasn't easy to find near The Drive. Thelma's had greasy burgers and cheap beer, top shelf liquor that wasn't overpriced, which was a small miracle on South Beach where things were as expensive as New York City. Some places even more expensive.

Jude invited a girl to join us, Sammie Silvers. When he mentioned that a woman named Sammie would be joining us, Will had asked if she was a date. Jude had responded, "Our relations are indeterminate at this point."

I had wanted to ask him exactly what he meant, but I was afraid to show any interest. The kiss had left an awkward space between us. Jude acted the same — warm, friendly, calm — when I saw him at school. But when he had come by one night during the week to study with Will and me, I kept catching him looking at me.

Maybe I had been looking at him too.

So, I was glad when Will had asked, "Dude, what the fuck. Indeterminate relations sound so… indeterminate. We want to know if you're hooking up. You like being the obscure artist." He chuckled.

Jude gave us his dashing grin. "It means exactly what it sounds like it means. I don't know what it is yet. Nothing has happened, *yet*, but I believe there is a mutual connection that will be consummated soon."

I felt my jaw tense up. *That's me and Will, indeterminate relations. Somewhere between friendship and romance. OK, closer to friendship, but still undefined. Or maybe not. Jude will consummate with a near stranger, while Will and I will remain in a perpetual state of sitting nearly on top of each other, maintaining the eye contact of two lovers, and what? Nothing more. No intimate touching, no sleepovers, no… sex. Maybe I am fooling myself into believing it's more than it is.*

Jude and Will talking about Sammie, a potential *date*, left me feeling more confused about Will and me, and more impatient.

I wanted a guy that wanted me. No more limbo guys. I tapped my fingers along my beer mug, feeling restless. There was no way I was making the first move.

Sammie Silvers arrived wearing a white dress around her voluptuous body that fit as tight as a nylon stocking. Jude caught her eye as she came in the door. She slinked over, swaying her hips to-and-fro, her breasts nearly popping out of the top of her dress, her hair, long, dark and pin straight. "Hi darling." She kissed Jude's cheek.

"You look amazing." He wrapped his arm around her back and introduced her to Will and me.

She spoke to Will and me for about ten minutes. She told us that she worked in a retail store on Lincoln Road. "But that's just for extra cash, until my modeling career takes off, ya know."

Will nodded politely and asked, "Do you do any modeling now?"

Honestly, she looked a little rough to be a model. There was something attractive behind all the ostentation. Maybe she looked different without so much makeup.

"I've been doing swimsuit ads." She showed Will a series of pictures of herself on her phone.

I leaned over his shoulder to look. Sammie had a curvy body. Not too many people could pull off a white string bikini. "You look great." I smiled at her.

"Thanks, darling." She smiled back.

Then she showed Will and me a couple of photos of her topless. "They pay very well for these. A few more gigs like that, and I'll be able to quit the old day job."

"Great," Will said, looking slightly awkward as he handed her phone back to her.

She seems satisfied that Will saw her photos, I thought as I observed their exchange. Sammie said, "Excuse me," then turned her back to us to give Jude her full attention. The two of them huddled together in conversation, leaving Will and me to our own accord.

Will's face was still flushed.

"You looked embarrassed," I said.

"She caught me off guard. Girls here in Miami can be very audacious. In Mauston, people tend to be more conservative in their demeanor."

I laughed. "People *everywhere* are more conservative than on South Beach. She has a gorgeous body, though. Why not show it off?"

"Her breasts are fake. I prefer a more natural look." He stared into my eyes, took a few strands of my hair and wrapped them behind my ear. Heat coursed through my body. Our faces were close. He was going to kiss me. I felt it. The small space between our lips became smaller as we inched toward each other. He moved his head forward. My heart fluttered. Just as I expected his lips to fall on mine, he broke the moment. "You want to get some food?"

What the fuck? He's doing this on purpose. "No. I'm not hungry."

"I'm going to get a burger. You sure you don't want something?"

"Uh, yes."

"You want another beer?" He leaned over the bar to get the bartender's attention. His arm rested right against mine. I was going to lose it. This thing, whatever it was that hung between us, was making me nuts. He was taunting me on purpose. Looking at his arm on mine, I felt my face burning. If he wasn't going to kiss me, I needed to go. I felt words hanging on the tip of my tongue, irritated words. "I want to go." I wanted to be as far away from Will as possible.

"What's wrong?"

"Nothing. I suddenly got tired."

He looked at me curiously, then looked over to Jude and Sammie who were sitting close, talking, unaware of their surroundings.

"I'll go with you. You shouldn't walk home alone."

"No. Stay." I gave him a sharp look. I knew he could read the distress in my eyes, but I didn't care. For the first time in the couple of months of knowing Will, I didn't care. I didn't want him. I didn't want a guy who I had to work so hard to be with. Or wasn't sure of me. Someone "ambivalent," as Michael had pointed out.

"I'm going with you. We could sit down by the pool or something."

"I'm tired, *Will.*" I pierced him with my eyes. "I'm done hanging out for the night. I'll see you tomorrow." I threw some cash on the bar. Said goodnight to Jude and Sammie, who were now kissing at the bar — *at least Jude acted on his desire, jeez* — and rushed out before Will could pay the tab and follow me, torturing me with this crazy intimacy-non-intimacy dance.

As I walked briskly through the swarms of people toward my apartment building, fuming, I wondered if my empowerment would last. And why was I so mesmerized by Will anyway? You should only fall in love with someone whose arms are open and strong enough to catch you. I was not going to want someone who could not open their arms fully.

Jude liked Sammie, so he asked her out, and there they were in an *indeterminate relationship* that was soon to become less indeterminate. That's the way it happened. Things started indeterminate but didn't stay that way.

I picked up my pace. I was almost running, barely noticing the crowds of people, loud people, passing by in hordes. I sucked in the humid air, trying to clear my mind, as I came up to my apartment building.

Passing by the pool, I saw it was empty. I needed to burn off my angst. I debated going upstairs to change, but Carter could be home, and I didn't want to talk. I wanted to be enveloped in water, in the place where I felt safe. I slipped off my sundress and dove in with my black bra and panties. I felt liberated doing it.

The water surrounded me, quickly quieting my mind. If I could depend on one thing to relieve me, it was swimming. I felt better as my arms tore through the water and the chlorine entered my nose.

Then, I felt a wave move across the water, the muffled sound of a splash as the trickles of water dispersed around me. I wasn't alone anymore. My haven was intruded upon. And I knew who it was.

God forbid, he would give me time to myself to process my emotions. No, he would continue to entice me, like the last cookie in the cookie jar, he would continue to make me want him. And he would continue not following through.

I thought he was sweet, but he wasn't.

I continued to swim.

He swam next to me, eventually getting me to stop for a minute. When I poked my head out of the water to face the inevitable exchange with him, the dim moonlight shined off his face and he looked so handsome.

"Come here," he said, looking right into my eyes with that look that I must've been mistaking for desire.

"No," I said, even though every inch of me wanted to be near him.

"Just – um, I'm sorry."

"For what?"

"Come here. Let's talk."

"I'm not in the mood to talk. Not tonight."

He moved closer to me. "Alex," he whispered, then took my hand.

I stood frozen, wondering what he was going to do. I felt simultaneously sexy and awkward as I faced him in my panties and bra, both soaked and no longer firmly against my body.

"I'm sorry."

"For what?"

"For waiting so long to do this." He placed his hands softly on my cheeks and kissed my lips. He slowly guided me toward the wall of the pool and then kissed me again, this time opening his mouth against mine and slipping his tongue in.

The kiss was electric. I felt it everywhere in my body, like a firecracker that moved from my head all the way down to my toes. His arms were solid around me, and the longer we kissed the more I wanted to feel my naked body against his. I couldn't take it. It was that type of desire that was painful and unfathomable and delicious all at once. I unfastened my bra and threw it on the side of the pool. He looked down at my bare breasts, touching them delicately, circling them with his fingers, then he rubbed his hand along the inside of my thighs, touching me sensually exactly how I had imagined he would. The kissing became fierce, almost desperate. He pulled me closer and I could feel he was aroused too.

"You want to go upstairs?" He whispered.

"No. It's nice out here." I looked up at him.

He ran his fingers through my hair and tucked strands behind my ear, his eyes wandering around my face and to my exposed breasts. "Let's go in the hot tub."

"'Kay," I whispered in his ear.

We quickly scooted out of the pool and went into the hot tub which sat adjacent to the pool. I had never felt so free. I walked across to the hot tub without my bra, covering my breasts with only my hands.

Stars scattered across the darkness, and the palm trees bustled in the ocean breeze. Will turned the whirlpool on and came in beside me, kissing my neck, my shoulders and my breasts. He stuck his head under the whirling steamy water and kissed my thighs.

He reached under my panties and massaged me. When he came back up from under the water, he stared into my eyes intensely, as he removed my panties, then he leaned against me, kissing me hard. I loved the feeling of our lips merging. I felt so close to him in that moment and I wanted him to slip inside of me, to feel him deeply against me.

I pulled at the top of his boxers under the water. He smiled at me, and leaned his nose on mine, as I removed them.

We made love in the hot tub.

Afterward, we stayed in the hot tub, caressing. I loved feeling close to him like this – finally. We barely said a word while we were out there. Instead of filling in the moment with words, we just enjoyed the fullness that swelled between us. There was nothing like that night, feeling so completely close with someone that for just a little while the world seemed small and safe. And I didn't feel alone.

Later, we went up to his apartment. When he opened the door, I saw *it* immediately. We had painted a chalkboard on his wall a couple of weeks before. And there it was in big white letters on the chalkboard: *ALEX, YOU ARE BEAUTIFUL.*

I felt all the blood rush to my face as I looked at him with a shy, flirtatious grin. "Were you planning on my seeing this?"

"Yes. And. No. I guess, I was hoping you would and afraid you would at the same time. I have wanted to tell you but didn't know how."

"You couldn't tell I was interested?"

"I could, yes. He diverted eye contact. "I'm not good with words."

"Actually, you are very good with words. That's part of what I like about you."

"Words are easy when you are talking through intellectual theories or dissecting someone else's internal world. I'm not good at saying words describing my own emotions. When I feel something deeply, it's hard for me to say. I'm working on that."

"That means that you mean them. Sharing your deepest feelings shouldn't be easy to say. I never trust people when they say things too easily. I guess, sometimes writing is easier than talking." I smiled again at his note on the board.

He took a piece of chalk and wrote: "*I hope I don't let you down.*"

"*You won't,*" I wrote, looking at him through the glazed idealism of love.

That night we slept with our bodies wrapped around each other in Will's bed. I felt completely contented and positive that our relationship status had moved to defined romantic, blossoming intimate partner status.

Section II
Fresh Perspectives

"You filled in the holes I tried but failed to cover, your love's embrace like no other I've ever known before."
—Alex

Chapter 8

Alex

"Morning," Will whispered in my ear.

I nestled against him. "Morning," I gazed up at him with my eyes only half opened.

There was no first time sleepover awkwardness with Will. I felt like I had found something that I didn't know I was looking for. Something maybe I wouldn't let myself want because I was afraid I wouldn't find it.

He ran his fingers delicately over my naked body, arousing me. He placed his fingers inside of me, massaging me until I was breathless, then he made love to me.

Afterward, we sat in bed feeding each other buttered English muffins, sipping coffee and musing about life. I had never experienced this level of intimacy before. I know it probably sounds strange for a thirty-year-old woman, but Zach and I weren't the "lay in bed and talk for hours" type of couple. What I realized from spending time with Will was that Zach and I didn't have enough in common to spend hours engaged in intimate conversations. With Zach, I was a girl in love for the first time. Instead of figuring out who I was, I was molding myself into something I wasn't. Someone I had thought he wanted.

Will saw inside of me without me having to say a word. I hadn't even realized how alone I had felt until Will filled a hole that I didn't even know I had. Laying there with him, I felt a part of myself come alive. Something stirred within me, some type of truth about who I was.

I looked up at him as he spoke, admiring his face. He was gorgeous, like a stallion, strong, masculine, athletic. He noticed me looking at him admiringly and he smiled, pulling me against his chest. I felt his heart beating against mine. If this wasn't love, I would never understand what was.

But it was way too soon to say that word: LOVE. So, I lay with him quietly, a soft smile across my face, thinking, *I think I love you.*

Will began talking about the book *Into the Wild*, by Jon Krakauer, and Thoreau's influence on the boy in the story, Chris McCandless. I loved that book. As I rested my head on his chest and he twirled tendrils of my hair, I said, "If I really think about it, the world is overwhelming. The rules made by governing bodies are skewed in the direction of profiting only the governing bodies. There's too much meaningless noise, and the things that do have meaning aren't valued by mainstream culture. Like art, why are there so many struggling artists? Art is where the truth is, and yet so many people must give up their calling or they would starve. If I were courageous, I would do what he did. I would disregard my worldly possessions and comforts and go live in the wildness for a while."

Will kissed the top of my head. "Interesting, the concept of the starving artist, 'cause, personally, I think true artists are the least hungry."

I looked up at him. "You love that play on words. Don't you? You said that to me when I called myself a starving graduate student."

"I like it, yes. But it is true. When people confuse value with money, they will always be hungry." That's where greed comes from. Without value, people think they need more."

"Are you referring to me?" I propped my head up on my bent arm. "You had said that maybe because I called myself starving, but wasn't literally, maybe I was hungry." His musing had a self-righteous quality, but I respected him. How utterly fabulous to be free enough to speak the truth.

And how sexy.

"No. Of course not. You do have things. I mean, so do I. It's not only about abandoning possessions, it's also about valuing what you have." He looked at me admiringly, touching my cheek.

Did I value what I had? I thought I did. I hoped I did.

"What are you thinking? Your eyes turn greener when you contemplate deeply, did you know that?"

"No, I didn't." I nestled against him. "I was thinking about Chris McCandless. It makes me sad that he died. He probably would have contributed a lot to the world. He saw things."

"He died, true, but he also lived, right? Just like Thoreau, he sought truth in nature. He traveled all through the West abandoning comforts to find the truth of life. It reminds me of one of my favorite Thoreau quotes: 'I went to the woods because I wished to live deliberately, to front only the essential facts of life, and see if I could not learn what it had to teach, and not, when I came to die, discover that I had not lived.'"

"I can't believe how many quotes you can recite verbatim like that."

"When I like something, it's easy to remember."

"What do your parents do? You never mention them. I bet they are in academia or something intellectual."

"No, nothing like that. I'm the only person in my family to even graduate from college, never mind going on for my graduate degree. I'm — different than my family. I don't really want to talk about them."

"I hope you tell me about them some time. I just want to know you more."

He played with strands of my hair. "I don't always think it's words that help people know each other. I think when we know someone, it's an unspoken connection."

"That's interesting coming from someone training to be a shrink," I teased him.

"I'm not saying words aren't valuable for understanding yourself and others. Talking is important. Sharing is important." He looked at me affectionately, then kissed me. "I just think when it comes to deep connections, it's less about words and more of a visceral knowing."

"Your heart knows what your brain wants."

"Maybe the heart is the brain," he said, letting his nose rest against mine. "I'm thinking more and more that I won't pursue the clinical work. I'm more interested in teaching and research. But we'll see." He kissed me before he even completed the sentence, and we made love again.

We finally got out of bed around noon and were preparing to go to the library when Will's phone rang. "It's Jude," he said to me as he picked up. For a moment I felt guilty about the kiss with Jude, even though it was before I knew Will's feelings. And Will never had to know the truth.

I observed the surprise and consternation on Will's face as he listened to Jude talking on the phone.

When he hung up, he had a look of astonishment.

"What is it?"

"Jude was arrested last night."

"For what?"

"His indeterminate relationship turned out to be very defined. Sammie Silvers is a call girl, and Jude was a customer. Only he didn't know their status until the cops busted them while at some bar near 11th or something, where call girls are known to bring clients."

"That's crazy. How could he not know?"

"How would he know if she didn't tell him? We didn't know."

"Right. But, still."

"Apparently, she liked Jude, so she didn't tell him the truth. They released him. One of the cops making the arrest has a young daughter who was in love with *Books*. Jude said he agreed to a dinner with the cop and his daughter, and the cop released him."

"That's crazy. Do you believe him?"

"Of course. This is the world we live in. This is how things work."

His tone sounded so intense, like it was personal.

"Right," I said, my eyes wandering over his face, curiously.

"I'm going to go meet him for lunch. He sounds shaken up."

"Ok. Let me go change really quick."

He kissed me, then said, "Just me. He sounded like he wanted to talk alone. Guy talk. Besides, maybe we shouldn't say anything about *this* to anyone yet?"

"This?"

"Us."

"Ooookaaay," I said, looking at him, confused. "Why?"

"I like to maintain my privacy. Our program is small. Once one or two people find out, it will spread around, and everyone will know our business."

"No, they won't. Knowing we're hanging out or seeing each other isn't knowing intimate details of our business."

"Whatever they don't know, they will fill in. You have no idea how fast gossip can travel in a small program."

"I think you're worrying too much. But, OK. We won't say anything. For how long though? People, Jude especially, may figure it out."

"I don't know. A couple of weeks. Let's enjoy the privacy of our relationship for a little while."

He went to the blackboard and wrote: *I like you, Alex Daily. And I don't want anything to mess this up.*

Me neither. I like you too. Lots.

Actually, I was sure I loved him, but I wouldn't say it first.

Chapter 9

Will

As soon as they separated, and he felt the absence of her presence, he knew he loved her. *Shit.* He had been afraid of this and yet, part of him had wanted it to happen. The mind often wanted two very different things, *ambivalence*. But ambivalence when it came to romantic relationships usually meant someone would get hurt. Or always. Maybe things would be different this time. If there was a *this* time. He didn't know if he could ever really try again, love again, in the way that love was meant to be experienced — with abandon.

Jude hadn't asked that Alex not join them. Will had made that part up, because he needed some distance between them. He had tried to wrestle away the feelings that were developing over those first couple of months. He wanted to be with her, and he didn't want to be with her. Both feelings pulling him as strongly as the other, like he had a tight rope in his stomach, in his brain, in his heart, pulling him in opposite directions.

One thing that always shooed ambivalence away, at least temporarily, was fear. Fear of losing the person. And that's exactly how it went down this time. When he saw how determined her face was to leave him the night before at Thelma's, he knew he'd lose her — and the thought of that sent a sharp pierce along his back — if he didn't do something. He ran, literally ran, back to their building to find her.

Now what? They had slept together. And it wasn't just fucking either. He could have stayed in bed talking with her and having sex all day. Kissing her. It was good that Jude had called and gave him a believable excuse. As soon as he knew he could fall for her, he should have stayed away from her.

That first night he had met her in the pool, he was attracted to her determination. He knew that type of drive he saw in her swimming. She was someone who knew the value of the pursuit of something greater, to push the limit, to find one's potential, to leave the realm of comfort. Just like him. Just like Chris McCandless. In fact, he would have bet a thousand dollars that she had read his book and Thoreau's work too.

He would have won that bet because, as it turned out, she had read it.

It was nice to feel understood by someone he didn't have to explain himself to. After everything he had had to deal with growing up, what a relief to feel like he could say what he wanted. None of his father's: *Tone it down, William. No one wants to hear your bullshit ideas. Why are you reading those stupid books?* This coming from a man who hadn't graduated high school and didn't value education for the sake of enriching life through learning. School was a means to an end. And that was to work and make money. Nothing more.

When he saw her without her swim cap and goggles for the first time, she looked incredibly sexy in a nondescript sort of way. Sexy, without trying to be sexy, and naturally beautiful. Tall and thin, nice greenish eyes, dark hair that hung down the middle of her back in loose waves. She had a beauty mark on the side of her nose that added to her attractiveness.

Underneath her proud, sexy way of carrying herself, he sensed her self-consciousness. If he had never spoken with her, he probably would have assumed that she was a bitch, but once he did, he could tell by the way she diverted eye contact and fiddled with the strap on her bag or a string on her shirt, or the way she hesitated with her words sometimes, that she felt nervous around people.

He felt like he knew her. And their rapport had been so smooth, so effortless. It would have been better if he hadn't been physically attracted to her too. He should have known it would go down this road eventually. How long did he really think he could carry on as friends with a beautiful woman who he could talk to about so many things?

And he had written that note to her on the board, hoping she would see it and make the first move, because then, if (or when), things didn't work out, he could blame it all on her and not suffer more guilt over his own mistakes.

Bethany died —— was killed. And it was his fault. That's what happened to people who he let get close.

§

Jude sat at a table outside of The Gallery on Lincoln Road, with a beer and a shot glass in front of him. His shirt hung out of his pants, and his hair looked messy. Will approached the table. "Hey, man, you alright?"

"A couple more of these and I will be." Jude held up the two beverages.

"Where did you go after they released you?"

"Club 39. That late-night, members only place, I told you about off Washington. Got there when it was almost morning. Drank with some guys, but I don't remember a lot. I got wasted, I guess, because right before I called you, I woke up under the boardwalk north of here. No clue how I got there or why I didn't just walk home. My apartment's closer than that."

"We should eat. You need food more than alcohol. Don't sweat it. You weren't charged. And it was an honest mistake."

Jude pulled the front of his hair off his forehead, then released it. "It's fucked up that it happened. I wouldn't've cared that she was a call girl. I liked her enough to hang out with for a while. Pisses me off that she lied. It reminds me of the type of drama I used to experience all the time in LA. I'm trying to change my life. I don't mean to sound like a martyr, but do you ever feel like bad shit just happens to you no matter how hard you try to get it right?"

"No. I think if the same stuff keeps happening over and over, then we must be playing some kind of role in it. Maybe today is not a good day for big life considerations."

"You've never made mistakes?"

"Of course, dude. Many. Everyone's made mistakes. You've got to think about choices. I mean, why Sammie? She didn't seem overly cerebral or artistic. Not to make a quick judgment."

"I met her at the gym. Honestly, I liked the way she looked. She was friendly. I assumed that she was the type of woman who I could have a short, uncomplicated fling with. I mean, we are on fucking South Beach. And in case you haven't noticed, there aren't many rules on this island. I thought I'd explore some of the offerings while I'm here."

"And that's the change you want to make to your life. Maybe you need to be a little more selective, think more before you act. I dunno, dude. You've got to live your own way. Not mine."

"Maybe you're right." He cleared his throat. "On a different note, what happened between you and Alex last night?"

Will's face grew hot. How could he know anything happened? "Whaddaya mean?"

"She ran out, and then you left right after her. She looked upset. You have a fight?"

"Nah. We decided to go back and hang out by the pool. She went ahead to grab some beer and change." It sounded like a ridiculous story as it came out of his mouth. He debated telling Jude the truth, but before he said anything, Jude responded with, "You're fucking her, aren't you?"

Will didn't like the word fucking associated with Alex. "What if I were?"

"I'd say you're a lucky guy. She's seems the type that doesn't give it up easily. You've got to work for a woman like her."

Will sucked in some air. "We hooked up last night."

"How was it?"

"It was… she's cool."

"You like her too."

"I guess. It's nothing serious, though. We hooked up. That's all. Don't say anything. I asked her not to say anything. I don't want it to get around school."

"I won't say a word. And nothing about my debacle last night."

"Of course not. Let's get the waiter and eat."

§

After they ate, they walked back toward Will's apartment. "You want to do something later?" Jude asked.

"I'm supposed to study with Alex. You want to come with us?"

"Yeah. I should probably focus more on my classes and less on the South Beach scene, huh?"

"You're spending time and money on grad school. Studying is the only way you're ever going to earn your degree. The program is hard. You can't skate through."

"You sure you don't want to be alone with Alex?" Jude asked, with a teasing glint in his eyes.

"It's fine." Will gave him a steely look. "Remember, *dude*, it's no big deal and it's private."

"Maybe I'm a little jealous."

"Why? You were interested? I thought you said she wasn't your type."

"She's not. Not really. Jealous, more that you found yourself a good girl, someone who wouldn't lie to you and have you arrested."

"Make a better choice next time. You didn't really like that girl anyway."

Jude nodded in agreement.

"Come by my place at six o'clock. We can eat something at the café downstairs and maybe study at my place or at Alex's if her roommate's out."

"Perfect. See you later."

Chapter 10

Alex

Will called to let me know that Jude would be joining us at the café in our building for dinner. The café was a diner-style restaurant, a bunch of booths lined up along the walls, round tables and chairs in the middle. A few times a week they had retro night, playing music from the Eighties with the servers dressed in Eighties garb. Sunday was one of those nights.

When I walked in, I noticed all the teased hair and the cropped shirts, a girl with a banana clip and another one with a cutup sweatshirt hanging off her shoulder. The hostess sported a small Rubik's cube on a string hanging around her neck, and leg warmers. "One?" she asked with a wad of gum in her mouth. She wore bright pink lipstick and matching eye shadow.

"I'm meeting people." I looked around, finally spying Will and Jude seated at a back booth. "They're there." I pointed and smiled politely at her.

"Here." She handed me a menu and blew a big bubble with her gum.

Walking toward the table, I felt mildly anxious. To be fair, I am a bit of a neurotic, so mildly anxious is almost a baseline for me. I had kissed Jude. I knew I was probably making it more of a deal than it was, but it made me feel awkward around him, especially now that I had slept with Will.

Maybe I was too uptight. But messy emotions held consequences. I knew what it felt like to have my heart smashed to pieces by easy words and careless behaviors.

I never should have kissed Jude, knowing something (hopefully) would happen with Will. *Thank God, I didn't have sex with him,* I thought right as I approached the table and Will and Jude both looked up with big smiles.

I locked eyes with Will, but he quickly broke the gaze with a casual, "Hey." Meanwhile, I felt Jude's eyes pasted to my skin. Will scooted over so I could sit next to him. My leg brushed his as I sat and electricity coursed through me. Then Jude looked into my eyes with that piercing magnetic look he had and asked, "What's up, Alllexxx?"

He said my name differently. It sounded flirty. I fought off a smile and looked away from him, pretending there was a loose string on the sleeve of my shirt. "Nothing much. Just finished a long swim. I'm starving. How are you doing?" I asked, looking up at Jude again.

The gaze in his eyes when he looked at me felt enveloping.

I narrowed my focus to his chin.

"Better. What do you know about Kendra Willows?"

"Nothing beyond what you know. You introduced her to us at Mary Jane's party. I said hi to her in the hallway when I saw her this week. Why?"

"She called me today to talk."

"About her husband's career?"

"Sort of, I guess. I probably shouldn't say too much. She asked that I keep the conversation confidential. She's having a hard time is all. And I'm trying to figure out what she wants from me."

"A listening ear. You offered your ear at the party."

"Yeah," he said trailing off. His eyes turned pensive, then after a long pause, he changed the subject to the catalog of Eighties music that played at the café and the overabundance of hairspray. "Trend wise the Eighties was the cheesiest."

"I think it has an irresistible allure, a loud and bold quality. Although, I wouldn't wear my hair like that if you paid me." I shook my head, letting my hair cascade across my shoulders.

"You like the free flowing, unpolished look of the Sixties." Jude shot me his magnanimous smile. "It's a good look."

I played with my fingers in my lap, fighting off a smile.

"She has her own look." Will looked at me, and I saw the affection in his eyes.

Will and Jude continued to discuss the trends in music of the Eighties. Will's leg rested completely against mine. I could not wait for the night to end, for Jude to go home, so Will and I could be alone.

But as the night went on, Will acted more and more distant toward me. At first, I had thought I was over-reading his behavior. You know, as a daughter of two shrinks and as a shrink in training, this was a vulnerability — overanalyzing. And after that closeness-distance game Zach had played for the last year of our relationship, I knew I was sensitive to that dance, like a tango over a bed of nails.

I tried to talk myself out of what I felt to be a shield around him. But the voice of intuition would not relent. It felt like Will had a wall of bricks surrounding him.

Worse, once we were all back at his place working on our research methods and statistics homework, Jude was more attentive than Will.

Jude leaned over my shoulder and explained the formula for correlations. His aftershave entered my nose, strong, robust, masculine. I sniffled, trying to eliminate the scent and erase the feeling of having his body so close to mine from my mind.

I didn't even like Jude, but his sexuality was so palpable, it gripped me like the ripples of a turbulent river, drawing me toward him.

I struggled not to be pulled.

Meanwhile, Will kept his head buried in his own book, seeming not to notice.

Will and I had agreed that we were keeping our relationship discrete, at least temporarily. And that was OK, but this distance after being so intimate felt dismissive, especially since he hadn't acted like that when we were friends. Coupled with Jude's enveloping, unfathomable presence, I started to feel uncomfortable.

Jude pulled his chair next to mine and leaned over my shoulder.

I could taste his scent. I took a long sip of my iced tea.

"The number indicates how much each variable relates to the other. The higher the number, the greater the relationship," Jude continued.

"Yeah. I get that. I'm talking about all the extraneous components. There is no way all components of every variable can be reduced to one number — the correlation coefficient."

Jude laughed. "Ah, yes, the ubiquitous confounding variables. You can't eliminate all the gray areas. All you can do is try to control them the best that you can." His eyes twinkled when he looked at me. *That's the look that makes all the women swoon over him*, I thought. Then I brushed that thought out of my mind.

"Thanks," I said. "I think I got it from here." I leaned away from him.

"What've ya got to drink?" Jude went toward Will's refrigerator.

"Water, Gatorade, orange juice, iced tea."

"I meant alcoholic." He opened the fridge and surveyed the contents. "There's a couple of Coors in here. Mind if I have one?"

"Take whatever you want. I've got vodka and tequila. Over there." Will pointed to a cabinet. "You're done working on this?"

"Yeah. I know this stuff. I studied statistics in college."

Jude poured some tequila into a glass. "You guys want one."

"No, thanks," I said.

Will said, "Yes."

I looked at Will. He glanced at me and shrugged his shoulders. "The stuff's not due until Tuesday. Besides, you understand it better than you think. Let's take a break. You want some more iced tea?"

"Sure."

Within less than an hour, Jude and Will were buzzed and discussing the parade of women Jude had met while part of the LA music scene, the way he never could tell if any of them really cared about anything other than who he was. "It's not easy," he said, "never knowing if anyone ever really sees who you are behind the veneer of the performance, or if anyone cares. It's easy to forget who you were before you became the image you portray." He looked pained when he talked about it. And I thought, for the first time, that I saw something real in his expression, something vulnerable and even troubled. It made him more attractive.

I enjoyed watching Will listening to his story and providing an empathic ear. Will's sensitivity was intoxicating. I decided to take a shot of tequila as I watched them go back-and-forth in their dialogue. Jude asked if I could offer a woman's opinion on what women really want from a guy.

"I think it's different for different women. Be yourself and the right woman will come along." *How cliché, Alex*, I admonished myself. But it was the truth. And I wondered how a guy as attractive and talented as Jude could be so lost when it came to women.

"Well, how about you? What do you like?" I heard Will rustle in his chair when Jude asked me that.

"I— uh," What did I like? "I like intelligence, someone who thinks about things, someone sensitive. Also, when I like who I am when I'm with him." I paused for a moment thinking about what I had said, then continued, "We all have different parts of ourselves. Different people bring out different sides. You have to like who you are, what side of yourself comes to life, with him." I expressed my sentiments only coming to these conclusions as the words came out of my mouth. I realized then that I had already learned about myself from knowing Will. I continued as if my mouth held command over my mind. "Maybe you even learn to know yourself in a new way because the person sees you more clearly than you could ever see yourself."

I noticed Will and Jude staring at me, and I felt a flush across my face. I had recited a monologue forgetting my audience: Will, the guy I liked. A lot. Maybe even loved. Will, the guy I had been intimate with less than twenty-four hours ago. And Jude, the hot, sophisticated, older guy who seemed to be a bit of a mystery, and whom I had rolled my tongue around with last week. I poured another shot and downed it.

The shot eased my nerves, then Jude asked, "How old were you when you lost your virginity?"

Will's eyes bugged-out. "*Dude*, that's a personal question. You can't ask her that."

Noticing Will rescuing me from an awkward question, I smiled.

Jude said, "Don't you think we need to be open about ourselves if we are asking people, patients, to be open and honest with us?"

Will said, "Different boundaries with professional relationships. And yes, we need to be able to tell the truth about ourselves to ourselves and maybe to others if it's appropriate. I'm not sure that question is appropriate."

"We are all friends," Jude responded.

"Stop it. It's no big deal. Why do you want to know?" I turned to Jude. "What will it tell you about me if I share?"

"Nothing, really. I'm just curious."

"I was 18 when I physically lost my virginity. It was a one-time thing. Emotionally, I lost it when I was 21 and met the guy I dated for seven years, my first serious boyfriend, and the guy who broke my heart." I said too much, my tongue was loose. "I won't get into it. Suffice it to say that I quickly recovered from the heartache and him. Satisfied?" I said sardonically, thinking, *what a lie*. I was over him, but I was still dealing with remnants of the heartbreak.

"Yes. Though, sorry the guy broke your heart."

"It's fine. I've come to realize that we weren't good together. I think, some choices can feel so right in the moment and turn out to be poor choices. Best we can hope is to learn from mistakes and not keep repeating the same ones over and over, you know, like Freud's repetition compulsion. If we want a different ending, we have to have a different beginning." As the sentence came out, Will stared at me with affection. I looked deep into his eyes. His distance was just him playing it cool in front of Jude.

I wished he would tell Jude, so Jude wouldn't be so flirty with me.

Jude poured another drink, then asked if we wanted to go down to the ocean to hang.

"It's getting late," Will said. *Thank goodness.*

But when it was midnight and they were still hanging around Will's talking, I decided that I had to go to sleep. "I'm going, you guys. It's late, and I have a long day tomorrow." Will got up to walk me to the door.

Jude kissed my cheek, leaving a wet spot. "Nite."

Standing at the open door, Will looked at me intensely, and said, "I'll see you tomorrow."

I wanted to kiss his lips, to feel his arms around me. But I felt that barrier between us. *Because he wants to keep our relations surreptitious*, I told myself.

"See you tomorrow." I leaned up and kissed his cheek. As soon as I released my lips, he crossed his arms over his chest, and said, "See ya."

For over an hour, I lay in bed wondering if Jude would leave and Will would call me. He didn't. That night, for the first time in a long time, I dreamed of Zach.

Chapter 11

Alex

When I walked into class the next morning, Will was already seated.

"Hey," he whispered, as I slid into the chair next to him

"Hey."

"Jude stayed until 3 a.m. last night."

"Wow. What'd you guys do after I left?"

"Same. Talked. He's had a lot of wild experiences."

I nodded my head in agreement.

Professor Constantine came in wearing her usual tan suit. Her speckled-gray hair was up in a bun so tight it looked like it pulled her whole face back. "Let's talk about narcissistic personality disorder."

Alana, a skinny girl with dark hair and thick glasses, shot her hand up and spoke before her hand was acknowledged. "The president is the epitome of narcissism."

I saw Mary Jane's hand shoot up and thought that Alana had cracked open Pandora's box — and I was not wrong.

"We can't diagnose people based on their public persona. It's careless." Before anyone could add to the conversation, Mary Jane continued. "Diagnosing without a full evaluation is just irresponsible. And honestly, I don't even like them. Diagnoses eliminate the use of context and nuance."

Alana shot back, "There has been a lot of material released about him. Enough to diagnose."

While Mary Jane debated the dangers of diagnoses, my mind wandered, preoccupied by the feeling of Will next to me. Out of my periphery, I could see his long legs stretched out under the desk. Then my phone buzzed with a text from him. *Swim and dinner tonight?*

I smiled at the phone, then texted him back: *I'd love to.*

I peered at him out of the corner of my eye. He peered back at me and we shared a sly Cheshire grin.

§

We met at the pool at 6:00 and swam together for an hour, then on our way up to Will's to make some chicken and vegetables for dinner, I said, "I should stop by my place and change out of my bathing suit?"

"You can, or I can give you a T-shirt." His eyes shined.

I felt the pull between us. "OK."

As soon as we got to his apartment, he pulled me close, kissing me hard. Will's passionate nature became clear through his kiss. He pushed me against the wall, and I reveled against him as the kissing grew more and more intense.

He guided me toward his bedroom, pulling off my bathing suit before he laid me down on the bed. He kissed my naked body from the neck down, slowly, gently, circling my skin with his tongue as he moved to my thighs making my body flourish before him. No one's touch brought me to life the way Will's did. I came as soon as he made it all the way inside.

Lying together afterward felt as good as the sex. He stroked my hair, letting his fingers get caught in some of the tangles the chlorine had left. "You want to take a shower?" he whispered, and the feeling of his breath in my ear sent a tickle up my spine.

"Together?" A shower was taking the intimacy up another notch.

"Only if you want to."

"I do."

"Good." He kissed me, then walked toward the bathroom. "Tell me how you like the temperature," he called to me over the pound of the water.

I pulled a T-shirt over my naked body and followed him into the bathroom. Will stood naked with a hand under the water. "How's this?"

I checked. "A little warmer. I like hot showers."

He made it hotter, then removed my T-shirt. "Go ahead." He watched me get in and then followed.

As I felt him washing my body and my hair, I thought that I had never felt this close to anyone before. It was so terrifying to want someone so completely and so electrifying. As soon as we finished showering, we moved back to the bed. He spread my legs and eyed my naked body. The desire I read on his face annihilated me. I wanted to lose myself in him. I pulled him on top of me and we made love again.

It was ten o'clock before we even thought about dinner.

§

I stayed at Will's for the next three nights. I went back to my apartment a couple of times to pick up some books, and changes of clothing. Other than that, we spent all our free time together.

No one was supposed to know — yet. But when Carter asked where I had been, with his knowing, raised eyebrows and the teasing lilt in his tone, I told him the truth: "I've been with Will."

"I knew that was coming. It's almost old news."

I smiled.

"You look really happy."

"I should say that our happiness should never be dependent on another person." This was my motto post-Zach. "But maybe the truth is that just because you feel happy around someone, doesn't mean you are dependent on them."

"Don't analyze love, just let yourself feel it."

"Love?"

He gave me a shrewd look. "Love."

I felt my face flush. "Like very much." I knew that I loved Will, but I would never say the truth aloud. Not until he said it first. If he said it. Or wrote it on the chalkboard.

"OK." He rolled his eyes on purpose. "Invite him to my birthday party. Oh, and invite Jude too." He gave me a teasing look.

"Jude is very straight."
"I know. There's nothing wrong with a little eye candy."
"I'll ask them."

§

Looking back, I wished I could have frozen time. Maybe everyone feels that way about certain moments. No one wants to believe that the jubilation or contentment, *the hope*, that they feel during a specific time will not last. That first week with Will felt easy and uncomplicated. Our indiscriminate relationship status seemed to have progressed to a defined relationship. We were together all the time. I let myself be open to a closeness that I had never felt before. I trusted in it. I trusted him.

And I let myself feel safe.

Something shifted in my personality too. My overly-controlled-scheduling-to-keep-order in-my-life-and-emotions self suddenly relaxed. I felt something that had been buried inside burgeon. I felt freer, more open. This was who I really was. This was me, Alex, the one who wasn't going to avoid closeness. Will pulled me out of my cave, out of the numbness, and with that I felt myself evolving.

Even Michael had commented one day when I ran into him at school. "You look radiant. Guess I was wrong about Will. He just needed a nudge, and so did you." He elbowed me.

I covered my smile with my hand. My cheeks felt hot.
"Ah, the blush of hot sex."
"*Michael.*"
"Just enjoy it."

"No one's supposed to know. How could you tell?"

He gave me a clever look. "*Really*? How could I not tell? Well maybe it's only obvious to me because I knew what was going on. But you two look close walking around together."

I nodded.

"I'm glad it's going well. Don't worry about what people know or don't know. People see what they want to see and what they don't actually see, they fill in anyway." He touched my shoulder.

Tension released from my neck. "Thanks, Michael. Of course, you're right. It's Will that wanted to keep it quiet for a while, but I guess it's sort of obvious."

Chapter 12

Alex

When Carter's thirty-sixth birthday party came on Saturday and Jude was going to join us, I said, "I think we should tell him about us. It's going to be hard to hide alcohol-related-flirtations. Don't you think? Anyway, I'm sick of pretending."

His eyes developed a heavy look. "We are not pretending, we are protecting."

I raised my brow. "Protecting?"

"Our privacy."

I took a heavy breath. "Will." I sat on the chair and leaned forward. "Please tell me what happened to you. This need for privacy seems overdetermined."

"Now you're going to throw a Freudian term on me like I'm your patient. It's not overdetermined. It's not linked back to some unresolved childhood issue. Or even if it is, it doesn't make the reality of what I feel any less valid. People can hurt your life if they want to."

"Who hurt you?"

His eyes looked pained as he stared at me, his mouth parted like he was about to say something.

I took his hands in mine. "You can tell me. I would never hurt you."

"You can never promise that. Once you let yourself close to someone, they can hurt you. Even more, you can hurt them. I don't want to hurt you."

"Then don't."

"It's not that simple. We hurt without intention. The only way to protect against that is to not let anyone get too close."

"What are you saying? You are going to keep what's happening between us from evolving?" I wanted to say that I thought we were already close, but I felt too vulnerable in that moment. He had found my relationship Achilles' heel.

"No. NO. I didn't mean that. See. I told you, I'm not good with expressing my feelings. My childhood was shitty. Worse than shitty. OK? Is that what you want to hear? You want to hear that I grew up in a family where I was different from everyone else? And it messed with my emotions. You would never believe that a kid could be punished and ostracized for being intelligent and ambitious, for wanting to learn and be educated. You want to hear how I had to protect myself from being beat down for being who I am?" His eyes welled.

"I'm sorry. Come here." I pulled him close and hugged him tight. I kissed his face, trying to ease the pain I felt hidden inside of him. A lot of pain. I wanted to know more. I wanted to know every inch of his pain, every word of his story, but I didn't want to push him into an area he wasn't ready to go. "I didn't mean to push you. But I am always here to listen."

He kissed my cheek, almost perfunctorily, then backed away slightly. His distance felt solid. "It's not your fault. It's mine. Sometime, I will tell you more. But not now."

"OK," I said, trying to sound convincing, but what I really wanted was to know what he had trapped inside of him. The things I felt that he carried, that kept him locked in.

He looked at me. "Don't get mad. OK?"

"At what?"

"Jude knows. I told him."

"What did you say?"

"I told him when we hooked up that first night. And I told him we've been hanging out a lot."

"Why would I be upset. You're the one who wants to keep this a secret." And I thought, *Yikes, I hope Jude didn't say anything about that kiss. He wouldn't.* "Did he say anything?"

"No. Nothing really. He said you were a nice girl and that I was lucky."

I felt my shoulders relax. It was ridiculous to think Jude would ever disclose that kiss. Will's wall dropped, and he pulled me in for a hug.

"I mentioned it to Carter. He was wondering where I had been sleeping." I contemplated telling him that Michael knew, too, but stopped myself. I thought that would piss Will off. A couple of times after we had slept together he asked me how well I knew Michael and how often we talked. I had just said, "Not too well. I met him the first weekend I moved here. We've hung out a few times. I mostly talk to him at school." I felt Will tighten when I had said that, and I couldn't be sure if I was making it up or not, because he didn't say anything, but I got the feeling that he was a little jealous when it came to Michael.

"Of course. I figured you told him. I guess we shouldn't hide or pretend. If people ask, we'll just say we're seeing each other."

"OK. And when you're ready to talk, I'm ready to listen."

"I know." His eyes looked sad again, then he changed the subject. "You want a beer while we wait for Jude?"

"Sure."

§

Carter's party was out back by the pool. He decorated the area with a Hawaiian luau theme. Guests were encouraged to dress in Hawaiian fashion. Will and I wore Hawaiian leis around our neck: mine, red; his, blue. Jude showed up in a white shirt with big black palm trees scattered all over it. I wrapped a red lei around his neck. "Perfect." I laughed.

Jude's eyes shined with a devious expression when he told me that he had invited Kendra. "She's going through a tough time. She wanted to hang out. I figured since it was outside, it wouldn't be a big deal. It's OK, right?"

"It's late to ask." I gave him a sharp look, but softened, "I'm sure it's fine."

Jude smiled, devilishly. "I think she might be interested in me."

Will gave him a steely look. "Dude, remember our talk. You don't want to go down that road. She's married."

"There's nothing wrong with making a new friend."

Will took in an audible breath. "As long as you can keep it that way, but that sly look in your eyes makes me wonder if you can or even want to. I'm just sayin', think about your choices before you act."

"Nothing's going to happen."

As we moseyed downstairs to the party, Jude received a text from Kendra asking if she could bring Mary Jane. "I'm sure it's fine," I said when he asked me, "but let me just double-check with Carter."

The pool area was packed and hopping when we got downstairs. An assortment of colorful Hawaiian shirts, shrill talking and laughter and equally loud music. The smell of the torch lights mixed with the faint scent of alcohol. Carter greeted us holding a huge plastic cocktail glass. "Hello, Alex and friends. Thanks for coming to my twenty-ninth birthday bash." He smirked. "Ya'll need a drink." A guy jumped into the pool, splashing water all around. A group of guys laughed at him, clapping.

People were already drunk, it seemed.

I asked Carter if Mary Jane and Kendra could come, to which he said, "Fine, as long as they bring a gift." He laughed. "I'm just kidding. Sure, it's fine. You didn't need to ask."

"I try to be polite when I can."

"Ah, a cover for your usual caustic demeanor." He put his arm around me, eyeing Jude conspicuously. "What do ya'll want to drink? This table back here is for mixed tropical cocktails. You want a piña colada?"

"I'll have one," I said. Will and Jude grabbed beers.

Carter had a guy named Larry — a pretty boy with muscles bulging out of his tight shirt — make my drink. Carter left to go mingle. Will, Jude and I found seats toward the back of the crowd. Club music thumped from the speakers. A few people grinded on a makeshift dance floor right near the sand. We had to yell to each other over the reverberating bass. More and more people jumped into the pool. Will raised an eyebrow at me and teased me with a crooked smile.

"No," I said, "no swimming tonight. Not with alcohol in me and a full pool."

It was nice to be out with him at a party. There was something romantic about feeling close with him while in a crowd of people. I kissed his lips. "I have to pee." I got up to go to the bathroom.

Jude said, "I'll walk with you. Kendra just texted. She's parking. I'm going to go out front and get her."

As I walked toward the building with Jude, he said, "So you and Will, huh?"

"Yeah."

"You like him?"

"Yeah." I crossed my arms around my chest, suddenly feeling uncomfortable. The sounds of the party had become a distance noise. The breeze blew strands of my hair over my face. Jude leaned in and gently moved them away. "He's lucky." He looked deep into my eyes.

It gave me a shiver.

My neck felt warm. Jude had the uncanny ability to completely disarm me with his eyes. Just like he disarmed all the other women he interacted with.

"Thank you," I said politely, then I turned away, "I gotta pee."

"Alllexx."

"What?" I looked back at him, tentatively.

"Nothing." He looked at me intensely. I could see in his eyes that it wasn't nothing. It was something all right. Something I didn't want to see. And it was totally weird. Jude liked me. Or he wanted me to think he liked me. Maybe it was that he wanted to sleep with me. No. We held eye contact. *He's interested in me, like, maybe, genuinely interested. Why would he like me? I'm not his type. I'm so fucking awkward.*

But even if I was his type, he knew I was with Will now. Was it that kiss at Mary Jane's? That impulsive, meaningless kiss? I was about to explain to him that I had liked Will from the beginning, just to clear up any possible confusion, when he broke my musing with, "I'm not who you think I am."

"Who do I think you are?"

"Some guy who likes to play around."

"I never said that."

"I can see it in your eyes. You don't trust me."

"I never said that."

"You didn't have to."

"Jude. You're Will's friend," I said, hoping he'd grasp the subtext.

"I thought *we* were friends too."

"We are. I hope I didn't give you the wrong idea that night at Mary Jane's. That kiss, it shouldn't have happened. I was interested in Will, you know what I mean." I couldn't believe *I* was trying to let *him* down easy. And as the words spilled from my mouth, he looked so vulnerable, and the vulnerability made him look sexy, sexier than he had already looked. "What do you want from me?"

"I want you to know who I am." He stared into my eyes.

I fought off an uncomfortable grin. I coughed so I had a reason to cover my mouth and hide my lips fighting off the awkward smile. I didn't want to be with him, but the gaze he bestowed upon me made me feel sexy. My back arched. *What are you doing?* I admonished myself. I squared my shoulders and said, "I'll learn who you are. We're friends."

Our eyes met.

"Of course," he broke the silence. He pecked my cheek, then said casually, "I'll meet you back there." He gave me that generous smile of his and rushed off to get Kendra. I stared at the empty space where he had just been, wondering how on earth I could feel so unnerved by his gazes when what I wanted was to be fully committed to Will.

When I went back out to the party, Will sat alone. I sat on his lap and hugged him. "I love it here."

"Me too." He kissed me. "You wanna get another drink?"

"Sure." We went to get more drinks. Mingling with some of Carter's friends, we lost track of time. After about an hour Will looked at his phone, then asked where I thought Jude went.

"I don't know. He went to get Kendra and Mary Jane and said he'd meet us back here."

Will texted him.

No response came.

Around 1:30 in the morning, the party was breaking up. Will and I helped Carter and a few of his friends clean up before going back up to Will's. We were slipping into bed around 2:30 a.m., when Will's phone buzzed with a text. We looked at each other both guessing it was Jude, and sure enough, it was.

I'm downstairs. Are you up? Too drunk to drive.

I squinted at the text, yawning. "Too drunk to drive? He lives close enough to walk, doesn't he?"

"It's a long walk from here. He's all the way north on Collins."

"Oh."

"You sound pissed?"

Was I pissed? "No, just tired." I wasn't pissed. I was uncomfortable thinking of Jude sleeping at Will's. The look in Jude's eyes when he brushed my hair off my face earlier passed through my mind.

You're being stupid, I told myself. Jude gave that look to lots of women, generously showering his attention like rain up north in April. "I'm not who you think I am," he had said. Meaning, he wasn't some guy who played around. I knew there was a lot more to Jude than one would imagine on first glance.

"I'm going to invite him to stay on the couch. Is that OK with you?"

"Sure. It's your place, anyway. But, yeah. And Will, thanks for asking."

I thought I should stay in Will's bedroom with the door closed and let Will talk with Jude, finding out where he disappeared to. But curiosity got the best of me. I slipped a pair of shorts on and went into the living room.

As soon as Jude entered and saw me, he looked deep into my eyes. "Hi. You OK?" I asked, trying not to let that look unnerve me.

"Fine. Better than fine. Fucking fantastic."

Will got Jude some water, sat on the chair and asked what happened.

"Nothing. Mary Jane came with Fred and the four of us went to Blue Tunnel for drinks. Kendra wanted to talk. Alone. And Fred's buddy works at Blue Tunnel. We stopped by to say hey to the dude and time just went by."

"You weren't alone. You were with Mary Jane and her boyfriend," Will said.

"Yeah. But Kendra and I took a long walk on the beach."

"Dude, what are you doing?"

"We're friends. Nothing happened. The woman is unhappy. It's human compassion. What the fuck are we studying to be psychologists for if we aren't offering compassion?"

Will raised his palms in the air. "You're right. Just looking out for you."

Jude wasn't wrong. But I did wonder why Kendra chose Jude to share her problems with. Sure, Jude understood the obstacles to having a public persona, but I couldn't help but think that it had more to do with his charisma.

Jude gave him a drunken wink and A-OK sign. "Dude, I got this."

Will nodded, then put a sheet over the couch and gave Jude a pillow and blanket. "Thanks, man," Jude said to Will as he removed his shirt, exposing his lean and chiseled torso and a tattoo covering the left side of his chest. I looked — no, I gaped. It was a big heart, partially cracked, trickles of blood coming out. It was like he disclosed a private part of himself. A part I wasn't ready to know. And the guy didn't have an ounce of fat.

I looked away and hugged Will around his waist as we walked back into the bedroom. "Did you see his tattoo?" I whispered once we closed the bedroom door.

"I think that's for his ex. She's the one he left the music scene for. The one who made him want to change his life."

Thinking of Jude as a forlorn lover made me sad. "He must feel permanently broken to get a big tattoo like that."

"Some heartbreak never heals. He may never be over it. Or maybe he's impulsive and got the tattoo based on how he felt in the moment, not thinking about the future."

"How freeing."

"Ha, good reframe." He wrapped his arms around me. I nestled against him, falling asleep in his arms so quickly, I didn't even remember closing my eyes.

§

The next morning, Mary Jane called and woke me up to apologize for never making it to the party. I heard Will and Jude talking in the living room. Mary Jane said, "I think Jude and Kendra hooked up last night."

"No. They're friends."

"Like you and Will are *friends*."

My face flushed. "What do you mean?"

"Come on. Give it up already. You two will be married before you ever come clean."

"Fine. Will and I are more than friends."

"Thank you." She sighed heavily into the phone. "I can finally relax now. He's a quiet one, but he seems like a good guy. How's the sex? I have to know."

"I don't kiss and tell, but off the record, amazing. It's not about sex with him though. I like him."

"Of course, you do. But never underestimate the power of a good fuck. And speaking of which, I'm guessing it's only a matter of time before Kendra and Jude do that. Unless they did it last night."

"Why do you say that?"

"Because I saw them together. And I think they like each other. Jude doesn't seem the type to wait. If you know what I mean."

"Yeah. I guess I do."

"Don't say anything to Jude when you see him."

"Why are you telling me at all?"

"Cause I'm worried about Jude. Kendra's husband is a powerful man."

"Jude knows what he's doing. I'm sure."

"I dunno. Kendra told me her husband thought she was having an affair once and threatened to have the guy killed."

"Whaaat? That's crazy. People don't mean things like that when they say them."

"Don't be so naïve, Alex. It happens all the time. And in Florida, every day. Fred and I found a dead body in a bush one day while out on a walk. I can't talk about it though. Never mind," her voiced cracked.

I scratched my head when I hung up. The last thing I wanted to do was get involved in Jude and Kendra's personal lives, especially if her husband was controlling and powerful. I thought I might tell Will what Mary Jane said, though.

When I walked into the living room and said good morning, Will and Jude both looked up and smiled. I went toward Will and hugged him. He hugged me back, tentatively. I felt his distance immediately. Jude noticed it too.

Will grabbed his basketball and said, "We're going to the court. I'll call you later."

"OK," I said, trying to sound casual. But in all honesty, I was annoyed. We had planned to go for an open water swim and then maybe to Key Biscayne for a barbecue. I wanted to say something, but there was no way I was going to make myself vulnerable, especially in front of Jude. In a measured tone, I said, "Have fun." I smiled at them both. I was pretty sure they could tell it was fake.

I moved through my day without giving too much thought to what had happened. Maybe he just wanted to hang out with a guy friend. We were probably spending too much time together anyway. I wished he had been a little less nonchalant about canceling our plans, but really, it wasn't *that* big a deal.

When my phone rang late in the afternoon, I assumed it was Will, but when I looked at the incoming number, I saw that it was Jude.

Chapter 13

Alex

Is there ever a moment that people can pinpoint when things start to change in a relationship? Whether it's moving forward or stepping back? Do most relationships move forward in a linear fashion? Or do they more closely resemble a zigzag or waves in the ocean moving up and down in a rhythmic, but unpredictable cadence?

I knew life was capricious. I knew that even the most stable relationships could break apart. My mother had explained once in one of her relationship seminars that when some relationships break apart, they come back together stronger. Other times, it's like a broken vase glued back together; tiny, unnoticeable pieces go missing that can never make the vase completely whole again. So, though the vase may appear repaired on its surface, water will seep through the invisible cracks. And like that vase, a relationship repaired imperfectly will allow subsequent breaks to be messier and easier to make.

The last line of that lecture stuck with me: *Maybe the only way to fix certain things is to leave them broken.* My mother had explained that sometimes relationships were broken beyond repair, but people keep trying to put it all back together. Sometimes, she had explained, the only way for reparation was to leave the relationship broken and for the couple to go their separate ways.

§

Jude called and invited me to the beach with Will and him. *Why was Jude calling and not Will?* was my thought throughout the entire three-minute conversation. They were picking up some beer. They were going to watch the sunset.

I wanted to ask whose idea it was to invite me, but the question sounded pathetic when I thought about it. I had spent the past year trying to recover my self-esteem from a seemingly unfathomable hole. My mind wandered, momentarily, as I wondered: *Who am I in this?* Was Will drawing an insecurity out of me that I believed I had put behind me?

I shook it off by telling myself I was being ridiculous. I wanted to join them. What did it matter who called? "Yes. Be down in ten minutes," I told Jude.

I threw on shorts and a tank top, swiped a line of brown under my eyes, a swash of mascara, and grabbed a sweatshirt and towel.

As I walked onto the sand outside behind the apartment building, I saw the scatterings of the evening beach dwellers. The sky already had magnificent hues of pink and yellow and purple. The light of the dipping sun hung over the beach, making the outlines of people look almost like shadows. The roar of the waves echoed through the air, sounding infinite.

My feet sunk into the warm mushy sand. I spied Will and Jude sitting on beach chairs. There was a third one empty for me. I felt that insecurity again as I walked toward them. I took a heavy breath. So what if he broke our plans. So what if Jude called instead of him. Why was I making such a big deal about it? I straightened my back as I approached them. "Hey, guys."

Jude looked up first. "Heeeey, Alllexx," he said and shot me his magnanimous smile that somehow felt simultaneously sincere and disingenuous.

"Hey." I smiled back. No matter how uncertain I felt about Jude's smile, it was nearly impossible not to respond to it. But, I quickly diverted my eye contact to Will, whose smile revealed how glad he was to see me.

So, I kissed him hello. He kissed me back, tentatively, his lips barely touching mine, but more than that, I felt his overall detached demeanor. I tried to shrug it off and not reveal my disappointment, my annoyance. I tried to be cool. Casual. Still, my intuition was spot on: Something was off. And again, I wondered if Jude had said something about that meaningless kiss. That bane of my existence.

I sat down. Jude handed me a beer and I took a long gulp. "What were you guys talking about?"

"Women," Jude said, teasingly and winked at me. "Woman," he corrected himself with a more austere expression. I noticed that realness I had seen glimmers of a few times now from Jude. As he continued explaining that they were discussing the demise of his relationship with his ex, he had this vulnerability about him that was inconveniently mesmerizing.

More than that, though, was Jude's warmness juxtaposed with Will's aloofness. Will's distance was so strong it felt tangible, like a physical barrier — impenetrable. The few times I thought to touch his leg or arm, or even get too close to him, his glare felt like daggers in my heart. I was supposedly dating this man. What was wrong? *Had Jude told him about that kiss, that meaningless kiss? Or was it something else?*

I had no clue what made him detach. And so, I was left to fill in the blanks. I told myself I would simply ask for an explanation when we were alone.

"I saw the tattoo on your chest. She really broke your heart, huh?" I continued talking with Jude.

Jude nodded as he took a swig from his bottle.

"What was it about her? I mean, you probably could have had anyone you wanted. And you picked her."

"This probably sounds cliché, but the truth is, Al," he shortened my name, and touched my knee for a second, then quickly retracted his hand. "I know that I'm physically attractive. And true, when I was in my twenties and early thirties, I was a dick. Irresponsible and careless with people's feelings. But as I got a little older, I knew none of the women I went out with really cared about me, either. Sure, they thought they did. But I never let anyone really know me. I was all show, all about the game. Nothing real. I started to feel empty. Lost. Alone. When I met Suzanna, she was working in a restaurant as a waitress to make extra money while going to graduate school for a doctorate in sociology. She didn't know who I was — Jude Booker, *Books*, the musician — and for the first few months, I didn't tell her. I told her I was in banking. I know. I lied. But I lied so that she would get to know the real me. You follow?"

"Yeah. I think I do."

He touched my knee again, and I could hear the emotion welling up, his voice quivering, "Because she didn't get to know the surface Jude, she was able to see the truth of who I was. Me. Me, beneath this fucking image. Me, beneath how I look. Just. Me." He spread his arms wide. "Emotional, sensitive, broody, moody, me. Flaws and all.

"We fell in love. Eventually, I had to tell her the truth. She was pissed at first, but when I explained my reasons, she forgave me. I believed the reason she forgave me was because she really knew me. She was the first person to ever really know me and to touch my heart. I'll always love her for that."

His eyes looked pained, and I reached out to him, taking one of his hands in mine and squeezing it. "I'm sorry that you lost her. And because of a media scandal that wasn't true. I'm sorry that she believed them over you."

"Yeah. Thanks. It's OK now," he said, coughing, trying to shake the emotion from his voice. "I think it was more that she was scared of the lifestyle and the fact that she could and would be exposed to such salacious bullshit than that she believed the story. I don't know for sure. But it made me rethink what I was doing and gave me the impetus to make changes. It was her final gift to me."

"Maybe you could call her and tell her that you've made changes."

"She's engaged. It's over. It's OK. I know what I want now." He gave me a heavy look. I felt bare. Was he saying he wanted me? And in that moment, something hung between us, and I allowed an uncomfortable thought to come fully formulated into my mind: Maybe I wanted him.

Will's voice broke my musing and, thankfully, the moment with Jude. "That's why you've got to be careful with Kendra. Hooking up with her would be like repeating the past you're trying to move away from."

Jude looked at Will. "Yes. And. No. I'm not saying I'm going to get involved with her as more than friends. But I do think she sees who I am. Our talks have been deep."

"Sometimes there's a real fine line between friendship and romance," Will said. I looked at him, but he didn't meet my eyes. Was he insinuating that about us? Stop. I was reading too much into things.

Then Jude said, "Friendship underlies all good romantic relationships."

"How long do you really think you can hang out with a woman you are attracted to, share intimate details of your lives, before something physical happens?"

A vein on the side of my head throbbed. First, he blows me off in the morning, then he's aloof, and now he's saying there's a thin line between friendship and romance. His obvious distance made me think he was talking about us. *He was, right?* Or were my insecurities getting the best of me? I looked at him again, still he didn't meet my eyes. A purposeful avoidance. *Screw him.*

"Why are you so worried about this?" Jude raised an eyebrow at Will. "It almost feels personal."

Will gave Jude a steely look. "I know how hard regret is. You have regrets. I have regrets. Alex has regrets."

Finally, he acknowledged my presence. I wasn't invisible. Still, he didn't look at me. Not even a freaking side glance!

"You said you want to make changes. I do too. I just don't want to see you fucked up over a woman. A married woman is bound to cause your life chaos." His eyes looked almost manic when he finished speaking.

Jude and I exchanged bewildered glances. Of course, Will was right about Kendra being married and not getting involved. But he seemed so impassioned. Too impassioned. *What happened to Will?* I saw that pain he buried deep within him and wanted to hug him, but I felt that wall around him. As I watched him sitting there, a heavy look in his eyes, I longed to reach behind that barrier and pull out the warm, sensitive, passionate man I knew was trapped inside.

There was nothing worse than feeling the potential that resided within him.

Things grew more irritating as the night came to a close. Jude was going home but needed to go up to Will's to gather his belongings. Standing in the elevator with them felt awkward. Unspoken words felt heavy on my tongue, but I wasn't going to go up without being invited. Will said, "Nite," as the elevator approached my floor.

"Nite," I said with a pinch in my tone.

"Nite, Alex," I heard Jude say as I walked out.

I opened the door to my apartment and took a long, frustrated breath. "Carter?" I called out, hoping he was home, so I could vent. I flicked the living room light on. The slightest scent of tomato sauce lingered in the air, and I noticed the pasta strainer in the sink. "Carter." I knocked on his closed bedroom door. No sounds came from his room. I dropped my shoulders. He wasn't home, no sympathetic ear to bitch to.

I called Michael, who didn't answer, but then he sent a quick text. *On a first date. Call you later?*

Sure, I responded back, wondering who the woman was. He hadn't mentioned anyone, but then again, I had been so busy with Will, we hadn't spoken at length in days.

I poured a glass of wine and plopped down on the sofa. How could he be one of the warmest people I had ever met, someone I felt I could drop my guard with, yet also be so cold? How could I fall for someone who was so disrespectful of my feelings?

And even though I wanted to say screw him and never let him near me again, I knew that this distant-Will wasn't who he really was. It was the pain from whatever had happened to him that pushed him to protect himself.

The question came again: *What had happened to Will?* He said he had done something bad. But what?

A knock at my door broke my musings. Even though Will had never shown up unannounced before, I thought it was him. When I walked over and looked out the peephole, I saw Jude standing there, shifting his weight from one foot to the other.

My stomach twisted. I was disappointed that it wasn't Will, and yet I was kind of glad that Jude was there. Maybe he could give me some advice or at the very least maybe he would stay for a drink, a welcome distraction. I opened the door. "Hey."

"Heeeey," he said with that dashing grin across his lips. We shared an intimate gaze. And I immediately felt the sexual tension between us. I polished off the wine I had carried to the door.

"You want a drink." I tried to sound light as I let him in.

"Sure. I'll have what you're having."

I poured him wine and refilled mine. "What's up?" I asked as we sat on the couch.

"I wanted to see if you were OK?"

"Why wouldn't I be?" I said, trying to sound nonchalant.

He tilted his head. "C'mon. You can talk to me."

I took a sharp breath. "About what?"

"Will." He moved closer to me on the couch, resting his hand on my thigh. Electricity coursed through me. I looked at his hand on my skin. I was dying. Even his hands were handsome. "I could tell you were upset tonight."

Our eyes locked. I could see the longing in them. He was irresistibly handsome, but it was his openness that made me want to kiss him. He put his hand on my cheek. While our faces drew closer, my head kept saying, *no, no… you're with Will; you've been sleeping with Will. This is all wrong.*

We both pulled back simultaneously. "Sorry," he said and took my hand in his, weaving his fingers through.

My body tingled at his touch. The room felt sweaty.

"What are you — doing?" I looked at his fingers through mine, I wanted to take my hand back, but didn't. Thankfully a second later, the door knob jiggled, and Carter's laughter echoed into the apartment as he entered.

"Alex." His eyes widened. "Jude." He looked surprised. "Uh, hey," he said trying to sound casual and like he hadn't just witnessed us in an obviously compromising moment.

"Hey." I smiled, awkwardly.

Carter was with a handsome man: tall, broad-shoulders, dark thick hair, dark eyes. A tight tank top revealed a chiseled body. "This is Charlie Duggan."

"Hi, I'm Alex. This is Jude. My *friend*." I added at the end to remind myself what our relationship status was. This was not an indiscriminate relationship. This was a defined relationship, and Carter just rescued me from making a huge mistake. I couldn't let my disappointment and frustration toward Will make me run into the arms of another man, albeit an undeniably attractive one.

Charlie looked Jude up and down, raised an eyebrow and smiled. "Great to meet you both."

Carter looked into my eyes questioning what was going on. I shook my head slightly, indicating that now was not the time to talk.

Charlie sat down on the chair next to the sofa, and Carter plopped on the couch, immediately deflating the mood between me and Jude that had been building only moments earlier. Charlie, a gregarious and animated hottie, was a waiter at The Delano and shared some wild stories about life on South Beach that had us all laughing. Jude kept looking at me. I kept trying not to meet his eyes.

Before Carter and Charlie decided to leave the living room, I said, "I need to go to sleep. This was fun, though." I looked at Jude, hoping he would know that that was his cue to leave and not an invitation into my bed.

"Walk me out?" Jude said as he got up.

I saw Carter observing the exchange, with an eye squinted and an eyebrow raised.

"Sure." I walked with Jude to the door and stepped into the hallway with him.

He searched my eyes. "I did really come down to see if you were OK. I read the disappointment on your face tonight while you were with Will."

"I'm OK."

I looked at him. He was painfully attractive, especially the sincerity I saw when he let his guard drop.

"You are a beautiful woman, Alllexx. Don't let someone treat you like an afterthought."

I felt my eyes well up at his accurate assessment of the situation. I did feel like an afterthought.

"I appreciate that," I said, crossing my arms.

"There's something between *us*. I know it's not just me."

I moved my body slightly away from him. I couldn't think straight when he stood so close. "I dunno what to say. There is an attraction, yes. But I've been with Will. I've been intimate with *him*. I need to remain loyal to that bond and see where it goes."

"You're a good woman." He kissed my cheek. "Good night."

I swallowed hard. "Nite." As he stepped into the elevator, I noticed how broad his shoulders looked from behind. I pulled at the neck of my T-shirt. As the doors closed on Jude staring at me from the elevator cart, I wondered why on earth he wanted me. Was it because he couldn't really have me?

I pulled my hair up into a ponytail. I felt confused. Maybe I loved Will. And though I certainly didn't love Jude, we definitely had a connection. Lust, maybe. Or was it something more?

Carter had his "do tell" face on as soon as I went back into the apartment.

"I don't know what happened. I mean, nothing happened. I don't know what's happening."

"It looked pretty clear to me, to us." He looked at Charlie, who nodded in agreement. "You were about to hook up. Sorry we interrupted."

"No, we weren't." I sat on the couch, put my hands between my knees. "Will was very distant tonight. I don't know why. Maybe he wants to end it but doesn't know how to tell me. Or maybe his distance has nothing to do with me. Jude noticed how cold Will was and came over to see how I was."

I gave them more of the details about the evening. "I want to be with Will. I think. I want the Will that I had all week."

"Personally, I think you should go for Jude," Carter said jokingly. "But seriously, if you feel that way about Will, you need to talk to him."

"That's the thing, I felt like I couldn't."

Carter gave me a pitying shake of his head. "Oh, baby doll, if you can't talk to him, he's probably not good for dating. Problems this early on aren't a good sign. Maybe give it a day. See if he comes to talk, then see how you feel."

"That's what I'm going to do. Thanks." I kissed his cheek, said good night to Charlie and turned in for the evening. I got into bed and stared at the ceiling waiting for sleep to whisk me away from my own thoughts. I could still feel the sensation of Jude's fingers intertwined with mine.

I looked at my phone wishing Will had texted to explain his behavior, but nothing. My last waking thought was how easy and open Jude was.

Chapter 14

Alex

I walked into the classroom, a cup of coffee in one hand, my books and tablet in the other. Will was already seated. As soon as I sat in my chair, he turned and smiled, whispering, "Hi," with a bright happy-to-see-you tone. I felt torn. Part of me was always happy to feel his warmth, the other part of me was irritated.

Driving over to school, my mind vacillated between feeling like he wanted to end the romance and feeling like the distance had to do with something independent of me. Looking at his expression, I decided it must be the latter. "Hi," I said wanting to say more, but feeling like it wasn't the right time.

"Are we swimming tonight?"

I raised an eyebrow. Now he was acting totally normal. He's like Dr. Jekyll and Mr. Hyde. Regardless, it still felt good to hear the warmth in his tone. "Sure," I said, and decided I would ask him about yesterday later in the day.

Waiting for the professor to arrive, Will and I talked about which TV series on Netflix we could binge-watch together. As we went back-and-forth in a teasing banter, it felt like yesterday was a minor wrench thrown into an otherwise nice progression in our relationship. Then I heard *it*: "*Alllexx*. Will," in a low, silky voice. It made me shiver.

Jude came into the room and sat in the empty seat beside me. He wasn't in our personality theories class but plopped down like he was. "What's up you two? Last night was a blast." He smiled at me, and his eyes looked so warm. I had that feeling again, like for a second the world stopped, and I was sucked into his gaze. I sat between them as they talked to each other about getting together to play basketball later in the week.

I was dying. I could feel them both beside me. Jude leaned toward me in order to talk with Will. His hand rested on my desk. I looked at his hand, then quickly shifted my gaze and met eyes with Mary Jane, who smiled and walked over.

"Hey guys. I'm having another intimate gathering this Friday. I hope you're free. Wouldn't be the same without your trio." She winked at Jude.

"I'll be there," I said.

Then Jude and Will nodded in agreement.

Thankfully, Jude got up. "Gotta get to class."

"See you," I said, my body relaxing as soon as he left.

"What's wrong?" Will looked at me.

"Oh, nothing." His questioning glance made me uncomfortable. I rested my hand on my neck, twisting it around like I had a knot, just to avert his gaze. When I turned back, I met eyes with Mary Jane, who raised her eyebrows like she knew something.

But there was nothing to know.

Nothing, other than the fact that Jude's presence affected me because of the way he looked at me. The same way he looked at all women. OK. OK. I was attracted to him, physically. But I didn't want to be with him. Besides, he shouldn't be making innuendos toward me about us; he was Will's friend. For a moment, I wondered if I was inviting it without meaning to. I did enjoy his attention when Will wasn't being attentive, as uncomfortable as it made me.

Walking with Will through the parking lot after class, I heard, "Hey," and I turned to see Michael waving toward us.

"Hey, you, what's up?" I waved back. "You have that rushed look."

"Running late for class. Traffic was awful. Talk to you later," he said, looking at his watch and picking up his pace.

"Sure. Catch up later," I called as Michael hurried off.

"How often do you talk to that guy?" Will asked with thinly veiled irritation.

"Once a week, maybe twice, depending if I run into him here. Why do you always ask me that?"

"What, I can't ask a question?"

I frowned. "You don't like him."

"I don't know him."

"You seem like you don't care for him. Are you jealous?" I elbowed him, teasingly.

He tensed up. "No."

"Jeez, I was joking." I locked my arms in his. "I wish we had come in one car, together."

He seemed distant again for a minute, then finally responded, "Me too. Let's meet at the grocery store and pick up a few things before we go home."

I nodded and smiled, ignoring the figurative whiplash I was suffering from his repeated 180-degree mood swings.

§

That night, Will was caring, available, open. We swam, made dinner, studied, then fell asleep wrapped around each other watching a movie. I decided not to bring up anything, because I didn't want to make everything heavy and serious. I mean, the very essence of *falling* in love is not knowing where you'll land. The uncertainty of it all.

As the weeks went by, Will and I settled into a rhythm. Whatever attraction I had felt for Jude passed. I believed it was only because I needed his attention in the face of Will's distance. Besides, who wouldn't be flattered by attention from Jude.

About a month later, Carter invited Will and me to a South Beach VIP party at an exclusive club called Illusion. Charlie knew the owner and was able to get our names on the list. Will had an exam the next day and couldn't go, so I went with Carter and Charlie.

White mist filled the club from a fog machine set to overdrive. Club music blasted from speakers, and people were grinding against each other wearing all sorts of wild, provocative clothing. One woman sporting a bikini, her butt cheeks bared for all to see, danced with a guy who had a huge white afro tinted like a rainbow. He squeezed her ass, pushing himself into her. Another guy came up behind her and rubbed up against her back; his crotch grinded against the other guy's hand which was still on the woman's ass. People were hooking up on the couches that surrounded the dance floor. One woman didn't have a shirt or bra on at all. And although I had been to numerous New York City clubs, I had never seen anything quite as wild, subversive and decadent as this.

"It's very free here," I yelled to Carter over the music.

"Isn't it fabulous?" he yelled back, taking my hand as we walked toward the VIP section. Smoke rose from the floor, blowing my dress above my thighs. I quickly smoothed it down my legs, following Carter through the thick crowd.

We stepped up into the VIP section. A small group of people lounged on the plush sofas. Various bottles of alcohol filled the tables. Everyone was dressed sexy and hip, unique. I looked down at my plain red dress and felt self-conscious. It was a silky dress with thin straps. When I had left the apartment, I thought I looked good, but in the presence of the people wearing things like platform boots that reached up to their knees, short shorts and halters showing off their perfectly sculpted bodies, I felt out of place. And awkward.

Carter handed me a drink.

"Whoa, girl," he said, as he watched me down it.

He gave me another and said, "Here, let me introduce you," gesturing toward two men seated on a big, white couch. "This is Victor, and this is Rock." He turned toward them and said, "This is my beautiful, fabulous and charming roommate, Alex."

Victor wore a white button-down shirt and washed out jeans, black shoes that looked expensive. His hair was dark, and his eyes were blue. The candles that lit the VIP area flickered off his face, revealing his chiseled cheekbones. Everyone who was into the club scene on South Beach was impossibly beautiful.

They smiled with welcoming faces. I sat. The three of us chatted for a couple of minutes until Rock suddenly kissed Victor on the lips and they hurried off to the bathroom.

Victor returned ten or so minutes later without Rock. I noticed him eyeing me. I sipped my drink nervously, then to fill the space I asked, "So, how long have you two been together?"

"Me and Rock," he shook his head, "we're not really together."

"Oh, sorry. I saw you kiss. I just thought. Never mind. So, tell me about your work. You said you were a photographer. What's that like?"

"It's wonderful. Especially down here. I often do modeling shoots on the beach or along The Drive." He put his hand on my thigh. "Maybe I can take your photo?" He smiled. The flickering light gave the illusion that his eyes had a flirtatious spark in them.

I looked at his hand on my thigh and inched away.

Then he took tendrils of my hair and ran them through his fingers. "Your hair is naturally wavy. Stunning. With the right stylist, you would look like a cover model. Your cheekbones are nice too." He moved my face side-to-side, observing me with detached curiosity.

My cheeks burned. He inspected me like a fine piece of art. And although, I thought he was just being nice — I definitely did not look like a model, not even close — I enjoyed the compliment. "I'm not photogenic. But, thank you."

"You are. Believe me. This is my profession."

I laughed generously. "I really appreciate that. You have made my day."

Then he gazed into my eyes intensely. "I'm not gay."

"But I thought... I mean, I don't care, and it's none of my business, but I thought I saw you kissing, Rock."

"Ah, yes. It's a messy situation with Rock. He is interested, and we work together. I've tried to let him down easy, but he just keeps trying."

"But didn't you two go to the bathroom to have sex?"

"You know the saying: What stays in Club Illusion bathrooms stays in Club Illusion bathrooms." Then he waved it off. "But that doesn't matter." Then, he took my hand, wove his fingers through and unabashedly said, "I like you. You're very natural. I appreciate that. And smart. I like an educated woman."

Our palms were touching, and I felt uncomfortable. I looked over at Carter, who was making out with Charlie on a couch. "I'm dating someone, but I appreciate the compliment." I unlocked my hand from his and moved slightly away from him.

"Is it serious?"

"Yes. I think so."

Rock came back, thankfully, smiling at Victor with bedroom eyes. The whole thing perplexed me, and although I didn't want to be rude, I got up abruptly and said, "Nice to meet you both."

Victor smiled but looked disappointed.

I went to the bathroom. When I came out, I found Carter and Charlie on the dance floor, so I joined them. I kept noticing Victor looking toward us, his gaze fixed on me. I kept moving behind other people to block his gape.

About a half hour later, suitably tipsy and tired, I decided to go home. I said goodbye to Carter and Charlie, sneaking out without having to converse with Victor again. His ogle made me feel grubby, like his sweaty palms were wandering along my skin.

As soon as I stepped outside, the ring of quiet filled my ears. I texted Will and asked if he wanted to come over. I felt lonely. Clubs did that to me. The atmosphere was so pumped, so thick with people, and yet there was no real connection.

My walk home was under five minutes. Will still hadn't texted back by the time I got home. It was midnight, so I assumed he was sleeping. I started to get ready for bed, pulling at my ear lobes, trying to shake out the lingering whistle.

I was changing when I heard Carter and Charlie laughing as they walked into the living room. "Hi guys," I hollered from my bedroom.

I had just slipped into a black satin nightshirt and boy shorts when there was a knock on the front door. I smiled. *It must be Will*, I thought. I heard muffled voices, then a knock on my bedroom door.

"Come in."

The door creaked open, and my jaw dropped. Victor stood in my bedroom. "What are you doing here?" I pulled a sweatshirt on and zipped it all the way up. I could feel the intensity coming off him, his penetrating blue eyes undressing me.

He stepped in. "Can we sit? I wanted to talk with you."

"How did you know where I lived?"

"I followed you."

"What?"

"I can't remember ever being so taken with a woman. And I'm around beautiful women all the time. You have an allure, Alex. You don't know how beautiful you are, and that has me captivated."

My brain spun. Here was this successful, older (I thought early 40's), dignified, beautiful man saying these flattering things, but I was sure he had kissed Rock. Maybe he was bisexual. He must be. "I really appreciate your attention. I am flattered. Really. But I am dating someone. Remember."

"It's because of Rock, isn't it? I explained that. I prefer women."

"I don't care about that. Sexuality can be gray. It's not about Rock, it's about Will, the guy I'm with."

He moved closer, crossing the line into my personal space. "He's a very lucky man." He moved closer, and I could smell his minty breath. I backed away. He leaned in, kissing my cheek right as Carter shouted, "Alex?" He sounded uncertain. The wetness from the kiss lingered on my skin.

"What?"

"Um…"

I turned, and Will stood in the doorway. His face creased with anguished confusion, as he swung his gaze between Victor and me.

"Will. Hi." My eyes shot open. The look of agony splayed across Will's face made me feel like I was guilty of something even though I hadn't done anything wrong.

His eyes were fixed on mine.

"Will." I reached for his hand.

He shook off my grasp.

Victor slipped out of the bedroom door. Will glared at him until he disappeared into the hallway. The tension, so palpable, you could slice it. Sweat broke out along my neck, as I stared helplessly at Will. "It's not what it looks like."

He didn't budge. "What is *it* then?" His face turned red. He spoke in a measured tone, but I could tell he was about to explode. "You invited me down, and I walk in on you with another man in your bedroom. You're wearing short shorts. What the fuck? Who are you?"

"Will." I pulled on him, desperate for him to listen to me. "Please. You know I would never do that. Ever. The guy followed me home."

As we argued, I heard a man yelling in the living room, and Carter trying to quell the commotion. "Where is *he*?"

I heard the voice coming closer toward my bedroom. "I know he's here." Rock, the guy from the bar who was with Victor, stormed into my bedroom flailing his arms and showing a crazed look.

Carter tried to buffer with, "He's not. Calm down. Have a drink." He put his arm around Rock, trying to maneuver him out of my bedroom.

Rock shook Carter off.

Will's jaw tightened, and his hands were clenched at his side.

Rock, with his feral eyes, said, "I followed him. I saw how you draped yourself all over him. Where is *he*?"

Will turned purple. "You lied. You just lied to my face."

"No. I didn't. This is all a big, crazy misunderstanding."

Carter said to Will, "Let's just all sit down and work this out."

"Hell no. I want to know what that guy was doing here, *Alex*."

Rock said, "She," he pointed a furious finger at me, "spent all night with him, flirting with her long hair and teasing eyes. Victor followed her home, and who knows what happened. I'm guessing they had sex." He pierced me with his eyes.

"*That* is not what happened," I begged, my voice catching. "He was coming on to me and I told him I was with someone, someone I really liked." I looked at Will, feeling totally vulnerable as the words spilled out. "But he followed me home anyway. Why would I text you to come over if there was someone else here?"

Rock said again, "Where is he?"

Carter rested his hand on Rock's shoulder and said, "He's not here. Look." He waved his arm around my bedroom. "Let's have a drink, and you'll call him."

Rock shook his head and with a sour look gave a defeated sounding, "Fine." He walked out with Carter.

I looked up at Will waiting for him to answer me.

"Because you probably thought I'd call or text first and then you could get him out before I came. I can't think. I can't talk to you." He gave me another angry, pained glare and said, "And to think I trusted you. I am so fucking stupid. I thought I knew you. My mistake." He threw his arms into the air and turned to leave.

I pulled on him, tears stung behind my eyes. "Will, you do know me. That's what I'm saying. Think, think. Why would I hurt you like this?"

"I can't talk to you right now." He moved away from me. "Don't call me." I watched as he walked away.

"Will," I called after him in a weak voice, knowing he was already gone.

What just happened? I didn't do anything. And despite trying to fight the tears, they trickled down my cheeks.

§

I paced in my bedroom, trying to piece together what the hell just happened. Did Will overreact? Carter had said it was all a *big misunderstanding* and I should go upstairs and talk to Will, even though he had told me not to call him. I walked back and forth across my bedroom floor, trying to figure out what to do. I kept seeing the pained look on his face, the creases of anguish. I decided I should go upstairs and try to explain what happened — again. I threw on longer shorts and went up.

My stomach knotted as I knocked on his door. "Will. Please. Let me explain."

My stomach jumped all around. I shifted my weight back and forth. I knocked again, harder this time, my voice catching, "Will. It's all a big misunderstanding."

I put my ear up to the door but heard nothing.

I knocked one more time, leaning my head against the door. "Please, talk to me," I said, my voice languishing, "that guy stormed into my bedroom uninvited. He came onto me. Think about how I feel." Tears stung behind my eyes. I couldn't believe he wouldn't open the door and it started to piss me off. "You know, I am just as upset as you are that he came into my bedroom. I can't believe you don't see what really happened."

I dragged my feet into the elevator, defeated, but anger sat in my stomach. His dismissiveness was getting under my skin. It would be nice to have a man who would protect me instead of one who was too busy protecting himself.

Chapter 15

Will

He heard her banging and banging, calling his name. He stood very close to the door. He wanted to open it but wouldn't let himself.

She stood in short shorts with another guy. What the fuck? He had let her close and now look what happened. Exactly what he knew would. Someone got hurt. This time it was him. More than that was her audacity, the way it happened. How could she text him to come over while the other guy was still there?

Wait. Wait. Wait. Chill out, Will, chill out. He knew sometimes when it came to girls his mind would spiral down the path to the worst-case scenario. His therapist had told him that that was called catastrophizing: anticipating (and then fucking worrying about) the worst-case scenario. A cognitive distortion, Dr. Jon Ballad, his therapist, had taught him. Now, of course, Will knew the term from studying psychology. But back in the day, it was Jon, the guy who practically saved his life, who explained the term.

The other thing he learned all too well was that knowing something intellectually, rationally, was very different than knowing something emotionally. Alex continued to knock at the door. The banging made it impossible for him not to feel pulled toward her. Man, she was right outside the door. All he had to do was open it, reach out to her and he could be wrapped around her.

At the same time, he was pissed at her. Whatever actually happened downstairs with that wealthy older guy — grow up in poverty and you can smell money from a mile away — he couldn't be sure. He thought he knew Alex. And he was usually good at intuiting who people were. Partially a gift, as Jon would say — being intuitive — and partially a heightened sense he needed to navigate his way around his home growing up.

The more he could sense the way his family wanted him to act, to be, the better he was at not getting yelled at or hit. The yelling was way worse than the hitting. His father's diatribes could last days, especially when he felt Will *was not listening.* And according to the philosophy of Dave Easton, listening meant not doing what Will wanted, and only doing what his father wanted. Quit school, so he could work at the factory and help out at home with money. Will was in 8th grade when these fights started.

Bang, bang, bang. "Will. Please." He heard her calling through the door. He ran his hand over his face and took a heavy breath. She would have to be an entirely different person than he had thought she was for her to have been having sex with that guy. But if they weren't hooking up, what the fuck was he doing there? When he saw her, half dressed, her hair cascading down her shoulders in that wavy stream he found so attractive, with another man, it felt like a knife sliced through his chest. Then he felt the impulse to punch the guy in his face. This thing with Alex had already gone too far.

Yet, he wanted to fling open that door and be with her. She had looked so sexy. He loved when she wore short shorts or better yet when she was naked. He loved feeling her bare skin under his fingers. She belonged to him in those moments.

He kept having flashes of punching the guy and seeing a splatter of blood come out of his silvered-spooned nose. But, he didn't want to let himself explode like that. Even if she hadn't slept with the guy — the thought made him want to throw something — she never should have been alone with him dressed like that in her bedroom.

Fuck that.

He had to stay away from her.

He looked over at the door as she continued to bang, his jaw tight, his eyes heavy. He felt himself wanting to open the door and be with her.

Be strong, he admonished himself. *Go away. Please. Just go. Leave me the fuck alone.* Then, as if she heard him, the knocking stopped. He heard the shuffling of her feet as she walked away. A wave of relief washed over him. But when he heard the elevator door open and the sound of her feet getting on, all he wanted was for her to come back and try again.

He spent the whole night tossing and turning, thinking about her.

Chapter 16

Alex

When I woke up, if you could call it waking up when I had barely slept, I ambled into the kitchen for a strong cup of coffee. My eyes were half closed and aching. I had a splitting headache and a queasy stomach. Suffice it to say, it was not a good morning. I scooped out the coffee grinds, poured the water in, then hit the "on" button. As the coffee brewed, I popped two Advil and downed a bunch of Gatorade.

I didn't want to go to class. I didn't want to do anything, except lay in bed watching cheesy television or reading a trashy novel, indulgences that I never had time for during the semester. The last thing I wanted to do was to see Will.

I had spent the night going around and around and around about what had happened. I wish I could tell you that I hadn't. I wish I could tell you that I was one of those women who could simply say, "Fuck him. If he's not willing to talk, then I've got nothing to say to him."

But that's not how I felt. Or who I was. I had always been a sensitive person with tons of little cracks, and as strong and self-reliant as I could act, it took very little for someone to slip through those cracks and hurt me.

That being said, in the mess of my ruminations, tears and stomach knots, I did realize that Will controlled the intimacy with his tendency to distance. I didn't know if it was something I could accept long term.

I had aged five years in my restless sleep as I contemplated every last detail of our relationship, trying to figure out what I felt. What I wanted. And why he seemed to be able to affect me so much.

So, I tossed it around and around, but like a leaf caught in the wind, the thoughts circled all around, but ultimately like the leaf that landed back where it started — on the ground — my thoughts ended where they started, with me not knowing what to do or how I felt.

I wanted someone who would fight for me.

And yet, I loved him. And I wanted him.

When the coffee was ready, I poured a mug and went onto the balcony. It was close to eight in the morning. The air was warm and moist, and the sun was bright. The constant sound of crashing waves and blowing palm trees was broken by the occasional staccato of chirping birds. I inhaled the warm, humid air, taking in the freshness of morning.

I peeked out at the pool, pretending to myself that I wasn't looking to see if Will was swimming, even though I was.

He wasn't.

I sipped my coffee, barely tasting it. I had to push myself to go to class. I could not let this guy (love him or not) affect my future.

I made myself eat oatmeal. I poured a ton of maple syrup on, so it would be sure to go down. I showered and got dressed.

I went to all my classes in a haze. Will and I didn't have class together on Fridays, which was basically a relief. And yet, part of me wanted to see him. It's crazy how he made me want two contradictory things at the same time. I looked for him in the hallways, in the library, and to my chagrin, I kept checking my fucking phone thinking he would cool off and text me.

Nothing from him all day. He just vanished. I looked for him again by the pool when I arrived home after class. I kept fantasizing that he would come barreling toward me in a rush of passion.

I called Mary Jane. Kendra was having a party later. I had planned to go with Will and Jude, which obviously wasn't the plan anymore. And even though I knew there was a good chance that Will would still go, I wanted to go anyway, partially to get out and be around people, and partially because I wanted to see him.

I explained the whole story to Mary Jane, who said, "That sucks. But on the upside, Will must be falling for you. He only got that mad and overreacted cause he must feel something pretty intense."

"What good is that if he's not talking to me anymore? He told me not to call him. I think it's over. I'm not sure I can be with someone who has such a hard time talking." As the words spilled from my mouth, I remembered the conversation with Will when he had told me that he wasn't a good communicator. We had said that we would write things when we couldn't say them. Was I shutting the door too soon? Was I going back on the promise I had made to him? Or was I making excuses for him?

"Come to the party with me. He'll probably be there, and maybe it will work itself out. Sometimes the beginnings of relationships are the hardest. People always say the beginning is the easiest, but two people trying to let their guards down and be open to intimacy can be hard too. See what happens."

"If you were me, would you reach out to him again?" I asked.

"Hmmm... you know I don't believe in absolutes, so I can't say for sure. But with this guy, I think I would wait. He sounds like he needs some space."

"Yeah, I don't believe in absolutes either. I wish I did sometimes. It would make decisions like this easier."

"True. But then you would be rigid and conventional, and we wouldn't be friends."

We shared a laugh. "I guess I'll wait and see what he does."

"That's a good plan, chickee. We'll have fun tonight. Fred's going out with the guys. I'm flying solo. Come over and we can go together. She lives close by."

"Eight o'clock?"

"'Perfect. And puh-lease wear something sexy. Show off that perfect body of yours. We're all sick of wondering what's under those loose jeans. Besides, it will make it harder for Will to ignore you."

"Ha ha. True, but mystery is also good."

Feeling better after we hung up the phone, I decided to take a much-needed nap before the party.

Will

He had wanted to call her all day. In fact, he couldn't stop thinking about her, but he told himself no, no, no. He had to stay away from her. Even if she hadn't slept with that guy last night, she had let him into her room. She had been half-dressed. It made him furious, and he just could not pick up the phone to talk to her, though he wanted to. The girl made his head spin.

As the day wore on, he wondered why she didn't try to call him again. Maybe she didn't really care about him at all. Why didn't she try harder? She was the one who did something wrong, not him.

Jude called around six o'clock to find out what time Will and Alex wanted to leave.

"It's just me," Will said with a tight voice.

"Oh? What happened?"

He didn't want to get into it with Jude. It felt too private, although he would probably tell him eventually. "We had a… disagreement. It's done, man. I hope we can get past any awkwardness eventually and be friends again. It's gonna be a long four years if we can't."

"I'm sure you will. You were only hooking up for a couple of months."

"We hung out for a while as friends first. We were tight, man. But I can't be with her."

"Why?"

"It's not right. It's not what I want long-term." And when he said that, he realized that was the truth. He couldn't be with Alex long-term, because once she realized who he was, where he came from, she would leave him. That's what really had bothered him about the guy. That older, sophisticated, wealthy guy was who he pictured her with, not him. Heat coursed through him at the insight. He felt the humiliation that he had felt his whole life growing up with his family and the absolute mortification he experienced the night the whole ugly truth came out right in front of Bethany. His face creased as the memories of that night entered his mind. He shook his head to rid himself of the thoughts. "I don't love her," his lips twisted as the lie resisted coming out.

"Really, how do you know? You said yourself it's only been a couple months."

"Come on, Jude, you can tell if you're going to fall within two or three dates. It's not going to happen. Better to end it now before I get more involved. I mean, our lives are completely interwoven: school, friends, we live in the same building."

"Huh. I'm surprised, but I get it. Sometimes things seem perfect on paper, yet for some reason you don't feel it. Chemistry: one of the greatest mysteries of life," Jude joked to lighten the conversation and Will's heavy-sounding mood.

"Let's not talk about it anymore. What time you want to meet up?"

"Eight? Nine?"

"Come by at eight, and we'll go from here."

When he hung up with Jude, he wanted to go for a swim, but he felt exhausted from the lack of sleep. Figuring it was going to be a late night, he set his alarm for 7:30 and took a nap.

Chapter 17

Kendra

Kendra put red lipstick on, puckered her lips at the mirror and blew a kiss. George was away, so she put on a sexy outfit: a short skirt with a tight, sleeveless tank and red stiletto heels. At forty-nine, she had to admit, she looked pretty good. Looking good and feeling good were two different things, though. And the truth was, straddling the line of the BIG 50 was causing her emotions to be all over the place. She had always been a neat and tidy person, emotions included. Until last year, between noticing her skin slightly hanging in places it never did (she had been fit her whole life), George's political endeavors making her vulnerable to constant publicly posted photographs and George's affair with the young neighbor — he didn't know she knew, but she did (she even had pictures of some of their liaisons) — her emotions rode the roller coaster.

Ultimately, she did what she thought she should. George was away for a week, so she decided to have a big party. And good news: Will Easton, the young, handsome man from her statistics class, was coming. She had called Jude earlier to confirm and was thrilled to hear he would be there. She had a good rapport with Jude. He was easy to get to know. But Will, on the other hand, was quiet, reserved, guarded and very appealing. The man oozed masculinity. All she could think about when she looked at him was that he had a passion simmering beneath the surface of that quiet persona, and she wanted it to be unleashed toward her. She wanted to let him have access to every part of her.

She had only been with one other man besides George, a one-night stand right before George and she were engaged. She had wanted to experience another dick before she was tied down for the rest of her life. That man's name was Roger and the sex had been amazing. He was large and wide and smooth.

She had been faithful though their whole marriage, but now that she knew about George and Adeline, she decided that she wanted to experience another man. That man had remained faceless until Will Easton walked into their statistics class that first day. Wow. She took one look at him and thought: *Him.*

He wasn't easy, though. And he was always with that girl (yes, girl, she was barely developed, too thin, no tits). She had assumed they were only friends. A man who looked like that would never want a girl — woman — who didn't keep up with her appearance the way men liked. George's friends' wives all were polished and manicured.

Jude had mentioned a few things here and there, which made her realize that Will and Alex were lovers. She didn't care. She was still going to charm him into bed. Jude was dreamy, too, and she could tell he was just about dying to kiss her but held back. Probably because he thought she would say no. A married woman. She would kiss him, though. That was the beauty of her situation, she didn't have to worry about love or commitment. It was purely physical. A new tongue, a new dick, a new experience.

Yes, she would kiss Jude. She would sleep with him too. But she was more attracted to Will. Maybe it was because his stoicism intrigued her. She had spent her life around extroverted people and a lot of supercilious men in politics. Will seemed the antithesis. She wanted to see what he looked like underneath. She wanted to see him naked.

If he had this thing going with Alex, she would wait and see what happened. She'd never met a man who could keep their dick exclusive to one woman. If for some reason Will was the exception, she'd take Jude instead. As she put some mascara on, she thought maybe she'd have them both. Maybe even at the same time. She ought to take advantage of this time in her life when she knew she still looked sexy — dressed or otherwise.

Chapter 18

Alex

Driving to Mary Jane's, the traffic inching along on Collins Avenue at a snail's pace, thoughts of Will would not relent. I kept replaying the moment he came down and found me in my bedroom with Victor.

It didn't look good. Even Carter had said that it didn't look good. But he also said that Will overreacted. Carter had called Will "tight."

"Tight?" I had asked, not knowing what he had meant.

"He holds things in, you can feel his intensity, but he tries to come off calm and easy-going. You're really only just getting to know him."

"I guess," I had said. "But we've spent a lot of time together."

"And how much has he really shared about himself?"

I had contemplated. "Some. I never trust people who share everything right away. It shouldn't be easy to expose yourself."

He had tilted his head. "Fair enough. Let me ask you something. Do you know anything deeply personal about him other than his ideas about psychology and philosophy?"

I had nodded, reticently. He was right. "OK. Fine. But we have an intuitive connection. That's stronger than words."

"Maybe, but if he can't trust you enough to share things — fears, his past, what's upsetting him — or if you feel like he won't let you talk to him, you've got bigger problems than the initial 'falling in love' phase." He had put his arm around me to be reassuring. "I know deep down you must know what I'm saying."

I knew he was right, but it was confusing. It's rarely clear when it's about yourself. That's why therapists need therapists. There was no denying there was something strong between us, yet I knew there was something he had been keeping hidden. Pain buried behind a wall he had used to seclude himself. I didn't want to share that with Carter. But what Carter had said made me realize that Will had trust issues. He reacted to the Victor situation too intensely, because he already anticipated a trust violation. I knew if we were ever going to be in anything steady or solid, we would have to talk about that.

The look of agony on his face when he saw Victor in my room kept emerging into my consciousness, making me feel guilty and sorry for something I didn't even do. I released a frustrated breath.

This wasn't good for me. Will wasn't good for me. I didn't like feeling that he had this control over me. Maybe that's what falling in love really was, the precarious exhilaration of descending, weightless, free, enveloped in euphoric emotions, suspended in time, nothing outside of the feelings and relationship affecting your joy, only the two of you in a bubble of unfathomable passion — so helplessly enamored with each other.

Then — *plop* — reality hits. You can't float around without eventually landing. Maybe you can't choose who you fall into the amorous abyss with, either, but you can choose who you want to be with when you hit the ground.

§

Mary Jane was waiting right in front of her condo in a short, skin-tight, sky blue dress, matching shoes and handbag. Her hair looked wildly curly. "Hi, chickee." She scooted in and kissed my cheek. She looked me up and down while cracking her big wad of gum. "What is with you and the knee length skirts? Not that you don't look good, 'cause you do, but you could be much sexier, especially with those legs."

I tilted my head. "I'm not hiding. I'm just wearing what I am comfortable wearing. Just like you are. Right?"

Mary Jane puckered her lips like a tulip. "See. I told you we are similarly subversive. Just because we express it differently on the outside doesn't mean it's not the same on the inside."

"Can't judge a book by its cover."

"Very true," she said, then cocked her head. "So how are you feeling about the Will problem?"

"Better. I've decided to make it a non-problem."

"Oh?" she raised her eyebrows.

"Yeah. He's not right for me. I shouldn't be feeling like this. I've never had a man come so close then pull back so far. I can't believe that someone I'm the closest to is the same person I can feel the most distance with. I'm done."

"Interesting." Mary Jane raised a purposeful eyebrow.

"What?"

"That you think I would buy into that load of crap or that I would let you plunge yourself into a pool of denial."

"I'm not in denial."

"How can you deny being in denial? It's so obvious. Of course, this is one of the elements of psychoanalysis that perturbs me, anything can be a defense mechanism. But in this case, I know I'm right. I can tell by how strongly you're saying it. You care a lot."

"I didn't say that I didn't care. I can care and decide it's not right for me. It's called making good decisions. Listening to your head instead of your heart. Your heart can fool you."

"Your heart can also break. And I think your head is trying to seal back the little bit of your heart he has bruised and protect it from someone who could split it right down the middle. You don't want to play it safe."

She was right, but that didn't mean I was going to listen. I didn't like the way his distance made me feel. "I guess, we'll see what happens. In any case, I feel good." And I did. As long as I didn't think about him.

§

Kendra opened the front door. "Hi, girls," she said with a bright smile. She kissed and hugged both of us. "Come in."

We walked through a hallway into a living room with a high rounded ceiling and a long brown couch that wrapped around a big glass table; two love chairs sat on either side; a huge screen TV, modern artwork and some family photos hung along the walls.

Behind the living room, there were sliding doors to the outside. A long, wide pool, with wooden furniture surrounding it, sat in front of a huge lake. I saw the dark green water glistening from inside. A group of people were already outside. I wondered if Will was out there. I figured he'd come with Jude. Or maybe he wouldn't come at all. My stomach clenched with disappointment as the thought flitted through.

Kendra guided us into the kitchen, and said, "A few people are outside. There's beer out there. Mixed drinks and wine in here. So ladies, what's your poison?" She smiled warmly.

"Who's here already?" I asked, trying to sound nonchalant.

"A few women I do clinic hours with at the hospital. They're very nice. I'll introduce you. And Sylvia, Ricky, Gabby and Tory. I've invited at least 20 more people who said they were coming. Where's Jude and Will?"

I felt uncomfortable answering, but I had to say something. "I don't know exactly."

"Oh, I thought you were all coming together."

"I decided to come with Mary Jane."

Kendra looked into my eyes. "Are you OK, sweetie? You looked upset when you said that."

The thing with hanging around a bunch of graduate students in psychology, everyone was perceptive or thought they were, making it hard to get away with even small untruths, the kind that were only meant to protect privacy. Like this one.

"I'm fine. Just a long day. I need a cocktail. How about a margarita?"

"Coming right up."

Mary Jane asked for a blue martini to match her outfit, of course.

The bell rang just as Kendra finished with the drinks. "Go outside. I'll get the door and meet you out there. Go mingle."

"Alex and Mary Jane," Gabby greeted us with her raspy voice as soon as we stepped outside, and she kissed us both on the cheek. Tory, Sylvia and Ricky came over, as well. I didn't really know any of them other than to say hello in class or the hallways, except for Gabby who was in a clinical seminar with Mary Jane, Will, Jude and me.

"Did you bring your suits?" Gabby asked.

"I did." I said. "Although, I doubt I'll go in."

"I thought you were a swimmer."

"I am. But that doesn't mean I wade in the pool. Let me have a couple of drinks. I might change my mind."

Mary Jane said, "I didn't bring a suit. Who needs one." She chuckled. "If you all are uncomfortable and need me to cover myself, I'll go in my underwear. That's all a bathing suit is anyway, underwear."

"You crack me up." I put my arm around Mary Jane.

A few more people joined us out back. No one I knew well, just familiar faces from class. This was a good opportunity for me to meet new people to spend time with, now that it was over with Will.

"Hey," I heard Michael's voice from behind, as he wrapped his arm around my shoulder and planted a kiss on my cheek.

I looked up at him, smiling warmly. "I didn't think you were coming," I said, feeling relieved to see him. His brown eyes crinkled in the corners when he smiled.

"Gabby convinced me in class today to try and get someone to cover my shift at the restaurant. And I did. Where's—"

I gave him a severe look.

He shook his head knowingly, put his arm around me again and whispered in my ear, "You deserve someone who knows your value. Don't forget that."

I leaned my body against his.

Gabby walked over and the three of us started talking about school, gossiping about our professors, then about sports we enjoyed. Nothing deep; nothing complicated. Gabby weaved her arm around Michael's at one point. I wondered if she was interested in him, and if he would be interested in her. Michael dated a lot, but he said he hadn't been in a serious relationship in about three years, since he was thirty.

Michael asked Gabby and me if we wanted go surfing or waterskiing with him one day. "I've been asking Alex for weeks," he said, elbowing me. "I think she's scared but is too proud to admit it."

"I'm not scared. It's just been hard to schedule the time. I wanna try it."

Gabby chimed in, "Maybe I'll try. I'm not that athletic, but I am exceptionally skilled at hanging out on boats." She laughed, placing her arm on Michael's shoulder, affectionately.

As the evening wore on, more people arrived. Every time I heard the screen door, I felt a shiver of nervousness thinking it was Will. When it wasn't, I felt a twisted combination of relief and disappointment.

Around ten o'clock, people started going into the pool. That's when Kendra came out in a string bikini with a thin wrap. Will and Jude walked out beside her. My heart plummeted into my stomach as soon as I saw him.

I focused on Michael, narrowing my vision to his face, his lips, his eyes. Jude came right over and interrupted my concentration with his usual flirty, "Heeey, Alllexx." I smiled politely, but Jude's presence was now an extension of Will's, making me feel uncomfortable. I assumed he knew what had had happened.

Jude took Gabby's hand, and kissed the back of it. She smiled, flashing him her big doe eyes. Jude walked toward a table with her hand in his, as if they had come together.

I stood with Michael, feeling self-conscious, when I felt Will come up behind me. "Hello," he said to Michael, stiffly, then he locked eyes with mine and said, casually, "Alex. Hey."

"Hey." I looked up at him. I was dying to touch him, but I stood with my back straight and tried not to show an ounce of emotion. My nerves made my breath catch and my heart pound. *He* made my breath catch and my heart pound. I only hoped he didn't notice.

But he barely held my gaze, and without another word went and sat with Jude and Gabby. Kendra moved a chair over and joined them.

I didn't mean to hurt you, Will, but you are hurting me too! I watched as he moved his chair closer into the circle they sat in. I felt his distance even though he wasn't near me anymore, almost like he had left a tangible space. His absence was a presence. Who knew an empty space could take up so much room.

I talked with Michael, trying my hardest to stay focused on his words. I could tell he was trying to keep me entertained with South Beach stories: the celebrities and socialites that came into the bar he worked in, their dramas and entanglements; intimacies that people were more comfortable sharing with a stranger than those close to them. He had always said that being a bartender was good training for being a therapist. "People ask for my advice all the time. Some of my regulars even call me Doc."

In between his words, he kept giving me a warm, sympathetic look. A couple of times he shot a look over at Will, then he finally asked, "Are you alright? We could go for a walk if you want to talk."

I shrugged my shoulders. "Am I that easy to read?"

"I just know you. And your eyes look sad. Let's go for a walk."

"No. That's OK. I'm OK. I'm just over it, that's all."

Michael raised a disbelieving eyebrow, but let it go.

"You were telling me about your trip to Hawaii. I'm dying to go there. Tell me more." I begged him.

Michael's adventurous spirit made everything seem interesting, because he was so enlivened when he spoke about his experiences. I listened to him talk, trying my hardest to focus on his lips moving, the sound of his deep voice, but I couldn't control my eyes. They kept wandering back over toward Will.

Every time I looked at him, he stared back at me, sending a shiver down my spine. He would break the gaze first and go back to his conversation, and I would go back to mine.

A few minutes later I noticed that Kendra moved her chair closer to him, and he had angled his toward hers, their knees practically touching. It hurt to see his knee doing that dance with Kendra's the way he used to do with mine.

I shifted my position, so my back was to them, which was better, but I still felt his eyes boring a hole into my back. A few minutes later Michael asked me if I wanted to go inside and get another drink.

"Yes," I said with too much zeal, just relieved to be further away from Will. Michael looped his arm through mine, and although it felt awkward at first because I knew Will could see us, I let my arm relax into his. When we got into the kitchen, I heard Mary Jane arguing with someone.

Chapter 19

Will

He wanted not to care. But he couldn't force himself to not care. All he could do was try to hide his feelings. He was a master at that. He had learned to do that when he was young. He had become increasingly irritated that Alex didn't try to contact him again to explain what the deal was with her in her short shorts with the older guy. If she cared as much as she said she did, she would have called again. What the fuck? So never letting her see how he felt, that was an advantage here, because if she wasn't going to let him see how she really felt, then he wasn't going to show her either.

Besides, it was never going to be a long-term thing with her. Two different worlds. She would eventually figure out that he came from a poor, uneducated family, and that he had run away from those roots when he came to Miami. He felt the ugly memory of the night his father pulled the gun out at the party and shot Saul Hanger. The night Bethany died.

He shook that memory out of his mind when he walked over to say hello to her. She looked beautiful. Her legs peeked out of that knee length skirt, teasing him. He loved that she wore clothing that hinted at her sexiness without being too obvious, especially since he knew what she looked like underneath all that fabric. Her thin, taut body was long, with curves in places you couldn't see in clothing, only in a bathing suit or when she was naked. He tried to shake those thoughts off too, but when he looked deep into her eyes he wanted to kiss her lips. They were so full, and she wore a hint of red lipstick that for some reason made the green in her eyes sparkle more than usual, even in the dim lights.

She stood with that frat-looking-boy Michael Cameron. After he sat, he did his best to talk with Jude and Gabby and Kendra, but his eyes kept drifting back toward them. She kept looking over at him, while trying to act nonchalant and interested in whatever Michael was saying, but their eyes kept meeting. *That's right, Mike, you may be talking to her, but she's looking at me.*

Kendra sat beside him, her knee practically touching his. He felt some sort of invitation hanging between them. She flirted with him in this subtle manner and it turned him off. She was a married woman, sitting in that string bikini — granted she had great tits and looked good — playing *knees* with him. He knew when knees touched over and over at a party, it was a sort of intimate, yet understated, message of interest.

He wasn't interested in Kendra and honestly, he wondered what the fuck she was doing and what she wanted. Jude and Gabby were in their own world. Maybe it was Kendra's way of trying to get Jude's attention, flirting with him. It didn't matter, because he let his knee go back and forth with hers while he watched Alex talking to Frat-Boy-Mike.

The longer this discussion went on, the angrier he became about the whole thing. And the angrier he felt, the more he knew he had to stay away from her. He felt too much. He hated how hard he fell when he did. Guys were not supposed to lose control over a woman, he knew this from the time he was like four or five. His father had drilled it into his head. *Never let a woman see she's got you*, he would tell Will.

Problem was that Will had all this restless, bottled-up passion, and when he let someone in, he would lose control. No, he wasn't going to let that happen. "So where are your kids?" Will tried his best to focus on the conversation with Kendra. So, he asked a question reminding her of her marital status and responsibilities.

"Oh, Paulina is in college, a freshman, and George Jr. is staying at a friend's. He's a senior in high school."

"Is that why you decided to go back to school? Because they are getting older and more independent."

"Yes. It's something I always wanted, but between the kids and George, taking care of everyone, I just didn't feel like I had the time to commit to it. It's hard to make decisions about your own life when you're a mother, because for many years your life isn't really your own. Now it's time for me to refocus on things I had set aside."

Kendra continued, but Will stopped hearing her words, only the droning sound of her voice, because Frat-Boy-Mike weaved his arm through Alex's as they walked inside together. Anger coursed through him.

"Tell me about you? What made you come here for school?" Kendra asked.

What the fuck? He couldn't believe she took another guy's arm right in front of him. They had been fucking only two days ago. Naked and spending hours and hours in bed. She didn't even come up for air. She wasted no time jumping from him to Michael. And it made Will burn.

Kendra put her hand on his thigh. "Are you OK?"

He looked at her hand there, then up at Alex and Frat-Boy's back as they disappeared inside. He was fuming.

"I'm fine," he said to Kendra. "I need another drink."

"Let's go get one." She took his hand, and they walked inside.

Alex was talking with Mary Jane, while Frat-Boy stood beside her.

"I'm sorry. Fred can be a royal pain in the arse. You know how men can be." She looked at Michael and said, "Sorry. No offense."

"None taken."

"Anyway. I need to pick him up. I can't have him driving drunk. I had a feeling he would do this."

"OK. I'll drive you home to get your car."

"I'll get an Uber. Stay. Hang out with Michael." Mary Jane looked at Frat-Boy, who said, predictably, "Stay." He smiled at Alex.

Will felt a furious knot in his stomach. He let Kendra take his hand and guide him to the bar. He made sure Alex saw too. He knew he got back at her when he saw her face fall.

Alex turned to Mary Jane. "No. I'll take you,"

Good. Go. Or I might wind up punching this guy.

Then Frat-Boy took her hand and said, "Stay for a little while."

Alex glanced over at Will before she responded, "OK."

He was about to blow a gasket. She was doing this on purpose. She was using Mike to try to make him jealous. Fuck her.

Alex walked Mary Jane to the door, leaving Frat-Boy in the kitchen with Kendra and him. An awkward air hung in the room. Frat-Boy must have felt it because he said, "I'll see you outside," and slipped out the sliding door.

Kendra leaned against Will, her breast brushing his arm. "What do you want me to mix you?"

He moved his arm away from her breast. "Um, I'll have tequila. Let's do a shot."

"Perfect."

Will put salt on his hand and some on Kendra's. "Like this." He went to lick his own hand, and expected Kendra to lick her own, but she licked his hand instead. And right as her tongue went over his hand, Alex walked into the kitchen, her eyes widened the moment she saw Kendra licking Will's hand.

Will and Alex locked eyes. She looked like she was going to cry. He wanted to grab her and hug her. *What am*

I doing? He thought as he felt the moistness on his hand from Kendra's tongue. He wanted Alex.

Before he could even figure out what to say or if he wanted to say anything, she gave him a heavy, pained look, then said to Kendra, "I've decided to leave. I'm tired. Thank you for a fun party. Tell the others I said good night." Her voice shook on the last words. She turned and quickly left.

For a moment, Will felt the air thin and a wave of relief wash over him. A second later, all he wanted was for her to come back.

Chapter 20

Alex

Mary Jane was gone by the time I got outside, which was just as well. I didn't want her to see the tears streaming down my cheeks. Will was a total dick. Mean. Cold. Distant. What had I ever seen in him? He wasn't the warm, sensitive guy I had thought.

I felt disgusted thinking of Kendra licking him. Why did I have to be exposed to that? I could see her tongue stroking his hand in my mind. I closed my eyes and shook my head to get rid of the image.

I took long, quick strides to my car. Thankfully, I hadn't had that second drink with Michael and was fine to drive. By the time I got home, the tears had stopped, but I felt anxious. I couldn't stop fidgeting.

I decided to walk along the beach to shake off the restless energy. I ambled down to the sand, took my platforms off and let the grains seep between my toes. I loved the feeling of sand around my feet.

Where You'll Land

I walked down to the water. I noticed a small number of people on the beach. A group of college kids were knocking back forties, laughing and talking. A few random couples strolled along the water hand in hand. The sight of a man and woman sauntering past me, arms around each other, made the tears stream down my cheeks again. No matter what a dick he was, I loved him.

I realized he was going to take a while to get over. I wanted to kick myself for not sticking to my plan of no relationships while I was at school in Miami.

Michael popped into my head, and it suddenly occurred to me that I had left without even saying goodbye. I went to text him and saw that he had left a text: *No goodbye? Call if you want to talk.*

Michael was a natural therapist. Even seeing his text was comforting, but I wasn't in the mood to talk, dissect, or go over what had happened. I just wanted to clear my head. And I wanted to be able to get over this situation on my own. It reminded me of my ex, Zach, the distance, the pain, the uncertainty, the way I was questioning myself.

I texted him back: *Suffering from mild overreaction syndro*me. :) *Call you tomorrow.*

Maybe I should've gone for Michael after that drunken debacle. He was surer of himself, not that he was at all interested in me. He wasn't. Besides, as cute as he was, there was really no chemistry once the alcohol had dissipated.

The thing with Michael or even with Jude was that I found them attractive, charming and interesting. I enjoyed their company. But it wasn't love. Love was feeling the person everywhere: under your skin, in every strand of your hair, in your heart, in your bones, in the tone of your voice when you said their name. Love wasn't always about being with the person, it was feeling that your world was better just because they lived. Even if you weren't ever going to be together, he was the air you breathed, invisible but everywhere.

And I loved Will. Even if we weren't ever going to be together, even if I was hurt, I loved him.

I walked and walked. The breeze blowing through my hair felt good, like gentle fingers soothing my distress. Sand stuck to my legs, my feet sinking into the beach. The expansiveness of night stretched out before me. Waves crashing. The endless blackness reminding me that I was just a small part of something greater. This soothed me. All of this with Will was meant to teach me something greater about life. And even if it hurt like hell to love him right now, I told myself that somehow it was important to go through it.

I pushed some unruly strands of hair off my face, letting the breeze stroke my cheeks. I stood there, just letting the rushes of air wash over me. I swallowed the salty ocean air, took some deep breaths and turned toward home.

Strolling back toward my apartment building, my mind felt quieted. The dim lights around the pool made shadows along the sand as I neared the complex. And as if he came from out of nowhere, I saw his shadowy figure. Although he was just a silhouette against the night, I knew from the gallant stride that it was Will. It was as if everything I had thought about earlier had disappeared into a compartment in my mind, locked up and unavailable. I felt helpless. The pull of my feelings, of our connection, took hold of me. I walked toward him, closing the space between us.

Before I could speak (not that I knew what I was going to say anyway), he pulled me toward him, kissed my lips hard, passionately, then lifted my feet off the ground.

I opened my mouth to ask what he was doing, but the words hung on the tip of my tongue. He pulled me into a tight hug and kissed my neck, my cheeks, my ears. He took my face so gently, kissing my lips over and over, like he was lost in me.

I leaned into him, whisked away by the moment. Whatever the consequence, I didn't care. We kissed fiercely. The passion, raw and insatiable, like a bottomless hunger. I couldn't get him close enough, and I kept pulling him in tighter. He ran his hand across my cheek, momentarily pausing the kisses. I saw the desire in his eyes. "I'm sorry, Alex," he whispered.

"Me too," I said, my knees feeling weak from the intensity. I never would have known that I was capable of feeling so overpowered by my emotions.

"Let's go over there." He weaved his fingers through mine and walked toward the lifeguard stand down toward the water.

I looked up at him. "You want to swim?"

He looked at me affectionately, and with a teasing tone said, "That's not exactly what I had in mind."

When we reached the lifeguard stand, which had a three-way enclosure, he gestured for us to go inside. He stood behind me as I climbed up, then he came behind me, wrapping his arms around my whole body.

The breeze blew my hair all around. As he pulled it off my face, he said, "You are the most beautiful woman I have ever seen. It's not easy for me to let you in."

I searched his face. I wanted to ask why. I wanted to know what he kept trapped inside himself, but I just kissed him.

I love you, flitted through my mind. I felt it hanging between us, as we skirted around love with the experience of passion. "Nothing happened with that guy. He followed me home and surprised me." I also wanted to say, *I don't want to be with anyone else.* But that comment needed to come from him. Not that I intended to be with anyone else. As long as I was with him, as far as I was concerned we were exclusive. "And then he wouldn't go. I didn't—" Will put his fingers to my lips.

"It's hard to trust sometimes, but I want to."

"You can."

He admitted what I had thought, that he had trust problems. Problem with people who have trust problems is you shouldn't trust them with your emotions. And even though I knew this from years of my mother telling me and from studying psychology, I had to trust enough for both of us. Maybe if I could do that, he would come to trust me and then be trustworthy. No amount of psychobabble was going to talk me out of giving myself to him completely.

"I'm going to try." He smiled, lovingly. His expression quickly turned intense, as he began exploring my body with his hands, stirring my skin with his touch. He ran his fingers up my skirt, along my inner thigh and under my panties. He took them off and slipped his fingers inside me.

The kissing grew more intense. My shirt hung off my shoulder, my skirt partially raised, as he continued to stroke me to arousal. I wanted him, right there outside on the beach. I opened the button of his jeans and pulled his pants down to his knees. His boxers followed.

When I felt him enter me, my stomach clenched. My whole body shook against his. My legs wrapped around him, my back against the wall of the enclosure. He squeezed me tight and pushed in deeper. My panting grew heavier with each thrust until finally, I released with a feral groan. He breathed heavily through his kisses and climaxed a moment later. Our bodies went limp with a final sigh of satisfaction.

He held both of my cheeks and gazed into my eyes before kissing me again. These kisses were passionate and incredibly intimate. I felt the heat of his body against mine as we kissed, arms wrapped around each other. So entwined in the moment, I didn't know where he ended, and I began. Everything else was gone, the world was small and safe, and we were one. I was lost in him. It was a moment that stood out among all other moments because that type of intensity can't last. You have to hold onto it, remember it, let it absorb, before the real world interrupts.

A piercing screech popped our perfect bubble. "Heeeelp. Someone. Please."

Looking out toward the voice, I saw a panicked woman in a white one-piece bathing suit running up from the water, screaming wildly.

The woman's voice was desperate and harrowing.

"He's drowning. He drowned. Oh. My. God. Help," The woman screamed out to an empty beach, then ran down toward the ocean. The waves were big.

Without a word, Will pulled his pants up and jumped out of the lifeguard stand. He ran toward the water. I threw my clothes on, following while still pulling my skirt down. By the time I got to the water's edge, Will was already in the water up to his waist, the waves crashing in a loud rhythm.

The screaming woman was in the water now. "There he is." She looked at Will and pointed to the tumult. "Oh, mister, there he is. Help. Please."

It was dark, but I saw the guy's head bobbing and his arms flailing before a voluminous wave swallowed him. Will dove into that wave. My heart raced, my breathing turned shallow. I walked into the water toward Will.

Another wave came up and I saw Will's head. "Will!" I yelled. The wave crashed on my legs and I walked in deeper. Where was Will? I lost sight of him again. The water was too loud, my calls out to him echoed into the infinite night air. I just kept telling myself that he was a strong swimmer and would save that guy and himself.

This time when the wave came up, I didn't see either of them. The ocean seemed huge and ominous. I went in deeper and was about to dive under when I saw Will walking out of the water, holding the guy in his arms like a baby. The woman ran toward them. "George. Oh. My. God. Is he alive?" she screamed.

Will nearly breathless, said, "Yes."

Will made it to the edge of the water, laid the guy on the sand and dropped to his knees. "Katarina," the man said weakly, gasping for breath. He held out his arm. "I'm OK."

The woman, Katarina, kneeled beside him, then dropped her whole body on top of his. "Thank God."

"Thank you." She looked at Will through big eyes.

"What happened?" Will asked, sitting on the sand beside the man.

"We went in too deep. Usually he's a good swimmer, but we had been drinking. It was very stupid. He could have died."

"I had it under control," George said, unconvincingly.

She grabbed his arm. "You can be so stupid when you drink. *So stupid*. I should hit you." She turned to Will. "He gets overly confident, and I can't get him to listen."

Will nodded. "Happens to all of us. Sometimes. But you should never underestimate the power of the ocean, especially on a night when there's a storm coming toward us. You need to be more careful."

"Please let us give you money or take you to dinner or something. Something to show our gratitude."

"That's not necessary. Just don't drink and go in the ocean again."

George now sat up. He shook Will's hand. "Thanks, man."

"You're welcome. Don't drink and swim." He took my hand and turned to walk away, when Katarina asked, "What's your name anyway? You're our hero."

"I'm Will. And this is Alex."

"I'm Katarina Tremble and this is my irresponsible, but gorgeous boyfriend George Willows."

Chapter 21

Will

It took a second when he heard the name, but he eventually realized it was George Jr., Kendra's son. He would say "what a coincidence," but he didn't believe in accident or chance occurrences. Coincidence was a lazy term used when the deeper meaning or connection was unobservable.

He wouldn't have even known who he was if he hadn't spoken to Kendra at the party. Kendra had talked about George, spending a solid ten minutes discussing Katarina, her son's beautiful girlfriend. Kendra had tried to contain her antipathy toward the girl, but Will could tell how much she disliked her by her tone. It wasn't what she said about Katarina, it was how she said it. "Katarina is beautiful, *very beautiful*. George Jr. loves her. We all do. She can be flighty and frivolous, sometimes, but that's her age. You remember how that was. Nothing is permanent. Live carefree." Her mouth had puckered when she finished like she'd sucked on a lemon, then she released a purposeful, haughty cough.

Kendra had this whole way about her. Excellent decorum. Put together. The type of person who rarely had a hair out of place. People like Kendra always made him wonder how they looked so perfect and made it look effortless. Underneath her usual demeanor, he felt something else, something simmering. Anger. Discontentment. Like a prisoner to her propriety.

He knew George and Katarina were too young to be drinking. And he wanted to say something, but he really didn't want to get involved in someone else's domestic affairs. He hated all of that from back home. When he had carried George out of the water, Alex stood waiting in water up to her waist. It was dark, but he saw the outline of her body. George was heavy. But he wanted Alex to see his strength, so he held George without cringing or groaning from the pain.

As soon as he made it onto the sand and put George down, Will looked up at her. Alex's expression held concern then quickly morphed into glowing admiration. It felt good. Real good. There was nothing like the way she looked at him, such radiance across her face, like his very existence lit her up.

All he wanted was to get her upstairs and naked. George was safe, and Katarina promised to take him home. And the last thing he wanted was for Kendra to know he had been involved.

When Alex had left the party, he had felt such an overwhelming desire to go after her, he couldn't even think straight. He had never felt such little ability to talk himself out of doing something. He wanted her to come back, but he knew she was gone for the night. He had tried to tell himself to wait and see how he felt tomorrow. He had told himself it was just about sex, that their relationship wasn't going anywhere.

It was bullshit. He wanted to have her naked and underneath him. And no, it wasn't just about having sex, seeing her naked or anything like that. He wanted to be the man that she let inside her, the one she opened herself to. He didn't like the thought of Frat-Boy-Mike ever knowing her the way he did.

Will considered going after her when she practically ran out of Kendra's, but he held back. He tormented himself with an internal back-and-forth, the type of mental ricocheting that could drive a person insane. He wanted to go but tried to stop himself. Volleying thoughts made his head feel like a tennis ball knocked about between two players. While he talked to Kendra about the drink she had mixed, barely paying attention to what she said, all he could do was think about Alex.

Then Kendra had turned to him, looked into his eyes, grabbed his crotch over his jeans and rubbed. He couldn't fucking believe it. There had been absolutely no subtlety. She reached in his pants, groped him and whispered, "Let's take this to the bedroom." It felt good. Not that he was attracted to her, but her touch brought on the physical reaction.

"You like?" she had asked and leaned into him, pushing her breasts into his chest.

He didn't know what to say. For a minute the sexual invitation aroused him. She had that little bikini on, and he could almost see her nipples. She kissed his chest, then stood on her toes and looked up at him, lips puckered and waiting for a kiss from him. He stared at her lips. Kendra's longing for him showed in her eyes, which snapped him out of the moment. She was a married woman. Erection or not, he had enough sense that he wouldn't kiss her. Wouldn't cross that line. Besides, all he really wanted was Alex — now more than ever. He took her hand off his dick. "You're married Kendra. Don't do something you'll regret."

She looked hurt or angry, maybe a little of both. He gave her a half smile. "I think I should go."

"Oh, don't be silly. Stay." She looked like she might grab him again.

"No. I need to go." It wasn't only to get out of the uncomfortable space with her, it was his desire to be with Alex. "I'm going to slip out. But I'll see you in school."

She regained her composure then said as casually as possible, "Yeah. See you then."

As he hurried out, he still couldn't believe she had grabbed his dick. She was trouble, with a capital T. In his rush to leave, he had ditched Jude, but he was pretty sure he wouldn't care. He and Gabby looked pretty cozy.

He texted Jude: *I snuck out. Will explain tomorrow.*

He got an Uber. As soon as he got to their apartment building, he rushed up to Alex's apartment. When no one answered he thought he would try the pool. When she wasn't there, he looked out toward the ocean and saw her tall, thin frame walking toward him. She had the most graceful walk he had ever seen; even on the uneven sand she had the posture and elegance of a ballerina. He felt like running toward her and grabbing her everywhere. But instead he walked slowly, trying to keep that passion that burned inside of him under control. He didn't want to lose himself in this. No words were exchanged, but they didn't need them. He pulled her close, smelling the ocean scent that weaved through her hair. He touched her smooth skin.

He wanted all of her. The ocean had roared as he moved inside of her, feeling her clenched around him. Now they were hand in hand, lives and feelings woven together. He couldn't wait to get her upstairs and take off all her clothes. He wanted her again. This time he would go slowly, exploring and ravishing every inch of her body.

But Will had to put that part of the plan on the backburner until he put this rescue behind them. It had sapped a lot of energy from him. Yet, the feeling of saving someone and seeing how Alex had reacted to his heroic action invigorated him.

And just as they were ready to go to his apartment, Alex turned back to Katarina and George and blurted, "I think we know your mother. Is her name Kendra?"

Will's neck muscles tightened. *Shit.*

George's eyes widened. Katarina sighed then said, "Sure. Now this will be another thing for her to hold against me. She'll blame me."

George rubbed Katarina's hand. "We won't tell her." He turned to Alex. "Yes. How do you know my mom?"

"We're in school with her."

George rolled his eyes. "It's like she has people out watching me. You can't tell her. I know it's a lot to ask, but I'm supposed to be at my friend Julio's. She'll go apeshit."

Alex looked at Will with uncertainty. "I don't know. I mean, George could have died out there."

Will tugged on Alex's hand. "Let's go. He won't do it again." He gave George a steely look. "Right?"

"Right. No. Never. That was fucking scary. I've learned my lesson."

Alex hesitated. Will squeezed her hand, said softly, "Come on. They'll be fine."

"I don't know." Alex looked at him, anxiety written all over her face. "I don't know if I can hide the truth like that. It's her kid."

"And he's fine now." Will gave her a warm smile. He appreciated her moral consideration. He found it a turn-on, especially piggybacking Kendra, married with kids, grabbing his dick. But he did not want to be involved in the Willows' domestic problems. The whole thing made him uncomfortable. Ultimately, Will felt sure he had lost the battle.

Suddenly, Alex turned to George and said, "OK. OK. Fine. But you must promise you will never do this again. If I find out you did, I will tell her about tonight."

Katarina said, "He won't be doing this again. I can promise you."

Alex glared at George waiting for his answer.

"I promise. And thank you. I love my mom, but she can be tough."

Will felt a wave of relief as he and Alex turned to go up to his apartment to continue their evening together.

Chapter 22

Alex

As soon as the elevator door closed, he pulled me close and kissed me, caressing my cheeks and running his fingers through my hair. I pushed into him. I couldn't believe that he dove into the ocean without reservation to help George. Will was brave. And strong. And passionate. "What you did back there was very brave," I whispered between kisses.

"I'm not brave." He looked into my eyes. "I just did what needed to be done."

We got off the elevator.

"Not everyone would do that. Weren't you scared? The waves were huge, and it's so dark."

"I wasn't scared because I wasn't thinking. My adrenalin was pumping. It was all action. No thought."

I looked at him wondering if I could ever love him more than I did in that moment.

With an ingenuous expression, he said, "You looked worried when I got out. Sorry, I worried you."

"Don't be sorry. I was worried, yes. But I was equally proud."

He squeezed my hand, then unlocked the door and we went into his apartment.

"I still feel funny about not saying anything to Kendra. He's just a kid."

He shook his head. "I hear you, but I feel like it's not our place. Where I'm from, interfering in other people's family matters can cause unnecessary problems."

"It's not really interfering if we just report what's happened."

"It is, though. If we hadn't been there, she'd never know."

"If we hadn't been there, he could have died."

"Honestly, he was swimming. I think he just got spun around by the undertow and panicked. I helped, sure, but he would have been alright. Katarina yelling made it seem more dramatic."

"You carried him out like a baby. In your arms."

"C'mere." He pulled me close and gently rubbed my back, then he raised my shirt and removed it. "You're all wet."

I smiled coyly. "Not just there."

His eyes glistened. "Maybe I carried him out like that because I knew you were looking." He unfastened my bra.

"For me? To impress me?"

"To help him too. But once I got my hands on him and he shouted, I knew he was fine. Like a reflex, I picked him up and carried him. But I think in the back of my mind I knew it was because you were watching."

I searched his face. I couldn't believe he shared something so personal. It spilled out with uncharacteristic nonchalance. "You don't have to prove anything to me. I already love you."

I wanted to take the words back as soon as they were out. I stood topless before him. His eyes wandered across my face, down to my shoulders and then across my breasts. I saw desire, love. He took my skirt and panties off while looking into my eyes. His expression deepened, and he said, "Me too." He took strands of my damp hair and put them behind my ears.

He carried me to the bed. We spent the next hour kissing and touching each other all over before we made love, sealing every space that existed between us.

Lying with him afterward, I knew I would never be the same after that night. He opened something so deep within me, every part that felt empty or lonely filled with love, with our love.

The next few weeks with Will were like a dream, a beautiful, fabulous waking dream. This was what falling in love, *being in love,* felt like. What I had experienced with Zach was only about a tenth of this. I felt so connected to him and to the world. I was growing. We shared ideas. We shared intimate moments that were too deep for words but stayed with me even when we weren't together. Like when he twirled strands of my hair through his fingers, or when we slept interwoven, our hearts overflowing into each other's. I thought about things we would experience together in the future. We spent all of our time together too. Talking for hours and hours. Sometimes we would be up late, both drowsy, trying to stay awake just because we wanted to continue talking. A few times we fell asleep while in the middle of a conversation, only to continue as soon as we got up. Besides that, Will was an amazing lover. He awakened places on my body I didn't even know could be aroused to the touch.

The other thing about falling in love. The harder you fell, the easier it was to get hurt. Maybe that's why it was called *falling in love;* at some point there was a crash at the bottom that could shatter someone into a million pieces.

§

Monday afternoon. Will went to grab coffee with Jude. I sat in the library with my head buried in regression analysis formulas. A nightmare. Statistics was not my strength.

"Hey, Stranger," I recognized Michael's deep voice.

"Hi." I smiled up at him. "What's up?"

Michael and I had barely spoken since Kendra's party. We had shared "hellos" and "how are you doings," in school, and a few texts back and forth, but no real conversations. He knew I was back on with Will, and he had started dating a new woman, Julianne, a model he had met while bartending.

"Ah, stats. The psychology grad student's nightmare." He sat next to me.

"For me. Jude's actually really good at it. He's been helping me."

"I'm actually pretty good with stats too, although I don't usually admit that in public." He laughed.

"Didn't you double major in college, psychology and statistics?"

"Yep. I see you actually pay attention when I talk." He elbowed me. "I've always found the formulas measuring abstractions fascinating."

I smiled. "You had said. I do too, I just wish I understood the numbers more easily. Did you pick your dissertation topic yet?"

"Gang violence. You know it's a big problem."

"Yes, I think I mentioned that I had worked in the inner city in New Jersey. Newark."

"Yeah, briefly. Here." He pulled some papers out of his bag. "I'm going to apply for an externship at Dade County Juvenile Detention Center next year. You should apply there."

"I was going to do my first year of externship at the clinic here. But that sounds interesting."

"The externship not only involves psychotherapy and assessments, there's also a court advocacy component. I feel like so many of these kids fall into the gang because they just want to belong. They want a family. Then they become worse from going through the system. Here, you can have this to read. They still have two openings if you're interested in applying."

I scanned it. "Looks interesting." I looked at him. "So, how's it going with the new girl, Julianne?"

"It's good. She's the first woman in a while that I feel interested in. You?"

"Great. It all seems to have worked itself out. I was just being neurotic." I laughed. "We need to get together and catch up."

"That's on you. I'm tired of asking and being sidelined for your boyfriend."

I leaned against his arm in a gesture of warmth just as Will walked in with Jude carrying two coffees, one for him, one for me. Will's mouth tightened, his lips in a straight, stubborn line, as soon as he laid eyes on me. His gaze swung between Michael and me. I could feel his wall go up before he even stood next to me. My stomach clenched.

"Hey." He looked at Michael with piercing eyes.

"What's up, guys?" Michael, acting oblivious to the obvious tension, smiled at Will and Jude. "I was just telling Alex about an externship at Dade County Juvenile Detention." Michael got up. He stood as tall as Will and Jude. They all looked at each other. The tension brewed. Michael in his casual style said, "Talk to you later," to me, then turned to Will and Jude and said lightly, "See ya in class."

Will placed my coffee on the table. "Here. I'm going to the computer lab with Jude."

"I'll come." I closed my book.

He gave me a sharp look. "No. I'll catch up with you later." His aloofness felt like a slap in the face.

I stared into his eyes. "I— I wasn't doing anything. He was just showing me some stuff about the site."

"I didn't say you were doing anything. I'm just hanging out with Jude right now." I saw the pain in his eyes and I reached for his hand.

"Will."

He pulled his hand away from me. "Stop."

That killed me. We shared a burdensome exchange when our eyes met. I saw Jude out of my periphery looking as confused as I felt.

Will said, flatly, "I'll talk to you later."

Tears stung behind my eyes as I watched him exit the library. What the hell? I didn't do anything wrong. I thought we had gotten past his need to distance.

I stared at my book, trying to wrap my mind around what had just happened. In one instant, everything changed. And although my stomach knotted, I convinced myself that he had overreacted and that we would talk later.

But he barely spoke to me the entire day. We sat right beside each other in the two classes we had together and other than one "hey" and two "see yas", he basically dismissed me. Arguing about what was bothering him would have been a welcome alternative to his distance, which made me feel so small, so insignificant. Like I didn't matter.

Then I realized, maybe that's how he wanted me to feel.

In our personality theory class, he sat with his back to me talking with Tammi, a girl we barely knew. The two of them blabbed nonstop about nothing, until the professor came in and began the lecture. It felt awful. Here again, we had been so close and he made me more distant than a stranger.

I texted him.

Talk to me.

I saw him read the text, then set his phone to the side. My face burned. He ignored me, purposefully. My shoulders and neck tightened as my sadness turned to anger. Further inflaming my already tense emotional state, he walked out of the class with Tammi. I watched them go, Will swinging his arms like he hadn't a fucking care in the world. A seething rage permeated me, a rage so bottomless, a rage preserved only for someone who you've first loved. One that seeps into the very cracks of your being, replacing what was once all the possibility and promise of love.

I had experienced this with Zach, but not one iota of the intensity I felt in that moment. I wanted to scream or throw something. Maybe both. As the day wore on, the rage made me increasingly agitated. When I got home from class, I paced, vacillating, like an insane woman, between wanting to scream at him and wanting to try and fix things between us. I knew I hadn't done anything wrong — assuming his distance had to do with Michael, which was ridiculous. He was my friend. And I wasn't even flirting.

The part of me that was swept up in the love, the part of me that could not let go without a fight, had me taking responsibility for what had happened. When I thought of it that way, the rage receded, and the sadness returned. Will must feel insecure about how I felt. It was the only thing that made sense.

And with that, I decided that the only way to make this right was to swallow my pride, go upstairs and give him what he needed. Reassurance. I would tell him how much

I loved him. That my life was changed because of him. I paced in my living room going over what I would say, and conjuring the nerve to say it, then I hurried upstairs in a bit of a frenzy.

I knocked on his door. When he didn't answer, I banged. "Will. Please. Talk to me. I love you. Don't shut me out."

Nothing.

Still on a quest to resolve this and not thinking rationally, I went to look for him. I hurried outside and saw that his car was in his spot. Maybe he was on the beach. I walked toward the sand, and I couldn't help but notice all the places where we had made love or shared other intimate moments, talking, kissing, cuddling, as we had watched the waves meeting the sand. Tears stung behind my eyes.

No success finding him on the beach. Feeling more frazzled by the minute, I decided to check a few of the local places we frequented. Even asked a few of the bartenders and waiters if they saw him.

No, was the answer every time.

I sent him a text: *Talk to me.*

As soon as I hit send, I wanted to unsend it.

I felt defeated.

And angry.

And humiliated.

Will obviously didn't want me to find him.

What the fuck was I doing? My cheeks flushed with shame as tears streamed down my face. These tears weren't about him. These tears were about me, my loss of control, my feelings of losing my pride. Who I was before Will was crumbling around me.

I received no response all day or night from Will.

In the morning, when he still hadn't responded, that fury coursed through me again. He gave me nothing. No information. Not even a polite acknowledgement of my text message, like I mattered so little. He couldn't even take a minute to acknowledge my existence. I had given him my whole heart, my whole self, every inch of my body. And the only thing he gave me was his silence.

I should have known better. All the signs that he would do this again were there.

Hope was the delusion of the idealistic lover.

Tuesday, we had one class together. The same pitiful "hey" and "see ya," nothing more, like we barely knew each other. He cut my heart with his wordlessness, and his dismissive inaction. I told myself it didn't matter anymore, because I was moving on. I waved casually at him when he said "see ya" after our last class then turned and rolled my eyes. He was an asshole.

When I ambled out of the class, I ran into Mary Jane and Kendra in the hallway. Mary Jane took one look at me and said, "Chickee. You alright?"

"I'm fine," I said, unconvincingly.

Mary Jane pursed her lips. "You're going to have to do better than that. What's wrong?"

I looked at the two women. I really wanted someone to talk to. And even though I knew Will would probably be pissed if I shared too much of our business with classmates,

I needed to make his emotions less of a concern than my own. "It's Will. It's over, and it's rough having to see him. I hate men."

Mary Jane looped her arm with mine. "Come with us. We're going to have some coffee and hang out for a bit."

"I'd like that."

Chapter 23

Will

He knew he had overreacted. Interesting thing about overreacting, even if you know you're doing it, sometimes you can't stop yourself. He hated being so emotional. Isn't that what made his father nuts and his brother Timmy tease him? Not that he let them see his emotions, he hid them. But every so often they would bubble over, his insides would fill up, and he would feel too overwhelmed to hold his feelings in.

"Passion, Tim, is the heartbeat of the world. It's what makes everything matter. I'm not a pussy, I'm passionate," he would argue with Timmy.

Timmy would laugh, one of those laughs that could slice you right down the middle with its sharpness. "Riiiiight. Pining over a girl doesn't make the world tick, little brother. It makes you weak. Never ever let a girl see she's got you. You'd better man up or you'll be ruined."

Will knew this brotherly advice was total bullshit. But the thing about where he grew up was that everyone saw the world the same. Everyone was the same. If anyone was different they were ostracized for their uniqueness. Crazier than that need for homogeny was the awful truth: Will was the smart, exceptional kid, the one who had potential that no one in his family understood. They saw it as strange, as weak, as arrogance.

His father would say: "You and those stupid books. You and those stupid ideas. You're not better than anyone else. Just remember that. Men are supposed to care for the family. Understand. Reading those books doesn't make you a man. Going to work and earning a living, being a provider is what you should be doing."

It was Bethany who saw him. Her father was in the army and she had seen more of the world. She knew things were different. She knew there was more out there than what was seen in small town Mauston. Will's family thought she was annoying and arrogant. "She's one of those big heads," his father had said, and his mother nodded in agreement. Mom wasn't a big talker, and he suspected she didn't always agree with the old man. But she never went against him. Instead, she drank. In fact, his whole family was a bunch of drunks.

Sometimes their drinking got ugly too and bad things happened. Like the night his dad shot at Saul, inspiring the series of unfortunate events that led to Bethany's death.

Which was his fault.

So, he knew he overreacted when he walked into the library and saw Alex talking to Frat-Boy-Mike. But a wave of emotion coursed through him: jealously, anger, but mostly fear. And that was why he had to get far, far away from her. The fear. Fear that at some point she would leave him for some other guy, some guy like Frat-Boy-Mike. Someone who wasn't ashamed of their family, someone who didn't carry the burden of an awful truth.

He brooded in the computer lab as he sat with Jude working on statistics.

"You going to tell me what's up?" Jude asked.

"With what?"

"With you and Alex? You've been with her all the time and now what? You got pissed because she was talking to *Michael?* I think the girl really loves you."

"It's nothing. It's never been serious, and I just need space sometimes. *We* need space sometimes. You know how it is. You can enjoy someone's company without being in love. But if you spend too much time with them, it's a mixed message."

Jude raised a disbelieving eyebrow. "You're saying you aren't that into her, you've just been hanging out every single day and night?"

"Yeah. I like hanging out with her, but it's not more than that." He thought for sure his lips twisted as he felt the lie spill out, but it sounded convincing enough. He'd never tell Jude the truth.

"So, what? You're done *hanging out* with her?"

"Don't say it like that. Alex is cool. It's just not what I want long-term. I told you that."

"Right." Again, Jude shot him a look of disbelief. "You know, Alex isn't the type of girl to stick around forever. If you're playing some game with yourself, I'd get my shit together. Cause you'll lose her. Made that mistake myself before. And losing *that* girl is a killer."

"I hear you, man. But she is not *that* girl."

"You're sure?"

He felt a sick knot in his throat thinking about Alex's eyes looking up at him, sadness gleaming, confusion gleaming, when he glared at her in the library. He felt furious thinking about her talking to Frat-Boy and fearful that she just might go out with him. *Well, if that's what she wants, he wouldn't get in her way.* He had wanted to pull her into a tight embrace at the same time, run his hands up her shirt and feel the smoothness of her skin. *Stop. Stop. Stop.* "Absolutely. She is not *that* girl. I'm sure."

"Well, if that's the case, then maybe you want to hang out with Gabby's friend Lilane tomorrow night. I'm taking Gabby to dinner. She was asking about you for Lilane. I told her you were dating Alex. But since you're not. Maybe you want to come."

"What's she like?"

"I never met her. This is only my second time hanging out with Gabby. But Gabby said she's beautiful and smart. It's one dinner. Dude, sometimes you are way too serious."

"You're right. I'll go." It was probably just what he needed to distract himself from Alex. He had to stay away from her. "What's going on with Gabby anyway?"

"*We are just hanging out.*" He shot Will a shrewd look. "I like her, so we'll see."

§

Classes were awkward. Walking around the apartment complex was awkward. Their lives were interwoven. He didn't even swim or go to the café to study that night, a usual routine for him. For them. That night he went to Thelma's for a burger with Jude. The bartender took their order, then with her elbows on the bar and her head in her palms, she said, "That thin girl with the long hair who you're always with was looking for you earlier. She seemed upset."

"Thanks for letting me know."

Jude looked at him. "Were you straight with her about what's going on?"

Was he? No, he wasn't. And after hearing that from the bartender, he felt guilty. Maybe he would try to talk with her tomorrow, not to be with her, but maybe to explain his past and why this thing between them could never work.

"Maybe I could have been clearer. It's not easy to let someone down."

"It's better to let them down then to leave them hanging. Trust me on this. I've been through hell and back with a couple of women. Be honest with her. She's a good person."

Jude was right, Alex was a good person. And she deserved better. Maybe he was making a mistake. He had never let someone as close to him as her. And he couldn't believe he was able to feel anything for a woman since Bethany, never mind love. He would talk to her. But by the next day in class, he felt a wall surrounding him as soon as he saw her. She walked in looking sexy, and he felt himself close off.

Her eyes had a touch of sadness, but she had a smile on her face, her head high. She glanced at him. They exchanged hellos. Simple. Unemotional. Like she barely knew him. Then Frat-Boy Mike walked over to where she sat (next to Will) and asked her about that stupid externship site again. He heard them blabbing.

Alex tossed her hair off her shoulders. It rested along her back in a cascading stream. He saw from her profile that she smiled up at Michael. Out of his periphery, because he would not look that douche in the face, he saw Michael's big white teeth smiling back at Alex. What the fuck. He stiffened everywhere. And the wall grew more solid, any crack that may have let her in sealed. It was painful. Watching her chat casually with another guy was excruciating. His aloofness from her — wanting to touch her and feeling incapable — was painful. There was nothing worse than wanting to feel close to her yet feeling like he was trapped inside himself. He couldn't reach her from behind the shield surrounding him.

Kendra sat on his other side. Will turned toward her and struck up a conversation, even though he didn't really want to talk to her. Anything to get his eyes off the exchange between Alex and Michael. He felt his anger swell, but he didn't want his passion to take over. He'd say something he regretted, like, "Get the fuck away from her."

He could still hear them talking behind him.

Kendra blinked her long eyelashes. "We haven't talked much since my party."

Awkward, Will thought. She had grabbed his dick. A married woman. And then he found George Jr. in the ocean and never said anything. "It was a good party."

"It's been awhile since I laughed that hard. George and his friends are always so… proper."

Will nodded, stewing, distracted by the voices behind him.

"Maybe we could do something one night. Jude too. The three of us," he heard Kendra say. And he noticed her looking over his shoulder at Alex and Michael. Their voices seemed louder. Maybe Alex was talking loudly, trying to get his attention. Heat coursed through him.

"Yeah. I don't know, Kendra. Maybe one night. Talk to Jude." He didn't trust Kendra. At all. But he didn't want to be completely rude. One thing was certain. He would make sure never to be alone with her. Her eyes had this hunger in them, like she would devour him if he let her.

Chapter 24

Alex

I sat in Starbucks with Kendra and Mary Jane. Kendra placed her hand on my leg, warmly. "You've been seeing Will, but things aren't going well? Tell us."

Mary Jane added, "I thought everything was going well. You two are together all the time."

I looked at them both through weary eyes. "It's very confusing." I explained the intimacy, our time together and then how he reacted in the library. "Could he be doing this over me talking to Michael? It was just a simple conversation. I wasn't doing anything."

"He was jealous, obviously," Mary Jane said. "I told you this before. Will's into you. A guy only acts like that if he's into the girl."

"Right. But what good is it if we can't talk about it?" Again, I remembered our previous conversation about Will's problems communicating. Did I owe it to him to at least hear him out if and when he was ready to talk? No.

This distancing thing was too painful. "I can't deal with this. Or him. I'm angry, even though, I— well— "

"Love him." Mary Jane finished my sentence.

"Yes, love him." I looked Mary Jane square in the face.

Kendra chimed in. "Communication is everything. If you can't talk, it's only going to get worse. And you are a sweet girl, Alex. You want a man who's going to be able to tell you how he feels."

I thought of the night that Will rescued Kendra's son in the water. The first night we told each other we loved each other and the genuine affection I always read in his eyes when he looked at me. I had really believed that he meant what he said.

"He had been telling me how he felt, but then it just shifted and now he's barely speaking to me. He's pushed me too far. Now, I don't want to speak to him either."

Kendra said, "You want a strong man. Will looks strong. Physically. But love takes risk. Big risk. Sounds like Will doesn't have courage."

I felt annoyed by this statement. Will had courage. Will had a lot of courage. In fact, that night he dove into the ocean and saved Kendra's drunk, irresponsible son was one of the greatest acts of courage I had ever witnessed. Annoyed at Kendra's assessment, I spilled out what I had promised to keep a secret. "Will has courage," I said sharply. "In fact, he saved your son the night of your party."

Kendra's eyes widened. "What are you talking about? You don't know my son, do you?"

I explained the whole story. Kendra's jaw hung open, and her eyes grew stern as she listened. Then she spewed, "Katarina. I'm sure it was her idea. Will dove into the ocean that night and carried him out like a baby? And neither of you thought I had a right to know?"

"I'm sorry. Will promised George he wouldn't say anything. And honestly, if Will knew I told you he'd be furious. He has this thing about privacy. It's like over the top. Can I ask you not to say anything to him?"

Kendra leaned toward me, slightly, then with a pinch in her tone, said, "I just can't believe the two of you. Grown adults. Classmates. Didn't tell me what my son was up to. He could have drowned."

"No. I thought so too. But Will said it was Katarina making a big scene and George would have been OK. That's the thing. He dove in, not knowing George was swimming strongly. And then he admitted that he carried him out to— um … impress me." I gazed downward. "I shouldn't be saying any of this."

Mary Jane said, "I can't believe you didn't say anything, Alex. You should have told her anyway. You don't mess with someone's kid."

"Of course. I know. See, Will is not good for me. I went against my own judgment and did what he wanted. I'm sorry, Kendra." I looked hard into Kendra's eyes.

She placed her hand on my arm and took a heavy breath. "It's OK. That Katarina is trouble. I bet she made a big stink like Will said. But I will be talking to George about this. I have to. I won't say anything to Will." She zipped her lips with her thumb and finger.

"Thank you."

"And Alex, courage in romance is harder than running into the ocean at night when you're a strong swimmer."

"Yeah. Maybe. But I also believe the harder it is for someone to love, the deeper it is when it happens." That was true of me, and I wanted to believe it was the same for Will.

Mary Jane nodded. "I agree with that. But I also don't want to see you tortured by a man who's afraid of his own feelings. You know, Michael Cameron looks interested. And he's hot too, plus he seems to have his shit together. It's good to have a backup plan."

"Mary Jane, jeez, I can only handle one guy at a time. Michael and I have a flirty banter, but there's nothing at all romantic. He's a friend."

"That's what you said about Will in the beginning."

"That was different."

"Every beginning is different." She raised her eyebrows.

"Definitely not Michael. I think what I probably need is to be by myself and figure out my own life, but we'll see what happens."

"Let's hit the town. Have some girl time."

"Looks like my calendar's open now." I forced a smile, hoping it would make the ladies feel like they had helped me.

I did feel better after our conversation. I would give this thing with Will a couple of days and see what happened. If nothing happened, which would be the worst-case scenario

— it would be very painful for things to just fizzle out, no conversation, like it mattered too little for words — I would let it go. I would do my best to take his silence as a sign that he didn't want to be with me.

§

I studied alone that night. Cooked pasta in my apartment, alone. I wished Carter had been home for a short chat, just to ease the transition from being with Will all the time to the soundlessness of the empty apartment. The walls seemed to echo, matching the hollowness I had in my heart.

But, I would not let this break me. I buried my head in my personality theories book and took notes, absorbing the material. I had come to Miami to be a scholar. I didn't come to fall in love with Will Easton.

The next day in school, Will was still distant. At one point, as he sat next to me, I felt the strength of his presence. I turned to him and we met eyes, sharing a long, heavy gaze. He looked like he might say something, something important, something other than "hey," but he turned away and spoke to Robin, the girl that sat on his other side. I was dying but remained determined to not let his dismissal spiral me into the self-deprecating, self-questioning, berating insecurity of the broken-hearted.

I went home, downed a protein shake and headed out to the pool. Jumping in, the water felt refreshing as it enveloped me. This was my home. My place. My personal space.

After my swim, I enjoyed relaxing in the hot tub, watching the sky mix with pink and blue and purple as it settled, as if melting right into the sea. And as the sun relaxed, I calmed with it. Maybe I would see if Michael or Carter wanted to grab something to eat at the café.

Then right as I was getting out of the hot tub, I saw *them*. I slipped back into the swirling, bubbling water. *What the hell?* My eyes must be deceiving me. How could he? There was Jude and Gabby and Will with some curvy, blond girl. He wasn't holding her hand, thank God, but they walked close. I was sure it was a date.

Blood rushed to my head. I felt dizzy. And sick. Should I get out and confront him? Or should I pretend that I didn't see anything? Even if it was totally over, I could not believe his audacity, bringing another woman to our apartment complex.

Feeling frenetic, I got out of the hot tub and wrapped a towel around me. The foursome headed toward the beach. I followed them with my eyes, feeling queasy. Will was taking another woman onto the beach. The beach that we had spent so much intimate time on. Was I so easily replaced?

Feeling a rush of anger, I wanted him to see me. If nothing else, I wanted him to take responsibility for the demise of the relationship. Because as far as I was concerned it was officially over.

OVER!

In that moment, I realized how this guy had blinded me to reality. But not now. Like a slap in the face, he revealed who he really was, a complete dismissive, uncaring, weak man. No. A boy.

I hurried toward the sand. When I was within a few feet of them, I slowed and acted nonchalant, swinging my arms like I was on an evening stroll, all *lalala*-ish. I stepped onto the sand as they were taking their shoes off. I let my feet sink in and released a purposely loud sigh. Not an erotic sigh, but a pleasant sigh. I knew he would hear it because it was a familiar sound for him.

Will turned, his eyes bugged-out with a look of surprised horror, like he hadn't even considered the possibility of this scenario. For someone so book smart, he was obtuse when it came to relationships. I glared at him but kept my back straight and proud. In a measured tone, I said, "Hey guys." I even managed a smile.

Jude said, "Heeeey, Alllexx," not seeming uncomfortable at all.

Even under the dim light, I saw that Will looked white as a sheet. "Hi," he eked out.

I looked straight into his eyes. I saw him studying my face, trying to read my emotional state. "Have fun," I said, then smiled at him. I turned, and as gracefully as I had ever moved, I sauntered away.

I felt his eyes burrowing through my back. The pull to turn around was strong, but I resisted the desire. I was not going to give him the satisfaction of seeing me look back. I had given him enough of myself. And it was time for me to walk away, not look back on him or us.

I walked and walked, not even putting my shoes on when I got onto the concrete or into my building. I just kept walking, staring straight ahead until I got into my bedroom and collapsed onto my bed and cried so hard I could barely breathe.

§

Timing was an interesting topic of inquiry. One of those philosophical contemplations that Zach had called "useless" when I used to bring it up.

Seeing Will with another girl was the final straw. And she was blonde, reminding me of the night I spied Zach with the yellow-haired girl.

I stared up at the ceiling from my bed, feeling exhausted from crying, but the tears had stopped, and a numb sort of calm replaced the grief. I thought of the timing with a detached curiosity. If I hadn't been in the hot tub, I wouldn't have known that Will had gone out with another woman.

The rest of the evening likely would have played out much differently too.

Chapter 25

Will

Will walked through the sand, Lilane beside him. Jude had a six pack and Gabby had a bottle of tequila. Lilane made small talk. Will wasn't too fond of small talk, but he tried to be polite. It was going to be a long night, and his mind was preoccupied with what had just happened.

Alex caught him with Lilane.

She walked over with that ballerina posture and looked him right in the eye. He saw the pain on her face that was invisible to everyone, the creases around her mouth when she smiled as she fought a frown. He wanted to reach out to her, ease the pain, close the space that he had created. But he couldn't do it. He had to stay away from her.

"Don't you just love the beach at night?" Lilane asked, smiling up at him. She had a beautiful smile.

"Yes, I prefer it at night. It's quieter. More mysterious."

"Oh, I love it during the day too. I love the sun."

"Me too." Will forced himself to be cordial.

"What do ya'll do for fun in Mauston? It's always interesting to hear about people's lives in places that have four seasons. I've never even seen snow, you know."

"Really? Snow is something everyone should see. You've never been up north?"

"Only in the warmer weather. I hate the cold."

"Let's sit here," Jude said, bringing the group to a stop. Gabby rolled out a big blanket over the sand.

Will didn't want to sit all night on the blanket next to Lilane. He wanted to go back to his apartment and be alone.

"What's up?" Jude looked up at Will after the trio sat on the blanket, leaving Will standing alone.

His face burned with embarrassment as he quickly sat. He couldn't just ditch the date. Lilane scooted close to him, their shoulders nearly touching. Her feet spilled out in front of her. He stared at the red polish on her toes, pretending to listen to what she said. Thankfully, Jude was a talker. He, Gabby and Lilane all talked about different restaurants on South Beach. Will barely added anything to the conversation.

They each had a beer and a shot, then another round of both. Jude managed to carry the bulk of the conversation through the night, sharing stories of his life in LA. His tales always mesmerized people. There was something about being a musician — or maybe it was anyone who had reached a certain level of fame — that interested people.

Jude took Gabby's hand and kissed it, then asked her if she wanted to go for a walk. No surprise, she agreed. The woman salivated just looking at Jude. The dude definitely had a way with women.

As Jude and Gabby walked toward the water, Lilane made herself comfortable on the blanket. "Come closer." She tugged his shirt.

He laid down beside her. She nestled against him. He didn't know what he wanted. Part of him thought he should just hook up with her. Jude's "you're too serious" stuck in his head. Lilane wasn't really his type, but he found her attractive enough for one night.

He moved his head, resting it against hers. They lay like that for a few minutes. He felt her looking at him. He turned his body toward her, kissing her on the lips. She opened her mouth and their tongues rolled around each other's, both turning so their bodies touched. As Lilane pushed her breasts against his chest, he pulled her close so he could feel her more.

He kissed her and kissed her, but though her body was nice, he just couldn't get into it. Her kisses had no passion. They seemed perfunctory, sterile, passionless. She also started talking between kisses about her sister's boyfriend and how he cheated on her sister. "Why do guys do that?"

"I don't know," he responded, trying to get her to stop talking by kissing her more.

"Well, you're a guy. You must have an opinion. Besides you're training to be a therapist. Gabby said you're real astute too."

"People cheat for different reasons. I don't know your sister or her boyfriend. She should probably ask him." He held her face in his hands and kissed her again, trying to silence the conversation. The subject was making him uncomfortable, reminding him of that look on Alex's face when she saw him with Lilane. As his lips were locked with this woman he barely knew, all he could think about was the way Alex felt, the way Alex tasted. The way her hair flowed through his fingers like a warm, cascading stream, the smell of the ocean that lingered on her body after they swam in the sea.

"What's wrong?" Lilane perched up on an elbow and looked at him after he had abruptly stopped the kiss.

"I apologize."

"What is it?"

"It's nothing. I just… it's not you. I have a lot on my mind."

She looked confused. "You want to talk about it?"

"No. Not really."

She looked at him again, a mild look of hurt or maybe disappointment. "You're not attracted to me. You can say it."

"It's not that."

"Then what?"

"I've just got a lot on my mind."

"I can take your mind off of what's on it." She ran her fingers through his hair.

"Not tonight. OK? I really am sorry."

Lying back onto the blanket, she folded her arms in a huff. He looked at her. All he could think about was how to leave her so that he could go back to his apartment and call Alex.

Alex

I was surprised when I saw the number rolling across my phone screen. Michael and I rarely called each other; we usually texted. I quickly answered before it went to voicemail. "Hey. What's up?"

"Hey. So, Julianne's out with friends and I'm not working. Wanna grab a drink or burger, or both? The night's too beautiful to stay cooped up."

My eyes ached from crying. And I felt drained. But I enjoyed hearing his friendly, upbeat voice. "Yeah. I'd like that. I got upgraded to phone call status?"

"Maybe I just wanted to hear your voice." I could hear his smile.

"You're such a tease."

"I thought maybe you could use a friend."

"How'd you know."

"That look on your boyfriend's face in the library. I just took a guess. The dude is way too intense."

"Yeah. I guess."

"You like that about him, don't you?"

I contemplated. "Yeah. Maybe. It's over now, though. And no, I don't want to talk about him. Let's just go hang out."

"You want me to pick you up at your place?"

The last thing I needed was to run into Will with the blond while I was with Michael.

"No. That's OK. Let's just meet at Felicities." Felicities. A brewery on 11th. "Meet you there in a half hour?"

"Perfect. See you soon."

I took a quick shower, to rinse the chlorine off. I ran my eyes under freezing cold water to hopefully get the swelling to go down.

I did not look great when I left to meet Michael.

"You look tired." He wrapped his arm around my back and kissed my cheek as soon as he saw me, "but beautiful, as always."

"You're such a flirt." I leaned into him. "I'm glad you called."

Will

Jude and Gabby came back toward the blanket, fingers woven through each other's. "Hey, let's head back," Will said a little too anxiously. Lilane looked annoyed.

Jude looked at Will curiously, knowing something was up. Will gave him an obvious "dude, let's go" look.

Jude looked at Gabby. "Ready?"

Gabby hugged him and responded in a cutesy voice, "OK. Let's go get something to eat. Alcohol always makes me hungry."

Lilane held the blanket in her hands. "Watch out," she warned before she lifted it to shake the sand off.

She shook, then folded it. "Here, I'll carry it," Will said, reaching for it.

She handed it to him. "Thanks," she said flatly.

They walked back toward the apartment building. Will wanted to say he was going home, but he felt rude backing out of the night like that.

So, when Jude said, "Wanna go to Thelma's?"

Will said, "Sure."

Passing Felicities on their way over, Gabby said, "Oh, let's go there. I heard they have great burgers. I've always wanted to try it."

"How did you even hear of it?" Jude asked. "It's a South Beach hangout. Strictly locals."

"There was a write-up in the *Miami Herald* awhile back. Come on." She clasped her hands, looking up at Jude with pleading eyes.

Jude looked at Will, who shrugged his shoulder and said, "Whatever you girls want."

As soon as they walked in, before he even registered what he saw, heat coursed through his body. He wanted to fucking throw something.

How could she?

And to think he had spent the night thinking about her, missing her, dying to leave his date and go to her. The sadness he had thought he saw in her eyes must not have been there. Because she was doing exactly — EXACTLY — what he had feared. She was out with Frat-Boy-Mike.

Fuming, he walked over to their table. Passion burned through his skin. He was furious, but when her eyes widened as soon as she saw him, he wanted to grab her and kiss her.

"Hi." He looked deep into her eyes. He could see Frat-Boy watching out of his periphery. He couldn't quite make out his expression, but he assumed it was smug, thinking that he had won Alex over like she was some possession to be had.

"Hey," she said back, then swallowed so hard he heard it.

He also could tell that she had been crying. He knew every nuance of expression, every inch of her skin.

Alex and he stared at each other through pained eyes. He wanted *her* to get up, grab his arm and say they needed to talk. He wanted her to do all the things that he desperately wanted to do but felt like he couldn't. He wanted her, and yet, that wall, that invisible wall between them tightened. He wished she would at least say something to soften it.

And he still wanted to punch Michael in the face.

Instead, he said, "Hello, Michael," glaring at him like a bull ready to fight.

Jude came up behind him followed by Gabby and Lilane, making an uncomfortable situation nearly unbearable.

Will said, "See ya," went to a table and sat.

Lilane followed him. Jude and Gabby spoke to Alex and Frat-Boy for a couple of minutes before sitting with him and Lilane.

It took everything he had to sit there and act normal while Alex was out on a date with that guy. He didn't want any of them to know how bothered he was. Jude looked at him a couple of times curiously, as if to gauge Will's feelings about the whole thing.

Will kept his shoulders and face relaxed, laughing when something funny was said, making a few comments to feign interest in the conversation. The mortification burned through his skin. She never even looked over at him, as if suddenly she was now with Michael and Will became invisible. All he wanted was to go to her, grab her and take her home.

Actually, he wanted her to come grab him and ask him to take her home.

Alex

I was dying. Talk about *timing*. Will walked in with the blond girl while I sat having a beer with Michael. What were the chances? I had purposefully avoided Thelma's, so we wouldn't crash into each other.

When he came over to the table, all I wanted was to touch him. For him to pull me close, to run his fingers over my skin and through my hair, kiss me softly on the lips, letting the kiss linger before he touched my body.

He looked angry, maybe. But he showed no other emotion. Instead, he was cold and distant. It was getting predictable. And old. I responded to his coldness, to his aloofness, by being distant too. I kept looking over at the blond wondering if he kissed her, if he touched her. Did they hold hands? I felt sick thinking about it.

When he walked away, the air thinned, but I felt tears welling again. My eyes burned, but I pulled from my emotional resources and made myself focus on Michael. Michael, who always made me smile, because he was so easy-going.

Michael and I talked about our lives and about life in general. The whole time, I heard the others talking only a few tables away. Laughter broke out a couple of times, and I struggled not to turn and look.

I leaned across the table toward Michael to make sure I paid attention to him. Michael talked about his parents. "Both of my parents are physical therapists. Funny, when I was in high school I thought I would go into medicine, be a medical doctor or a physical therapist. I saw how much my parents helped people and I wanted to do the same. Once in college, I realized I was more interested in emotional well-being, morality and social issues than with the physical side of things."

"I thought I might go to med school too, but then realized I wasn't interested in the biological basis of mental distress. I was more interested in psychodynamics, which made the doctorate a better fit."

"Well, your parents are psychologists too, that must have influenced you."

"Of course. I believe everything can be traced back to early family relationships."

Michael nodded. "I believe personality traits have some biological basis, but yes, those early dynamics are the template for everything."

As interesting as this conversation would be on any other day, and as much as I enjoyed Michael's company, I was distracted by the voices from Will's table. I heard Jude telling one of his LA stories. And it hurt, it hurt because I should have been sitting with them.

Focus. Focus.

Michael gave me a sympathetic look, then whispered, "I know you said no talking about him, but I can see the distress on your face. You can talk to me."

"I am talking to you."

"You know what I mean. The guy is a dick to treat you like this."

"I know."

"What happened after the library?"

"Not sure, because instead of telling me how he felt, he became distant. Anyway, he's history. Clearly." I glared toward Will's table, then slumped back into my chair, crossed my arms over my chest and looked at Michael, whose face wore an expression of compassion.

Michael shook his head. "It's not over. It was clear from how he came by the table that this is far from over, at least for him."

"He's out with someone else." I fought off a frown, then sat up straight, squaring my shoulders. "And so am I."

He smiled at me and then reached for my hands across the table. "I hope it's over for you." He squinted his eyes. "But I get the feeling that whatever is between the two of you, you're not done yet. And that's OK. Sometimes we have to play things out, even when they're painful."

My eyes welled at his accuracy and I looked at him, hard. He cupped my hands in his and squeezed.

It was a moment. One of those moments that should have felt romantic, the possibility of something burgeoning sitting at the table between us. I had always found a man holding a woman's hand across a table — especially for the first time — to be one of the most romantic gestures.

But I didn't feel the desire, the nervous butterflies, or the excitement, only the warmth of his hands around mine, comforting my distress. Michael had this way about him, something I couldn't put my finger on, something honorable. I could feel the devotion in his hands and it made me want to feel his arms around me. I wanted to cry on his shoulder while he stilled my pain.

As I looked at him, I noticed the adoration mixed with compassion in his gaze and I felt myself smile, warmly. "Can we go? It's uncomfortable being here with them here."

"I was surprised you hadn't said something sooner."

Michael settled the bill. As we got up from the table, he took my hand and squeezed. I wanted to lean against him. His presence was so comforting, but I didn't want to do anything like that in front of Will, even though he hadn't given my feelings the same consideration. It felt wrong.

When we got outside, the air felt relieving.

He asked, "You want to go somewhere else?"

"Oh, thanks, but I think I need to go home. Nothing personal. I'm wiped out."

"I'll walk you home."

Michael weaved his fingers through mine and walked me home. Holding his hand felt nice. His warmth felt nice.

"So, how's it going with Julianne? And don't say good. I need details."

He swung our joined hands. "I don't kiss and tell."

"Ha ha."

"Seriously, it's been easy. She's got a busy schedule, so it's not too intense. Plus, she's not demanding of my time, which is good cause I don't have a lot of it to spare. She's smart. She speaks three languages; she's traveled all over for her modeling." He shrugged his shoulders. "We'll see. I never jump too far ahead. Everything is one step at a time."

"That's what I need, something easy. It shouldn't be this hard, should it?"

"No, I don't think it should." He squeezed my hand, as we arrived in front of my apartment building.

"Thanks, Michael." I looked at him and smiled.

He put his arm around me. "You can always talk to me."

I leaned into him. "I know. You are going to be a great therapist. I feel like I could tell you anything."

"Same here."

"See you in school. Call me if you need me."

"Yep."

§

I went upstairs and changed. It was just after midnight. Carter wasn't home. I put on some soft music, poured myself a half glass of wine and sat on the patio thinking. Thinking about Will and the blonde, and how I felt seeing him with another woman. Thinking about how betrayed I felt that he couldn't tell me how he felt. Thinking about how the whole scenario echoed painful memories of Zach. Trying to avoid emotional entanglements to protect myself from making the same mistake led me to a totally different man, but with the same result.

I thought about Michael. He was attractive, tall, athletic, with his warm eyes and inviting smile. I thought of the way his hand felt and the reassurance in his presence. I hadn't noticed that about him quite so clearly before tonight.

I wondered why nothing happened between us after that first drunken night, why I felt no passion toward him. It would have been so easy to fall into a rhythm with him.

I swirled the wine around, took a sip and listened to the ocean and the bustle of the palm trees. I was about to go in for a refill when I heard, *"Alex."*

I looked down the three stories from my balcony. Will stood looking up at me. My heart pattered wildly.

I was not letting my guard down. "What are you doing?" I asked sharply.

"Can I come up?"

"NO."

"Please. I have to talk to you."

I stared at him and my mind raced. I wanted answers. I also wanted to feel his arms around me. And I was afraid of him. Afraid of his distance. Hurt by his distance. Afraid that he could hurt me even more than he already had.

"Please," he pleaded from the courtyard.

"I don't know, Will. You hurt me. Badly. I can't keep doing this."

"Let me at least explain."

I shook my head and huffed at my own weakness. "OK. Fine. Come up. But *nothing* is happening other than us talking. Understand."

He nodded his head.

§

I convinced myself that I needed to set a boundary. He needed to be honest with me or I was not going to be open to even friendship at this point.

He knocked.

I opened the door.

Before I could say anything, he grabbed me, pulled me close and kissed me fiercely. He guided me toward my bedroom, holding my face, kissing me over and over, looking into my eyes in between kisses, with a fiery, almost desperate longing. The intensity made me dizzy.

I felt every emotion he did, concentrated and blazing. I should have stopped it. I should have tried to talk about what had happened. He had been cold. He had been out with another woman. I should've made him explain. But I didn't. And my boundaries went out the window.

I know it probably sounds weak, but the thing with passion is, you can't stop it. The ferocity between us drowned out any words, the desire filling every space between us, every crack within me, every crack within the relationship. And I forgot why I had even felt hurt. All I wanted was to merge with the same person who had broken me, thinking that he was the only one who could fill in all the little crevices making me feel whole again.

Within minutes I abandoned myself, helpless underneath him.

Chapter 26

Will

The phone rang. Will stirred in bed, Alex beside him. He rolled his body over hers and held her from behind. Her bare skin felt smooth and soft next to his. He kissed her neck. It was probably Jude calling about their plans to play basketball and study later. He wasn't sure of the time, but regardless, he wasn't ready to sever his body from hers. He also felt certain that he was going to have to tell her at least some of the truths about who he was.

He had gone to her in a rush of passion. As soon as the four of them had finished at Felicities, he hurried back toward their building. It was late. He had thought she might be in her apartment with Frat-Boy, which made him rush over filled with fury. He had planned to put a stop to it. Nuts, now thinking back. But that's the thing when you're driven by passion: nuts or not, it makes little difference once the emotion takes over.

He had walked past the balcony first, hoping she would be outside. She loved sitting there late at night. There she was, her hair rolling over the sides of her bare shoulders. As soon as she looked down, he knew it was going to be OK. She had seen him with Lilane, and he had seen her with Michael. It was messy, and it was his fault. But it wasn't too late to be fixed. And that's exactly what he had planned to do, until he got in her presence and all he could do was grab and kiss her. The woman made him helpless.

Now it was morning. Before they separated for the day, he felt he owed her some sort of explanation. He was terrified that he would be hurt again. Even more, now, he worried that the wall, that protective barrier, would emerge without intention. Maybe telling her would help them get through this.

She turned and buried her head in his chest. Moistness accumulated along his skin and he looked down at her, raising her chin with his finger. Tears brimmed her eyes as she looked up at him.

She sniffled. "Don't look at me."

"Why not? You're beautiful."

"I – I don't want you to see my emotions."

"I want to see them. I want to know that side of you."

"Then you need to tell me what's going on with you. I'm confused. And afraid."

She diverted her eyes, then rolled over so her back was to him.

He held her tight and whispered, "There are thing — things that I want to tell you but are not easy for me to say."

"Well, you can start with what you were doing with that woman? Who is she?"

"No one. Gabby's friend. I went out with her to try and get away from you."

She sat up, pulled the sheet over her breasts and said, "Why would you do that? Why are you putting up a wall between us?" Her eyes welled again. And he wrapped his arms around her, kissed her eyes and lips. "I will. But first, tell me what's going on with you and Michael."

"Nothing. *Nothing*. At. All. He's a friend. A classmate. You ignore me and then you think you have a right to ask me why I'm spending time with someone else."

His phone rang again, then a text came through from Jude.

"I wasn't ignoring you. I— " The text distracted him.

He read: *I'll come by around 1:00 for basketball. Talked to Kendra. She told me what you did for her son. Impressive.*

He read the text, confused at first, then he looked at Alex. "Kendra knows about what happened with her son? Did you say something? Or did George?"

She swallowed audibly, looked at him through regretful eyes.

"You told her," Will said, sharply, "even though we discussed that we would keep it private. What else did you tell her?"

"Nothing. It slipped out. I'm sorry."

"You know how I feel about keeping things private."

"I do. And it was a mistake. But what's the big deal?"

"The big deal is that I trusted you. You have no idea what it's like to have your trust violated, do you? I told how you hard it is for me to trust," he hollered. Heat coursed through him. How could she do that?

"You violated *my* trust. You told me you loved me, and I believed you. Then you acted like I was a stranger. Do you have any idea what that was like for me? You're not the only one in this relationship. You're not the only one with feelings."

"So, Michael was about getting me back!" His mouth tightened.

"No. NO. I would never do that."

He got up and pulled his boxers on and then his jeans.

Her eyes looked anguished. But he had to get away from her.

"I have to go. We'll talk about this later. I can't right now."

She pulled on him. "Please. Talk. To. Me. What happened to you? I love you. I want to know. Please."

"I can't right now. Later. I will. Later."

"Later's not good enough. You can't keep doing this. You can't keep running away from this. From whatever it is you're holding inside. From us. Tell me *now*." Her eyes were mixed with anguish and fury.

He felt words hanging on his tongue, but no sound came out. He had to get out of there. Even though part of him wanted to take off all his clothes, get back into bed with her and tell her the ugly truth about who he was, he rushed out before he said something he regretted.

He ran to his apartment, taking the stairs instead of the elevator to burn off some of his adrenalin. He was irate.

How could she spill the story after they agreed to keep it between them? What else would she share, offering a liberal look into their private lives?

He was sweating by the time he got into his apartment. He wanted to go swim and burn off some of his ire, but he feared she would be down at the pool. What a messy entanglement their lives had become. He couldn't even get away from her if he wanted to. Unless he left South Beach and graduate school.

Even as he thought the whole thing through — moving, switching programs — he kept looking at his door, waiting for her to knock, asking to come in and talk.

He had let her close, and now there was no turning back. He was out there. Just like the pussy his brother had called him. Maybe Timmy was right. As soon as he was gripped by his feelings, he couldn't contain himself. That's what happens when the whole narrative of your life is false. When your aunt is really your mother, and the woman who is supposed to love you the most — your mother — never loved you at all.

It made him cling too tight to women, he thought. If he had been told the truth when he was a kid, he would have been able to accept it. It was the secrecy, the hushed voices, the pieces of conversations he picked up on, making him think his mother didn't want him. He'd hear her on the phone with his aunt (who was his biological mother), arguing about taking him back. "*He's your responsibility, not mine,*" he had heard his mother say a couple times. He'd cried alone into his pillow, thinking she didn't want him for the same reasons the old man hated him — because he was different.

If only they had told him the truth. Timmy knew. Everyone knew. His ugly self was hung out on display for the whole town to see.

He looked at the door again, trying to will Alex to come knocking for him. He would let her in, even though he knew he shouldn't. He wanted her as much as he didn't want her.

At least if she came to him, he was a passive participant. He didn't have to take responsibility for hurting her if he did.

Or when.

Chapter 27

Alex

William left.

Again.

I lay under my sheets, naked, able to feel the warmth of where his body had just been. I tasted him on my tongue. I felt his fingers in my hair. A tangled web of emotions gripped me, as powerful as the undertow of the evening sea. Complex. Tangled. Relentless. I was furious. And Exhausted. Being tossed around by his emotional back-and-forth was tiring.

I was also heartbroken.

And angry with myself, because when I had told him he could come up last night, deep down I knew he would pull back again. This time I blamed myself as much as him.

That was the worst part. The self-blame. Feeling like I should have or could have stopped the spiral, but Will was the undertow pulling me back into the wild and volatile sea that was our relationship. I was helpless once he gripped me. And even though I was drowning, part of me didn't want to come up for air.

I wanted to go upstairs as insanely irrational as I knew it was. I wanted to scream and pound on his door, demanding that he talk to me. Demanding that he tell me the truth about what he was feeling. If only he told me what had happened to him, the barrier might fall, and we could finally be together.

Thing was, now I didn't trust him. It was the broken vase glued back together with cracks that couldn't be sealed completely. I didn't think the fissures in our relationship could be repaired. We would never be the solid, steadfast vase. The only way to save myself from cracking more completely was to leave all the broken pieces unfixed and walk away, no matter how hard it was.

I got up and got dressed. I paced in my room trying to figure out what I could do to release the anxious agitation, the pain, the anger, that I felt through every part of my body. If I didn't go out, I thought I would lose my resolve and go upstairs and scream, make a scene, a shameless public display of hysteria. I would be one of those women who made other women cringe, because we all fear that type of vulnerability in ourselves.

I did jumping jacks. I jogged in place. I picked up the phone to call Mary Jane, then hung up. I went out on my balcony. The empty pool glistened. And although I knew there was the possibility of seeing Will down there,

I promised myself I wouldn't try to speak to him. I was not going to allow him to take my space, my haven, my swims, from me.

I swam. My arms ripped through the water, and with every lap I felt stronger and calmer. The sun's rays kissed my back and my shoulders, which felt amazing, almost like a warm hand stroking me, soothing me as I swam.

When I got out of the pool and went for the sunscreen, I heard, "Hey, Alllexx."

I turned and saw Jude in long shorts, no shirt. Under the bright sun, I could see every muscle in his chest and abs. His blue eyes, clear as the Miami sky. He smiled.

A broad smile crossed my lips. But after the initial feeling of being in Jude's gaze passed, I felt uncomfortable. He must have known everything that had gone on between Will and me. He had been out with Will and that blond last night. And then I had slept with Will after he had been out with someone else, someone who he may or may not have hooked up with.

You are an idiot, I thought. I felt my face burning with humiliation, I said, "Hey, Jude," then quickly turned away from him and grabbed the bottle of sunscreen. I squirted some into my hand and then squirmed to reach my back.

"Here. I'll do it for you." Jude reached out.

I looked at him, hesitated, then handed him the bottle.

Jude rubbed sunscreen along my shoulders and back in slow, gentle circles. I saw our bodies in the shadow in front of me. His fingers felt warm and sensual and soothing. Given my compromised emotional state, I let him take his time, even though I knew my back was covered and safe from the sun.

His fingers still circled my back when I asked, "What are you doing here anyway?"

"I'm meeting Will to play basketball in an hour. I decided to come early and hang out by the pool and read." He motioned to his books on the table.

"Oh," I said in a small voice.

He massaged my shoulders and said, "Sorry about last night."

I turned to face him. "It's not your fault."

"I know. But I know how it feels to want to have a relationship with someone and have them want less than what you want."

I felt a knot in my throat. I swallowed hard, hoping my eyes didn't well. *Is that how Will felt?* And despite that I knew Will would probably be pissed off that I talked about our personal relations with Jude, I had to know the truth. Besides, it wasn't about him anymore. It was about me.

"Is that what he said?" I searched Jude's face.

"Let's sit."

We sat side-by-side. I adjusted my ponytail and looked at him through sharp eyes. "Tell me. The truth."

"He likes you. I mean, who wouldn't." He put his hand on my leg, then retracted it. "He just doesn't think it's going anywhere. It's always hard when that happens. You like someone a lot, but for some reason, you don't feel what you want to. It's always hard to let that person down. I've been on both sides of that equation. And they both suck."

"That's how he feels about me?"

"I told him to tell you."

I looked down at my lap. It didn't make sense. He would have to be an entirely different person than I had thought. Not haunted by a past demon, but almost manipulative. He had said that he loved me, and I had believed him.

"He's going to kill me for saying this." I looked at Jude, about to tell him that Will told me that he loved me but decided not to. "Never mind."

"What?"

"Oh, nothing. It's a very different version of what I thought was happening. And it's confusing."

"Relationships are confusing." He smiled at me, his eyes warm and charming, enchanting. And for a moment I forgot that he had just delivered a painful truth.

Will wasn't in love with me.

Which meant that he had been lying to me. I had given myself to someone who didn't want me the same way that I had wanted him.

Jude looked deep into my eyes, the blueness enveloping me like an unfathomable sea. I felt lost in his gaze as our faces hovered, and I felt the pull of a kiss. I quickly backed away and asked, "You wanna swim? I'm going back in for another fifteen minutes or so of laps." I needed to finish my swim and get back upstairs before Will came down.

"Sure." Jude jumped in, making a huge splash.

I jumped in after him. Despite how heartbroken I felt, having Jude there made it easier. Knowing the truth made it easier too.

As I swam with Jude, feeling the quiet companionship, I thought that he would be a good distraction, *If* he wasn't Will's friend. Our friend.

IF.

Section III
Here's Where Things Get Complicated

"Every day I wear my guilt and pain around my neck, a different noose, but the same self-inflicted punishment; the weight of it, a daily reminder that I'm responsible for a past I don't deserve to forget."
—Will

Chapter 28

Jude

While he swam with Alex all he could think about was how her lean, tight body was covered with only two pieces of spandex. He wanted to run his fingers down her legs. He wanted to kiss her collarbone. He loved women's collarbones, and Alex's was prominent.

He had backed off from pursuing Alex, because it seemed like Will was interested in her. She was certainly interested in him. But now, Will had told him that he wasn't romantically interested.

At first, he wasn't sure he had believed Will. He had this guarded way about him, and at first Jude had wondered if Will didn't want to admit to himself how much he felt for Alex. The guy was only twenty-five. How many times had Jude, at that age, acted too cool, not admitting to his buddies that some girl stole his heart. Too many. He had always fallen in love so easily back then. He was in love with being in love.

But after talking with Will that morning, he felt certain he just wasn't into her. When he asked about seeing her with Michael (he had been surprised by that, he thought it must have affected Will, even if he wasn't in love with Alex), all he had said was, "I don't own her, man. I have to know she'll go out with someone else, since I'm not going out with her anymore."

"So, you're definitely done?"

"Yeah. I mean, hopefully we'll be friends."

"Right."

That was that. Will and Alex were done, and Jude wanted to get closer to her before she got involved with someone else. She looked awfully cozy with Michael last night. He'd have to squeeze in before he scooped her up.

It was complicated because of the friendship between Will and him, he knew that. And he knew she had just wanted to kiss him and didn't. Probably because he was Will's friend.

So, before she left him down at the pool, he spilled the question: "Can I take you out tonight?"

She gave him a sharp look which he couldn't quite read, so he asked, "What is it?"

"Like a date?"

"Yeah. Like a date. Or *a* date."

"Jude. I'm flattered, but it's too weird. You're Will's friend. You're my friend."

"OK. Then not *a* date, a friendly dinner."

She hesitated, probably for about 30 seconds or so, but it felt longer.

"OK. Yeah. Dinner."

"I'll come by and pick you up at 6:00?"

"That's good. See you then." She turned and then turned back. "Are you going to tell Will about our 'friendly dinner?'"

"You want me to?"

"He's your friend. I feel bad."

"Don't feel bad. Feeling bad for someone who hurt you will only hurt you more."

"Jude, seriously, we are training to be therapists. Empathy."

"Empathy is good. Especially when you are listening to a story that you aren't personally involved in. In this situation, you need to practice self-compassion too."

Her eyes developed that pensive look Alex would often get that he found irresistible. "You're right. Sometimes I don't pay enough attention to what I need. My tragic flaw."

"Mine too. That's why I can see it in you."

She smiled. "Tell or don't tell. I'll leave it up to you. I guess it doesn't really matter."

"No. It probably doesn't."

Alex

It was 6:00 on the dot when Jude knocked. It was a *friendly dinner, not a date*. I had spent the day repeating those two lines over and over. I feared my vulnerability. I was so hurt by what Jude had told me earlier, about Will's feelings. I felt rejected. I felt betrayed. Used. Why hadn't he felt any responsibility to share the truth with me?

Jude made me nervous. I felt like I was looking forward to hanging out with him too much. I needed his attention, somehow, to make me feel better. The notion was simultaneously shameful and irresistible. That was not a good thing with a guy like Jude. A guy I had kissed. A guy that emanated charisma.

When I opened the door, Jude had one yellow rose. "I wanted to get you red, but since it's a *friendly dinner*, not a date, I thought yellow was more appropriate." He shot me that dashing smile.

My cheeks flushed as I saw him trying to fight off eyeing me up and down. I took the rose and let him in. His fresh scent overwhelmed my senses. I had to resist taking an obvious, deep inhale.

"Here, sit." I brought him into the living room. "What can I get you to drink?"

"Red wine?"

"Good choice." I went into the kitchen, which was adjacent to the living room, and retrieved the wine. Jude couldn't see my face because of the wall dividing the kitchen and living room. Knowing this, I asked, "So, did you tell Will we were sharing a friendly dinner?"

"No."

"No?"

"I was going to, but it didn't come up."

I walked back in with the wine and handed Jude his glass. We clinked glasses and each took a sip. "Don't guys talk about… stuff?"

"Stuff? You mean women?"

I shrugged my shoulders. "Well, yeah."

"Of course. You've heard some of our conversations. We are just having dinner. And you and Will aren't together. I didn't think I had to say anything. I mean, I would have had it come up, but he – h. It didn't come up."

My eyes narrowed. "What were you going to say?"

He moved closer to me on the couch and rested his hand on my leg. "I— I— " He took a heavy breath. "I didn't say anything because he was going out with Lilane again tonight."

"*Lilane*? Is that the blonde from last night?"

"Yes."

I looked down at the couch and took a deep breath. I felt tears piercing behind my eyes but stopped them.

I couldn't believe he dumped me without actually dumping me and was going out on a second date with that blond girl. I couldn't believe I had given myself to him last night! What an idiot I was for thinking the fact that he came to me after his date meant something.

I downed my wine. "You want another?"

Jude threw back the remainder of his red and handed me his glass. "Please. You alright? I didn't want to tell you."

"I'm fine. And thank you for telling me. Because *he* didn't. I've had a whole relationship developed in my head. And I guess all along it was a fling. The truth will set you free. And you have bestowed that upon me."

I went to refill the wine glasses. Something still bothered me though. What had Will tried to tell me over and over. Something had happened to him. Something bad. Something traumatic. Something that kept us apart.

No. That last sentence was made up. A made-up addendum to the Alex-Will story in order to avoid feeling rejected.

I brought out the refills and a whole new bottle. "So, what about you and Gabby?"

"Gabby told me last night that she lives with her boyfriend. She's not in love with him, supposedly, but doesn't plan on leaving him either. Something to do with her parents' expectations. Apparently, he fits the mold of the guy she's supposed to marry. It's fucked up. Parents imposing that sort of thing."

"That is messed up. What happened between you two?"

"I kissed her. I know. I probably shouldn't have. She told me she liked me and that she wanted to hang out more. But I don't want to get too involved. She's involved with someone else, whether or not her emotions are invested in him, doesn't matter. I'm looking for a relationship at this point in my life." He penetrated me with his eyes.

The severity of his gaze disarmed me. "I— I see," I broke the gaze. "Well, if that's the case, then yeah, why waste your time with that. Besides, the whole thing sounds like trouble to me. I mean, if her boyfriend found out, it could get ugly." The whole time I spoke, I still felt his eyes on me, as strong and penetrating as the rays of the Miami sun.

"Exactly. So, what are you in the mood for?"

I had no appetite. "I dunno. You?"

His eyes glistened. "I'll take you anywhere you want. But I did bring a surprise."

"Oh?"

"Yeah. It's in my car."

"What is it?"

"If I tell you, then it's not a surprise. Are you willing to let me take control over the evening plans? I had this whole thing planned that I thought you would enjoy, but I didn't want it to feel too much like a date. I don't want you to feel uncomfortable."

Wow, what a switch. Jude actually considered my feelings. Even though I knew he didn't want this to be a friendly dinner, he tried to stay at my comfort level. It was nice to be with a man who respected my needs. "I surrender to your plans." That came out wrong. Jesus. "I— um, meant, I trust you to keep our evening friendly and fun."

My cheeks felt hot.

§

When we got into Jude's car, I felt a wave of relief. Traversing the hallway in the building meant that we could have run into Will and Lilane, which would have been awful. And it probably would have ruined my night. Jude picked up a pizza and more wine, then drove out of South Beach.

Thank goodness.

About 25 minutes later, we arrived at Key Biscayne. It was dark and quiet. Jude found a secluded nook and parked. One of the things I loved about living in Miami was that it was possible to be outside all the time. In fact, Will and I spent most of our time outside, even studying.

"I've taken you for an earthy sort of gal. I thought instead of some fancy South Beach restaurant, we'd try something more rustic."

This was waaay more than a friendly dinner.

This was seduction.

"You've got me all figured out."

"Not all. Some. You and I are similar in a lot of ways."

"Yeah? I don't feel like I know you that well. I know who you were, cause you talk about that a lot, but I am less sure of who you are. Sometimes I think it's easier to hide behind stories about our pasts, rather than being in the moment and letting someone see who we are right now."

"Interesting." Jude pulled a huge blanket out of his trunk, along with his guitar. "This is the surprise. I thought it would be fun to play some live music. Here." He pulled out a small keyboard for me.

"Oh, my God, how fun." I took the keyboard from him. I sat on the blanket he'd rolled out while he got the pizza and wine from the car.

The moon was full and glistened off the water. Stars scattered across the sky, making loops and circles everywhere along the darkness.

We sat side-by-side facing the water, our legs spilling out in front of us. Jude's fingertips touched the edge of my hand. "Back to what you were saying earlier, past experiences define who we are. If you want to know who someone is now, you need to know some of who they were before. We are all a sum total of our past experiences. Right?"

"Yeeees. Riiiight." I nodded slowly as I contemplated. "I believe everything is traced back to our earlier experiences and relationships. I am of the psychoanalytic orientation. I just meant that sometimes I feel you hide behind that life, the one you had before. It's OK. I enjoy your LA stories. I'm not pushing you to say anything you're not ready to."

"I would tell you anything. All you have to do is ask."

Jude was easy to be with. Open, warm, honest.

No walls.

I had overlooked this Jude before, the realness of his in-the-moment self. Maybe his looks or his congenial manner had distracted me. Maybe I was afraid of seeing his realness because the combination of his genuine warmth combined with his vulnerability and handsome looks was beguiling.

"Maybe it's not so much what people say in the moment that tells us who they are, but what they do. How they interact. You know, the interpersonal process, rather than the content." As I finished the sentence my heart felt heavy. I had been listening to Will's words, *I love you.* But what he did, pulling back, going out with another woman, and going out with her after he had just slept with me, that was louder and clearer than anything he had said.

Something swelled between Jude and me. On that blanket, something grew. A deepening of our friendship, I told myself.

But when he reached for the pizza box, his arm brushed against mine, and I shivered.

"Here." He handed me a slice of pizza and a napkin.

"Napkins. Wow. You thought of everything."

"I try." He laughed.

Eating the pizza, we made light chitchat, talk that seemed insignificant but said a lot about a person. It's the little things. Our favorite pizza toppings. Whether movie popcorn had to have butter to taste good. Why coffee was better black. Why we both found seltzer blah, even with a hint of flavor.

We laughed together. It wasn't the laughter of something hilarious, it was the laughter of two people connecting. The type that happened when two people realized they agreed on these little everyday things. When he looked at me through our shared laughter his eyes were dreamy. I drank another glass of wine. It went down like water.

He moved closer to me. Our bodies nearly touched and the suggestion in the movement toward me made me giddy. I put my wine glass down, ran my fingers through my hair and shook my head up at the sky.

"Let's go in the water." I stood up, looking out at the gleaming bay. "I feel like doing something unexpected."

"Are you drunk?"

"No. Why? Am I usually a bore?"

"No. I— you seem different. I don't want you to do anything you will regret."

"Regret? You think I'll regret going in the bay with you. I am a swimmer."

He gave me a knowing look and took my hand in his. "C'mon, Alllexx."

I recognized the seriousness in his eyes. "Come on what?" I batted my eyelashes at him. His gaze made me feel sexy. Uninhibited. I turned away from him, stripped down to my bra and panties — a black silky set — and walked toward the water. I turned back and faced him, noticing the helpless expression on his face. "Come in with me." I splashed a little water at him.

He gave me a serious look.

I tilted my head, stepping backward a few steps deeper into the water.

He stripped down to his boxers and came toward me, taking my hand as we went all the way in. We frolicked around, splashing each other, dunking each other. Jude picked me up and tossed me through the air a few times. We laughed to the point of breathlessness. I looked up at the sky, catching my breath, feeling exhilarated. Then we locked eyes.

Jude picked me up in his arms, the laughter replaced by intensity. His arms felt sure, and his skin was hot. My bra hung loosely over my breasts, barely covering me. I rubbed against him, hoping it slipped off and exposed me.

I felt wild. Feminine. Free.

A liberation from my own mind, and freedom like I had never experienced before.

I stared deep into his eyes. A small intense pause, then our lips merged. His lips were soft and firm on mine, in a conversation so intense it nearly brought tears to my eyes.

We kissed and kissed. I felt those kisses everywhere in my body, even my fingers and toes.

Soon he carried me up to the blanket, both of us now laying in our soaked underwear, kissing and exploring each other's bodies with our hands. When his fingers wandered beneath my panties and he slipped his fingers inside, my stomach clenched. My whole body quivered at his touch. For a moment I thought I should stop it. It was too complicated. I needed to be responsible, careful, conscientious.

But Will had already unfastened the tightness I had had over my heart, freeing me for another. He opened me in a way that perhaps would never be closed. As Jude's fingers traveled inside me, I wanted him, desire permeating my body, almost painful.

I removed all my clothes, his eyes drifting slowly along my bare skin. He ran his lips and tongue from my shoulders, across my breasts, down my torso, over my vagina and along my legs. The wetness of his mouth lingered on my skin as he met my lips with his. He slipped his shorts off. By the time he entered me, I felt desperate for him.

§

Afterward, we laid together, sweating, unable to form words for a few minutes. I soon threw my T-shirt and shorts back on. Jude did the same. He came behind me, wrapping his arms and legs around me, pulling me tight against him. He was an amazing lover, and he felt warm around me.

And yet, tears stung behind my eyes. I had just done something that could never be undone. I gave myself to him, Will's friend. Even if it only happened this one time, I could never take back what had been given.

But I shouldn't concern myself with Will anymore. It was over. My feelings toward Jude were authentic. I didn't love him, that had been an act of pure unadulterated passion. And it felt fucking good.

I turned toward Jude and kissed him, rubbing my hand down his perfectly chiseled face, over the little bit of scruff along his temples and chin. The guy was perfection. Now, not only did I appreciate his good looks, I felt aroused being near him, knowing how he felt.

He put his hands on my face. "You are amazing, Alllexx."

His deep voice made me tingle. "Thanks." I blushed.

"How do you feel?"

"Good. How about you?"

"Perfect."

"Jude?"

"Yeah?"

"Why do you like me?" Jesus. I didn't mean to say that out loud.

He played with a few wet tendrils of my hair. "What's not to like. You are sexy, smart, interesting, athletic, artistic. More than any of that, though, you are easy to be with, easy to talk to. You're serious, but funny, and you are yourself. I don't have to guess with you, because I already know." He kissed me.

"Thanks." I nestled against his chest.

He played with my hair. "I'd like to do this again."

I laughed. "I bet."

"I didn't mean, *this*. Well, *this* too. I also meant, I would like to take you out again. If this was a friendly dinner, I could only imagine how an official date would go."

I chuckled. "I'd like that."

As we drove home, we talked and laughed. "We never played our music. You brought the instruments out and everything."

"Had I known you would seduce me, I wouldn't have bothered with them."

"Me, seduce you? You're the one who set the whole thing up, bringing me to a romantic, secluded area." I shot him a coy smile.

He chuckled. "Um, not to embarrass you, but you stripped down to that lacy poor excuse for a bra and panties, which barely covered you. What did you think would happen?"

"OK. Fine. It was mutual." I kissed his cheek as he drove.

When Jude dropped me off, I brought up the inevitable. "I don't mean to kill the night, but I don't know what we should do about Will? I know there's nothing serious between him and me, but honestly, I had been spending all my free time with him. And I can't help but feel some sense of obligation to tell him the truth."

"It's awkward regardless, I agree. We are all friends. And classmates. Maybe things will take off with Lilane. That would make it easier."

Now that the liberating wine was wearing off, I felt a small knot in my stomach when Jude mentioned Lilane. As much as I enjoyed Jude and was already looking forward to another sexy night with him, I still felt wrong about it. It happened the day after the last time I had been with Will.

"Can we agree not to say anything right now? I guess, I'm asking you not to say anything, since I'm not sure Will will talk to me again."

Jude nodded. "He'll talk to you again. But, yeah. Let's take this one day at a time."

"We'll see where this goes between us before saying anything. 'Kay?"

"Yes."

"I'll see you tomorrow in school."

"It's going to be hard to see you without kissing you."

I blushed and smiled. "You can do it. I have faith in your many talents."

I leaned in, and we shared a long kiss. "I had a great time. Nite." I opened the car door and stepped out.

"Nite."

Chapter 29

Alex

Will looked up at me and then looked away when I walked into class the next day. My heart sunk when I saw him.

"Hey," he said. His eyes looked pained, but his whole manner was detached. Meanwhile, my thoughts swung between the night with Jude, and wondering what had happened between Will and Lilane. My mind was a circus, too many emotions, incongruent colors bleeding into each other.

The thing with love. It didn't just go away because I was done with it, with Will, or because I wanted my feelings to remit. The feelings had a life of their own. The experience of being with him, of loving him, existed within me. The feelings burrowed into a corner of my heart and made a home there.

"Hi," I responded and buried my head in my tablet, making myself appear busy.

I felt his presence, though. I kept swinging my eyes all the way to my periphery, wondering if he was looking at me. He seemed not to care at all. The shared intimacy hanging in the space between us caused distance instead of closeness. Only human emotion was complex enough to maintain such a painful paradox.

Will's distance remained painful, but as the week went on, I tried to accept it. This was what happened when something was over, right? People had to separate, and with separation came distance. Meanwhile, Jude's openness and the easy intimacy between us eased the pain of losing Will. I knew running broken from one man straight into the arms of another probably wasn't a good idea. But we don't always do what's right, do we? Sometimes we do what feels good in the moment.

Jude and I shared a flirty banter. It was fun. And sexy. I hadn't had that with Will. Interspersed between the passion, Jude and I sent playful texts back and forth. I realized that these built intimacies too. Not everything had to be so intense. We hung out together twice that week. One night I slept at his place. He was growing on me. The openness. The ease.

And honestly, he was an attentive and passionate lover.

As much as Will's touch was gentle, sensual, and as much as he excited me, Jude took more control. There was something about the way he commanded my body, like a possession. I wanted him wildly. I wanted him to ravage me, split me open, break the shackles of judgment and fear

I trapped myself in, leaving me bare, exposing every ounce of my skin. I didn't want to be safe anymore.

"Take me," I had said the night I slept over. "All of me." I couldn't believe it came out, but it felt good, really fucking good. His eyes had filled with passion. An intensity swelled as he pulled my dress over my head and rolled my panties down my legs, leaving me bare in front of him. He pushed me onto the bed, spread my legs and went down on me, bringing me to the edge of climax, then stopping, making me gush with desire. He stood back, looking at me through lustful eyes as he slowly removed his boxers, revealing his perfect physique.

"Come here," I had raised my arms in the air, reaching out for him. He stood there, looking at me laying on the bed. I wanted him. Every part of me ached for his body. "Are you gonna make me beg?" I teased, feeling my stomach clenched and weak, waiting for him.

His eyes filled with passion so intense, the gaze penetrated my skin like a ray of the strongest sun. He spread my legs wide, picked me up, wrapped my legs around his body, kissing me hard and wild as he pushed me against the wall and thrusted into me, piercing me with an ecstasy I felt everywhere, even in my hair and toes.

I screamed and screamed. I had no control, my body shook against his over and over, my legs turning limp. He held me the whole time, kissing me while I released and released, then he carried me back to the bed, kissing me slowly all over.

I had spent that night in Jude's arms, fighting off the relentless tingles I felt cuddled against him. As soon as the sun peeked through the blinds, he took me again, twice before breakfast. I liked him. I mean, who wouldn't like a handsome, intelligent, artistic man who was also a passionate lover. Maybe our bodies can fall in love, even without our mind's consent.

Then one night while sitting alone on my balcony, I saw Will strolling down to the pool. He hadn't been swimming to the best of my knowledge. There he was, bronzed and shirtless and handsome. I thought of calling out to him, but what would I say? All the unsaid words? All the unresolved issues? Those were in my mind. Not between us, but within me.

I watched his long, smooth stroke once he eased into the water. He swam for about a half hour and I watched, like a spectator of his life, feeling the fullness of the love I had held for him. When he emerged from the water, his head bowed, pulling the string on his swim trunks, the dim light glowed around him. I stood to go inside before he saw me.

He looked up as if he knew I was looking at him. He smiled and waved. That smile from all the way out at the pool was the most he had given me in two weeks, since the morning he left my apartment. Who knew smiles were precious and not a given.

My lips twisted into a cautious smile, as I waved back.

He looked like he was going to walk over and talk to me from downstairs, but then he turned and walked toward the entrance of the building. I sat back down and rested my elbows on my knees. I should have been glad I dodged an awkward conversation. I *was* sleeping with Jude. But my stomach twisted into a knot of desire and anger, like a braid with two pieces woven together, I longed to feel close to him, and yet, I still felt angry with him.

I could never be with him again (a) because of what he had done to me, and (b) because I was sleeping with Jude. *Aye-aye-aye!.*

I heaved a sigh, one laden with all the emotional baggage left unresolved, and went inside to take a bubble bath.

About an hour later, Jude called to make plans for the following night.

"I'm going to cook for you. Any requests?" he asked with a teasing lilt in his tone.

"Surprise me," I tried to sound flirty, but I felt distracted. *What was I doing?* "Can we talk for a minute?"

"Sounds serious. What's wrong?"

"I— um, shit, I'm not even totally sure what's wrong. I guess, I feel like I'm not being honest with you or with Will." I took a sharp breath and blurted, "I still love him. I don't want to. And I love spending time with you. And it makes no sense at all because he doesn't want to be with me and I don't want to be with him, but I want you to know that I still love him."

"It's OK. I knew that already. People don't just stop loving someone because it's over."

"Exactly."

"What are you saying, really?"

"I dunno. I guess, I felt you should know how I felt. Otherwise it felt like I wasn't being honest. And I do like you and enjoy our time."

"One day at a time. OK, Alllexx?"

The way he said my name always made me shiver, and he was so much easier to talk to than Will.

Maybe in time it will be more.

"OK. I worry too much."

"You're perfect."

"I don't know about that. I do think you will have to tell Will if we continue."

"We will. In time."

"'Kay. See you tomorrow. Nite."

"Nite."

§

About an hour later, Carter called me from outside my bedroom door. "Alex?" I must have heard *it* in his voice, because my stomach clenched.

Shit.

"Yes?" I said, trying to hide the tremor in my throat.

"You have *company*," he said, sarcastically.

I cracked the door. Carter's eyes narrowed, as he peeked his head in, his brow furrowed. "Mr. Wonderful is here," he whispered.

"I kinda thought so."

"You want me to tell him you're sleeping?"

"I dunno. I don't know what to do." Carter didn't know about my ongoing relations with Jude. I hadn't told anyone, yet.

Before I could figure out how to handle this, Will came up behind Carter, intensity emanating off him. "*Alex.* I need to talk to you."

My whole body tightened, one big giant knot of angst. I could barely look into his eyes. But I felt him boring a hole into me as he glared forcefully, even desperately. "Not right now. OK? Tomorrow." I could not deal.

Carter said, "You heard her. Not now."

"Alex. *Please.*"

A fury developed in the pit of my stomach hearing his plea. "What the hell, Will?" I opened the door all the way, piercing him with my eyes. "It's OK," I said to Carter, who twisted his lips and rolled his eyes. "I'll be right in the other room. Just in case you need me," he said with a pinch. He turned to Will and said, "You know, being there for someone you care about, that's a foreign concept to you." He walked away.

Will looked at me as though he could see right into my soul. I saw the ache in his eyes.

"What do you want?" I threw my hands up in the air and turned away from him, then turned back. "You can't just come storming in here. It's ten thirty at night."

"I need to talk to you. Can I come in?"

"Fine." I motioned for him to enter the bedroom, then crossed my arms over my chest.

He went to sit on my bed. "No. There." I motioned for him to sit in the big lounge chair. I pulled my desk chair over to face his chair, leaned back and crossed my arms again. I was not going to let myself be vulnerable. I was not going to pretend he was safe. I was not going to get sucked back into this. Just because I loved him — even as I looked at him, I felt the twinges of the longing, the ache for him — didn't mean I wanted to be with him. Or could be with him.

It was a lesson he had taught me. One I never quite understood until he sat there in my bedroom with those heavy eyes trying to get me to pay attention. I loved him more than I had loved anyone, but I could not be with him. Loving someone didn't mean the relationship was right.

I crossed my arms tighter. "What is it? You finally decided to come break this off properly? Getting serious with Lilane and worried I'd find out?" Lilane's name twisted off my lips, leaving me with a sour taste. I sat up straighter, unwilling to let him see any of my feelings.

He leaned toward me and with that heavy gaze said, "There's nothing between Lilane and me. I hung out with her a few times— "

"That's *not* nothing."

"Let me finish. I hung out with her a few times to try and get away from you."

I stood, ramming my hands onto my hips, my eyes inflamed. "Why on earth would you do that? You have purposely hurt me by shutting me out. I can't talk to you. You just keep hurting me. Do you hear me? You have hurt me. Badly. And more than once."

"*Please*." His eyes pleaded. "I know. I'm totally fucked up. But it's because I was so afraid of how much I felt for you. Feel for you. It's not right. And it's not fair. But it is the truth. I want to tell you things. Things, that I don't normally tell people."

I sat back down. My neck began sweating, so I pulled my hair up and fanned myself. I almost didn't want to know anymore. As I looked at him, pained, serious, troubled, all I kept thinking was that no matter what he said, I was sleeping with Jude, and there was no way to go back to anything with Will. I didn't want him to trust me with his private life or his feelings. I wasn't trustworthy anymore. I would never trust him with my feelings either. I needed him to go.

But his pain was so palpable. It hung all around me. I felt it under my own skin, as if it were mine and just like that, the intimacy barrier was crossed. Before I could even rationalize myself out of it, I kneeled in front of him. "Tell me."

He swallowed audibly. "I lost my mother last year."

"I'm so sorry." I rubbed his leg, contemplating what he said. "Wait? You've spoken about your mother. I'm confused."

"Yes. It is confusing. My biological mother is who I thought was my aunt — so my aunt Renee is my mother. And who I had thought was my mother, Dottie, is my aunt. Dottie is the mother that raised me. My old man is a dick. He hates me and makes it obvious. He never understood me because I didn't think like him. He never told me the truth. He told my brother Timmy, but *no one* ever told me.

"Last year there was a party at the house. Everyone was drunk. Which was usual. My parents — when I say that, I mean my father and the woman who raised me, my mother's sister, Dottie — are drunks. They'd pass out on the floor and I would have to put them to bed, even when I was as young as five or six. They always teased me. They saw me as soft because of my gentleness and arrogant because of my intellectual sensibilities. I had this girlfriend, Bethany. Bethany was the first person I felt understood me. She came from an army family. She had traveled. She saw things. Knew things. We met in college and I had immediately fallen for her. She moved to Mauston to be with me. We were going to get married and move to Miami together.

"But that night, Saul, my father's friend came over. The guy was a total asshole. When he got drunk, he would get loud and rough. A few times he grabbed some of the women, women who were with other men. This night, he grabbed my mother's breasts. I went nuts. Ape shit. I punched him right in the face. Blood poured out of his nose. He looked furious. I thought he was going to hit me back, but he didn't. He laughed. A sinister, maniacal laugh.

"Then he said, 'fuck you, little Willy. That ain't yo mothah anyway. Stupid kid.' My father's eyes became slits. I looked at my old man and then Saul and then back. Then Saul spit it out. He told me the truth about who I was. My mother, Renee, who I thought was my aunt, abandoned me when she found out my father cheated on her with Dottie, her sister. I had overheard some conversations when I was younger, which made me think my mother didn't want me, but that wasn't the case. She wanted my biological mother to take responsibility for me. I always felt something, some sort of fear or confusion, but I had no idea that this — *this* — was my story. Are you following me?"

"Yes. My God, yes." I put my hand over my mouth, shocked. "How awful. To find out like that. To not know the truth for twenty-four years, that must have been devastating."

"It was. And is. But the story gets worse. Much worse."

I felt a lump in my throat. Will's eyes were all red. He looked like he was on the verge of tears.

He looked so vulnerable. I squeezed his hand. "Tell me. I'm here for you."

He continued in a whisper. "My father pulled out a shotgun and pointed it right at Saul's head, screaming, 'get out, mother fucker. Get out.' Saul glared at my father, blooding streaming out of his nose. Then he pulled a shot gun out from around his pants' leg, and my dad shot him in the arm to disable him. His gun landed on the floor, and my mother, my Aunt Dottie, went to call the police. At this point I was mortified. Embarrassed. Ashamed. I'm thinking, this is where I came from? This is who I am? My father shoots people. Like a bar fight in our house. And my mother isn't my mother. I'm not who I thought I was.

"Bethany was beside me crying hysterically, her hands around her cheeks, shaking her head in disbelief. I should have attended to her. I brought her there after my mother,

Dottie, begged that we come to the party. I hated their parties, but I was always trying to please my mother. And she'd married my loser dad, so I wanted to be there for her. I never should have exposed Bethany to their lifestyle.

"Bethany cried. I wanted to help *her*. But the news about my mother overwhelmed me. I ran. I ran out of that ugly mess. Away from the gross house I grew up in and all those people who knew the truth about who I was. Who knew that my mother didn't love me or want me.

"I ran. And ran. Soon I heard Bethany calling me, screaming through the streets, 'Will, come back. Talk to me. It's going to be OK. Will. *Please*.' Then I heard the worst sound I will ever hear in my life. A loud screech. A long piercing screech followed by the noise of metal colliding with something, a thump that I felt in my throat. Then total silence. Eerie silence.

"I turned and ran back. Everything was soundless, everything felt motionless, even my own body, like I dissociated. I ran a block back and saw her. Blood streaming in a web from her head, her body sprawled along the road in an X. The car, a light blue sedan in the distance, zooming, leaving the scene of the accident. Leaving Bethany. I ran over, checked her pulse, screamed for help. People came out of their houses. Some guy, Hank Farley, helped me. He called an ambulance, but it was too late. Bethany…" Tears fell down his cheeks. "Bethany was… gone. And it was my fault."

I had a huge lump in my throat as I watched tears streaming out of his eyes, his face scrunched in agony. I pulled him into a hug, rubbing his back over and over. I felt his woundedness against me. "It's OK. I'm here."

He finished through his tears, "To top it all off, when I called my mother, Renee, my biological mother, and confronted her, she said that in her mind I wasn't her kid. Never would be. She abandoned me twice. I'm still fucked up from it."

He looked into my eyes, a gaze so concentrated I felt it in my whole body. His pain. I kissed his head, his cheeks and then his lips.

"I— I— " his voice shook. "I was afraid to love you because I thought I would destroy you the way I destroyed Bethany. I thought you would hurt me the way my mother did. When your whole life is a lie, you fear. You fear that at any second, what you think is real will turn out to be false. I kept thinking you would leave. Turn your back on me. Once you saw who I was, you would pull away. It's not rational. But the feeling was so strong it made me act in ways I didn't want to. It made me hurt you. But then being with Lilane, a woman I felt nothing for, made me realize how foolish this was. You love me. And I love you back. I was running away from the first good thing in my life since I lost everything. My mother, my childhood, and Bethany. I'm so sorry. *So sorry.*" He pulled me tight and kissed me with painful intensity, his tears soaking my face and dribbling into my hair.

I kissed him back, his cheeks, his lips, his hair, his neck, trying to kiss away the pain, the pain that had left a barrier between us.

The wall was gone in that moment. I felt such an authentic closeness with him. No walls, no hesitation, a truth from him, more real than anything I could have imagined. I saw deep inside his soul, his broken, wounded, but warm and gentle soul.

We kissed and hugged like two people that had been separated for years and finally reunited, hungry kisses, desperate to fill any spaces between us. I was lost in that kiss for a few minutes, before the reality settled in, sending a piercing sensation up my back.

I had slept with Jude, abandoning Will, the man I had loved. Now I held a truth that would shatter his reality again. Another betrayal of his trust. Another false narrative.

And even though I knew it wasn't my fault — how could I have known what he was going through if he didn't share – his pain was so palpable, I couldn't help but feel guilt.

He was the first to break the silence. "Are you OK?"

"Yes," I whispered. "It's just so much. I wish you would have told me."

"I wanted to but didn't know how."

I nodded.

"Let's lay down." He held my hand and guided me toward the bed.

We lay together, holding each other. I felt him breathe in and out along my hair, my cheek, his heart beating against mine.

Will fell asleep in my arms.

When I heard the rhythm of his breathing change, I disentangled myself from his arms and stared at the ceiling, tears streaming out of my eyes.

What was I supposed to do? I hadn't a clue how to untangle the mess I was in. Worse, I didn't know what I wanted. Or who. The ceiling was a blanket of white and I stared at nothing, afraid to feel anything, because I had too many emotions all at once. Maybe I didn't even know who I was anymore. Or maybe I never did.

§

The morning provided no answers. Will woke up and hugged me from behind, whispering in my ear, "You feel good."

"You too," I responded, but the truth weighed on me. I had barely slept.

Then Will ran his fingers through my hair and said, "I'm exhausted, but I feel like a burden has been lifted. You're the only person outside of Mauston I have shared the truth about my life with."

I stared at the wall in front of me, the stark whiteness, the nothingness of the blank white wall, trying not to think passed the moment. "I'm glad you told me. None of that is your fault. None of that defines who you are. Those are things that happened to you, an awful chain of events that you could never have anticipated."

"And things in our environment define parts of us. Especially when you find out the narrative of your life wasn't what you'd thought. Especially when your careless actions hurt … took someone who you loved, someone who you should have been taking care of. I will never forgive myself completely. Therapy has helped some. But totally forgiving myself is out of the question. I didn't tell you because I need to work through it or even because I was looking for compassion. I told you because my past was keeping us apart. It was keeping me from letting you in. It was hurting both of us. And I knew telling you was the only way we would ever work."

I turned and faced him, looking into his eyes. I had never felt closer to anyone than I did to Will in that moment. I had never had someone share something so painful, so close to their heart, something that took real courage to share. I saw inside of him.

And yet, I felt something deep in my gut, a new expanse between us that could never be crossed without telling him the truth about Jude. I also wasn't sure I could trust that Will wouldn't pull away again, that I could feel open to him in the way that I had. If I gave him another chance and he distanced himself again, I would blame myself.

Something else occurred to me as my eyes wandered from his eyes down his neck to his bare chest. I had allowed myself to be open to Jude in part because of what Jude had told me that Will had told him: Will didn't want to be with me.

I didn't know whose story was the truth. Did Jude lie to me to get me to sleep with him? Or did Will lie to Jude?

I wanted to ask Will, but I didn't want to draw attention to anything having to do with Jude and me. I would ask Jude. Thinking that highlighted the easier connection with Jude.

Not closer. *Easier.*

Will wrapped his arms around me, pulling me close, my whole body tingling at his touch. Tears licked the corners of my eyes from the intensity of being near him combined with the truth about my relations with Jude.

We kissed.

And kissed.

An hour of kissing.

I became lost in him, like we went to a place, wandering and exploring together, so close. He removed all my clothes and ran his hands all over my body, slowly, circling my skin with his fingertips, watching me respond to his touch. As his eyes wandered across my naked body and I lay bare before him, I felt no need to cover myself. He had exposed himself to me and I wanted to give him the same. He took me in with his eyes, running his fingers along my lower abdomen, then he stuck his finger inside me, my back arching as I responded to him.

He took his clothes off, never taking his eyes off me. We made love. Not wild, passionate love. Deep, concentrated love, the type that happened when two people shared something so personal, it eliminated any boundaries between them.

Lying with him afterward, I knew I had to talk to Jude. I wasn't sure what I would say. Because as much as I didn't want to think about it while cradled in Will's arms, I wasn't sure what I wanted.

I wanted to go back in time. I wanted to have Will share these things before it created the circumstances that led me to make an irreversible decision. I wanted him to have shared these things before my hurt had turned to anger, an anger that still lingered on the periphery of my mind, almost like a dull, but relentless hangover.

Then Will said, "You want to do something today?"

"OK," I responded with a knot in my stomach. I needed to talk to Jude and STAT.

"I have to call Jude. I was supposed to meet up with him to work on statistics. I'll reschedule with him for tomorrow."

That little knot in my stomach expanded and felt like a boulder, the weight of the secret baring down deep inside. I had to tell Jude the truth before Will did.

"Don't call him now. Let's make breakfast first." My heart pumped wildly.

"It'll only take a minute."

Will picked up his phone and rang Jude. I felt the consternation in my whole body as I thought, *please don't pick up.*

"Voicemail," Will said to me. My shoulders relaxed.

"Hey, man. Change of plans. I need to reschedule our stats today. Can you meet up tomorrow? Call or text me."

He turned to me, his eyes morphing from animated to concern. "What's wrong." He moved closer to me.

"Nothing," I responded, too short and quick.

He tilted his head and the green of his eyes swirled around. "Tell me. Is it what I shared last night? Is it bothering you?"

"No. NO. I'm tired is all. It was a late night." I shrugged my shoulders and swallowed.

Will seemed satisfied and then asked, "Do you want to rest by the pool?"

I shrugged my shoulders.

"Wanna go to the zoo?"

"Sure. Let's do that."

§

Will went upstairs to take a shower. I ran to my phone, nearly tripping over the leg of the kitchen table. I rang Jude. *Please, pick up.* I went into my bedroom and paced, as his phone rang in what felt like an endless *brrrriiiinnng*.

"Heeeey."

"Hey," I said with a mix of relief and trepidation. Unformulated words sat on my tongue. I didn't want to say the wrong thing, but I didn't even know what the right thing was. The truth, I told myself. Don't lie. You are already prisoner to one big secret. "Um, so, something happened last night."

"Are you OK? You don't sound too good."

"I'm *not* OK," I said too emphatically, then continued in a more measured tone, "something happened with Will." I realized as the words came out, to my vexation, that I could not tell him *everything* Will had shared.

"Tell me."

"I— he. I'm sorry. He came down last night and apologized for being distant. We talked."

"Did you sleep with him?" Why was *this* the question he asked? Typical. Predictable. I wanted to cry. Having sex was easy. It was all my emotions that made this an impossible situation.

"Yes."

"*Oh*."

Silence.

"Jude. I'm sorry," I gushed. "I like you. A lot. And seriously, I love hanging out with you. You're so easy to be with."

"But that's not enough, right?" he sounded defensive.

"It was until— "

"You love him."

"You knew that."

"I did. So why are you telling me?"

"I don't know. Honestly, I'm not sure. I'm confused. But I wanted to tell you the truth. And I wanted to ask you to please not say anything to Will about you and me. If that is to come out, it should come from me."

"What did he say to you last night? Cause he's been acting like it's completely over between you two and that he never saw it going anywhere."

I bit my lip, hard. Why would Will tell Jude that and then tell me a whole different story? I felt certain that his sharing the truth about his life meant that he really loved me. Trusted me. And I wanted to trust him, but why would he lie to Jude?

And did he lie to Jude? Or was it me he was lying to?

My mouth twisted as I felt the betrayal of Will's trust releasing from my mouth. I needed to protect myself. And that meant telling Jude some of what he shared with me. I also needed Jude to keep everything discrete, until I figured out what to do.

"Will told me he loved me. He told me he had tried to fight it but couldn't. I know he told you something different and I don't know why. All I can guess is that he's adamant about privacy. Or maybe he was afraid to tell you the truth because he was afraid to expose himself. Whatever it was, I feel confused and guilty and awful."

"This isn't your fault. It's mine."

"How is it your fault?"

"He's my friend. Granted, I haven't known him for that long, but still. I shouldn't have pursued you so quickly. Fuck. You really think he was lying to me and not lying to you about how he feels?"

"I can't be sure. But, yes. And now I don't know what to do." I fought off the well of tears.

"I like you, Alex, but I'm not going to pursue this if what you really want is to be with him and he wants to be with you. If you guys are in love with each other, I'll never say a word about what happened between us."

Jude's reasonableness and maturity were attractive. Talking to him on the phone, his deep voice and the warmth, even given the content of the conversation, made me more confused.

"I do love him, but that's not enough reason to stay with someone at this point in my life. Love is a feeling. A great feeling. But I can't be with someone I love if they continue to hurt me."

"Of course not. But *we* can't continue until you figure out what you want. I can't wonder if when I'm not with you that you might be with him. And I can't wonder while I'm with you that somewhere deep inside, you're thinking of him."

"I need time."

"Then take it."

"God. I appreciate how levelheaded you are."

"Thanks."

"Talk later. OK?"

"Yeah. Sure."

I heard the deflation in his voice, and I felt regretful. But I couldn't be with Jude while trying to figure out what I wanted from Will. In fact, I probably could never be with Jude unless I was willing to tell Will the truth.

I didn't know if I could be with Will while carrying the burden of this secret either. I didn't know if I could be with either of them without the truth coming out.

Chapter 30

Alex

After the zoo, we went back to South Beach for dinner. Will had texted Jude to meet us. Thankfully, Jude had texted back that he already had plans. But I knew it was only a matter of days before I had to be with both of them together.

We went to Thelma's and sat at the bar. "Come here." He pulled my bar stool closer, then rested his hand on my leg.

Will had been unable to keep his hands off me all day.

His hesitancy was gone. That feeling I always had that he held back something was gone too. I felt all of him with me.

And it was terrifying.

I had never felt responsible for someone's emotions before, not like this. I knew I held his heart in my hands, and I knew there was a pretty good chance that I was going to hurt him.

I pushed Jude out of my mind and tried to enjoy Will. If I was ever to see if things between Will and me could work out, I needed to be fully present with him. But I kept leaning slightly away from him and I moved my chair a little, creating some physical space between us, both of which, I realized, had nothing to do with Jude. It was a sense that too much had happened. That he had hurt me too much and no matter how much I wanted to feel the way I had before, in love, I didn't know if I could get it back.

He put his hand on my leg. "I'd really like to be a vegetarian. Have you ever been?"

"I was for a few years. Then I cheated one day with a burger. I've always wanted to go back. It felt better when I wasn't eating meat. It's just more work to get the calories to fuel my training. When I swam competitively in college, I couldn't get enough food."

"You *still* eat a lot," he teased.

I laughed. "This coming from the man who eats like he's filling a bottomless pit."

"Ha! Touché. We could try cutting out meat together. We could get a vegetarian cookbook and try new dishes."

"That would be fun."

He took a tendril of my hair and ran it through his fingers. "We could go to the bookstore after this."

"It might be too late. And I feel like I need to start working on the personality theories paper."

"When is that due?"

"Two weeks. It's twenty pages with at least ten references. It's a lot of work."

"*We* probably should get started."

My stomach tossed around. Will slipped right back into a rhythm, like nothing had happened, like nothing had been broken between us. I wished I could slip easily back into it with him, but those fractures weren't gone. They needed time to heal, *if* they would heal.

"Will. Um, I am grateful that you shared such a private part of yourself with me. But we need to take this slow. I was hurt by your distance. I understand now why you pulled away when you did. But, my heart is still healing."

His eyes turned heavy. "The last thing I wanted to do was hurt you."

"I know. I forgive you. But sometimes too much happens, and you can't go back. I don't think that's the case with us. I think I just need time to ease back into this."

In the back of my mind, that secret rumbled, intruding like a dissonant noise that I had no control over.

"We'll go as slowly as you need." He squeezed my thigh.

I kissed his cheek. "Thanks. We should talk more about what you told me. It sounds like you still carry a lot of pain."

"I saw a therapist for a while. Sure, we can talk about it more. Probably should. I mean, it was an all-defining experience."

"Do you talk to your mother?"

"To Dottie? The mother that raised me, yes. There was some estrangement for a short time, but I have forgiven her. She was trying to do the right thing by me and make up for what my biological mother was incapable of. Renee is a child. We have almost no contact now. She sent a birthday card this year, Love, Aunt Renee. She had underlined 'Aunt' three times. Even though she knows I know the truth." Will's face turned red.

I placed my hand over his. "That's really terrible. But it's not your fault. It doesn't mean you aren't lovable, it means she can't love. You know that, right?"

"Sure. I know it, but sometimes it doesn't feel like that. Every once in a while, the feeling of being betrayed creeps in. I think sensing that something wasn't right but not being told the truth made it worse. It affected my ability to trust. It made me fear."

"Fear?"

"It's like a panic. A deep panic that somehow it will happen again. I will be betrayed. My trust will be broken. Telling you feels like a turning point. Like I released all of these secrets that made me afraid to be close with you." He took my hand and kissed it. I gulped. He could never ever know about Jude, regardless if we moved forward or not.

I realized within two days that there was no way to take something slow that had already emotionally evolved. Will and I were inseparable. No matter how much I tried to slow our pace, I couldn't. Jude avoided us in school. Will didn't notice because he didn't realize there was something to notice.

We only see what we look for.

On Friday, we sat in a deli around the corner from campus, eating avocado and hummus sandwiches, trying to be vegetarian, and drinking iced coffees. Our heads were buried in books. I felt him before I saw him. *Maybe we develop telepathy for people we have had recent sex with.* When I turned, Jude and I met eyes, a tingly sensation ran down my back. I'd like to tell you that it was all nervousness, because of our secret, but it wasn't. I felt our mutual chemistry as soon as he came over. "Heeeey," he said.

I smiled at him, but I had to look at his chin, in order to avoid his eyes and the penetrating gaze I could sense.

"Hey," I said, trying to keep my voice steady.

Will asked, "Did you finish the stat homework? Man, regression analysis is hard."

Jude nodded. "But learning the predictor variable is important for behavioral science research. Trying to figure out what traits predict outcomes are a fascinating part of the work."

"Or what environmental circumstances predict behaviors," Will said. "I get it. The theory behind it is fascinating, looking at the variables and making sense of the numbers is fascinating. It's the actual formulas that are hard."

"Like I was showing you, you can do it all on the computer. We can go over it again if you need more help," Jude said to Will.

Will looked at me.

"You go. I'm gonna go home. I think I know how to run the predictor variable. Not well enough to teach you, but well enough to get the homework done."

Will and Jude both watched me talk. I was warm, but I pulled my sweater around myself trying to cover the truth that seeped through my pours.

"Let's do something tonight," Will said to Jude. "Come out with us."

Jude looked at me, and I saw the thin lines of consternation around his eyes. He said to Will, smoothly, "I'm actually hanging out with Kendra tonight. She's having a few people over. Come."

"She didn't invite us," I said, assuming Kendra was still pissed about George Jr. and didn't want Will and me there.

"Don't be silly. It was last minute. She just decided about an hour ago when she found out her husband was staying the weekend in Chicago on business. I think the guy's having an affair, if you want my opinion. He's away a lot."

"Don't get close to her," Will admonished.

"We're friends. I like her. She's really easy to talk to. I am capable of being a woman's friend."

His eyes met mine. I was dying. I felt the ghost sensation of his fingers running down my body as he looked at me. Hot sex never leaves your skin, I decided.

"I gotta go." I gathered my books and tablet.

"What's wrong?" Will asked me. "You didn't even finish your sandwich."

"I'm going to swim. I don't want to overeat."

"I thought we were going to swim together."

"The stats are important. It's OK. Go with Jude. I'll catch up with you later."

Will looked perplexed. "Ooookaaay Let's go to Kendra's with Jude tonight."

"Really?"

"Why not? We haven't hung out with Jude in a while. It'll be fun."

Jude said, "MJ and Fred will be there."

"Maybe." I shrugged my shoulders. "Let me think about it. It's been a long week, and I'm exhausted." I kissed Will's cheek.

He looked puzzled.

I said, "See you later," to Jude.

The two of them watched me as I threw my bag over my shoulder and hurried out.

I almost fell getting into my car, distracted by the whirl of my tangled, indistinct thoughts.

I leaned forward, making sure to concentrate on the road, while attempting to shift through my web of thoughts. I felt the truth on the precipice of my conscious mind and kept trying to talk myself out of it, but I just kept coming back to the same thing.

I loved Will and I was attached to him, but something was broken between us, something I was hoping would repair itself, but hadn't. Worse, I had feelings for Jude too. And not just sexual feelings. Real feelings. Not love, but something.

Maybe the possibility of something.

I wanted to love Will enough to fix all the cracks in his broken heart, but the love felt different now. I loved him because he needed me.

And maybe I liked Jude because I needed him. He filled something that Will had left empty.

No. I pulled my hair up, flicking the air conditioning to its coolest setting, angling the vents directly on my face. I blasted the radio, bellowing words that didn't match the music, trying my best to not think anymore.

Maybe I didn't really love either of them. Maybe it had something to do with me.

Chapter 31

Kendra

Kendra leaned up and planted a kiss on Jude's lips. He had arrived early to help her set up for her little party. She wore a low-cut shirt, exposing her cleavage. Men liked tits. Hers were still nice. She might as well use them when she could. She had learned from George and his friends just how important it was for a woman to use her physical assets.

Jude hadn't made a move, and it was getting close to the time guests would begin arriving. She couldn't wait any longer, so she initiated. Nothing wrong with a woman who knew what she wanted. She wasn't looking for more than sex, so she really had nothing to lose.

Jude kissed her back, but she felt the tentativeness in his kiss. "What is it?" she looked at him, batting her eyelashes.

"You're a married woman."

"On paper, yes. But my husband is having an affair with a much younger woman. Quite honestly, to me, this means the covenant of the marriage no longer applies." She weaved her fingers through his. "We've been friends for a few months now. I feel like I can be frank with you about what I want."

Instead of playing the seductive woman role, she decided to tell the truth. It was a little trick she had learned from observing George. The truth disarmed people, because they never expected it.

"I've never been with another man. Only George." OK, so she had made a small fib by saying George had been the only man. It seemed smarter if she left the other sexual experience out. It was almost like she was a virgin. She knew how much men enjoyed penetrating a fresh pussy. "Finding out he broke our vows crushed me at first. I trusted him. But now I see it more as a liberation. Positive reframes are always good." She smiled. "I would like to experience another man. And I'd like it to be you."

When Jude wrapped his muscular arms around her, she felt a tingle in her vagina. She had felt nothing for George for the last year or so. Of course, the passion had dwindled over the years. The familiarity of his body made the sex less exciting, but there was a comfortable, safe intimacy that made their loving satisfying. Until she found out about Adeline. She felt nothing when he touched her now, even when he penetrated her. She wouldn't allow herself to feel anything. His dick was tarnished, as far as she was concerned. A dirty dick.

"You're an attractive woman, Kendra. And I like you as a person. I understand your situation, but my experience has been that you don't mess with a married woman."

His arms were wrapped around her as he said this, and his eyes betrayed his desire. He needed a nudge. She leaned into him, kissing his neck. "Show me what you're like," she whispered.

"You are making this really hard." His eyes narrowed, and she felt him grow — harden — against her. He pulled away. "I'm sorry. I can't."

She could tell he was lying. So, she opened the button of his jeans, pulled them and his boxers down, and took him in her mouth.

He groaned, throwing his head back and she knew she had him.

His dick was thick and juicy. And she opened her throat, bringing him as far back as she could without choking. She felt her nipples harden under her shirt. She gazed up at him with kittenish eyes. "Take me in the bedroom."

He looked down at her, trepidation splayed across his face. He let out another mild groan and then moved back, bent down to grab his boxers and pants which were around his knees. "I— I can't. I want to. A lot. But I can't."

His pants were up, and her skin felt hot. She was horrified.

She looked at him through sharp eyes. "George is having a full relationship with someone else. It's not wrong. And I could feel in my mouth how much you wanted me."

He pushed his hair off his forehead and took a heavy breath. "Let's sit. Let me mix you a drink. We'll talk. What do you want?"

She crossed her arms and, in a huff, leaned against the wall. "Gin and tonic"

He made the drinks quickly. "Let's sit outside."

Her lips were puckered and pushed to the side of her mouth. "Fine."

They sat, and he looked at her with those warm blue eyes. "Maybe you should think about filing for divorce. Your kids are grown. You're clearly not happy. Why not leave him. Start over."

"Aye. Someone else telling me what to do. George has been telling me what to do and how to act for the last twenty-five years. I'm sick of it."

"I'm not telling you what to do. I'm trying to be a good friend and make sure you don't do something you will regret — like have sex with me, or stay in something you are obviously unhappy in. You are an amazing woman. You leave him, you will find someone you can be with."

"But not you."

"You don't really want me. I'm just an act of convenience. I was here. It would be easy. But just because something is easy, doesn't mean it's right."

"George is in politics, a divorce would be public."

"He should've thought of that before he started his affair."

"He's all I've ever known," she looked away and said softly. "I don't think I'm strong enough to leave."

He leaned forward and took her hands. "Look at me," he said in a soothing voice.

She looked at him through glassy eyes.

"Yes. You. Are. We are always capable of more than we think. Complacency makes us think we aren't strong enough to change. I will stand by you as a friend."

"And that's it?" She attempted a coy smile, through the sadness that coated her eyes.

"I'm also trying to make changes. I'm looking for a relationship. Engaging in sex with a married woman — especially if she's someone I like and respect as a person — is a mistake. It's something I would have done in the past that would have been a selfish and immature decision."

"Oh. Leave it to me to try and have a casual fuck with Mr. Morality." She looked deep into his eyes. "Is there a woman in particular? You seem so… adamant."

He sucked in air and stared out at the water. "There is. But it's not going to work out."

"Oh?"

"Yeah," he said in a faraway voice.

She put her finger under his chin and turned his face toward her. "You can talk to me, you know."

"It's a mess. I probably shouldn't even get into it."

"Nonsense. You just helped me. You can talk to me." Kendra watched him pause for a moment, contemplating if he should reveal his secret, focusing on a distant building rather than meeting Kendra's gaze.

"It's… Alex. I think I love her." When he finally met Kendra's eyes, his were moist. "I know I love her."

Kendra nodded. "And she's back with Will again, isn't she? They are either together constantly or ignoring each other. It won't last. That type of thing won't last."

The thought of Will excited her. He was the one she had originally wanted to explore her sexuality with. When she had heard of his heroic act with George Jr. and realized how important discretion was to him, she realized he was perfect. It was probably a blessing in disguise that it hadn't gone further with Jude. If Jude was with Alex, that would leave Will free.

Jude sighed. "Something fucked up happened. You can never repeat this. I shouldn't even say it out loud, but I need to talk."

"You can tell me." She put a hand on his leg.

"Alex and I were hanging out for about a week. Truth is, I have liked her since the first day I met her. Gradually, I realized she was into Will. I didn't let that stop me until I realized that Will might be into her too. So, I didn't pursue. But Will and she were on and off. He told me at least four or five times that he wasn't into her. That it was over. He went out with a friend of Gabby's a few times. Then suddenly they're back on, and Will supposedly loves her but never said anything. So now, I've betrayed one friend and I'm in love with the other. I fucking come here and promise myself to make better decisions. And look. Shitty choices again. And now a secret that will always be there."

He leaned forward, resting his elbows on his knees. She rubbed his back, but he wiggled away from her fingers.

"I don't deserve consoling. I screwed over a friend. And the truth is, all I can think about is that I hope it doesn't work out between them. Isn't that awful? Hoping something doesn't work out for people you care about."

"It's human, Jude. You love her. I see what you mean, though. It is messy." She looked at him. He seemed so genuinely distraught. She took his hand, squeezed and then released it. She empathized with his distress, which brought a warmth to her heart that had been gone since she found out the truth about George and Adeline. "What are you going to do?"

"Nothing. Fight my feelings for Alex. Hope Will never finds out."

"Really? You're going to give up so easily on the woman you love?"

He shrugged his shoulders. "I think so."

Kendra squeezed his hand. "Mutual love does not come easily."

"No kidding, but even if I decided to disregard any loyalty, she wants him. Loves him. I screwed myself over by even becoming involved with a woman while she still loved another man."

"Nonsense. You took a risk. It's courageous."

"I'm not so sure."

"Are you sure she doesn't feel the same?"

"Yes. She said so."

"Perhaps *you* need another drink."

He nodded.

"About earlier," she touched his arm, then retracted, "I apologize. You're a good friend."

"I already forgot about it."

Will texted a few minutes later that he and Alex weren't coming.

Jude wrote back: *Why not? A better offer?*

Will wrote: *Alex isn't feeling well.*

Jude: *What's wrong? Is she OK?*

Will: *Tired and burnt out, I think. She just needs rest.*

Jude: *Why don't you come alone?*

Will: *I feel like I should stay in case she needs me. I'll text if I change my mind.*

Jude: *OK.*

"They're not coming. Alex doesn't feel well. I'm disappointed and relieved."

"I understand that. Did you tell her that you love her?"

"No. I didn't want to make her uncomfortable or come on too strong."

"Don't you think you should tell her, so she has all the information?"

"I don't know. She loves him, and he loves her. They're both friends. It's not simply putting my heart out there, it risks hurting Will, and it risks hurting Alex by making her feel guilty. Sometimes the greatest form of love is sacrifice."

"Don't be a martyr. You haven't known Will *that* long. Sometimes you have to go after what you want. I sat back my whole marriage. I let George dictate my life, down to how I would dress to impress his 'friends.' I didn't even let myself recognize the discontent until I found out about his affair. I regret not pursuing things I wanted early, like going for my doctorate. And honestly, I had always wished that I had had a relationship with a man before George. At least one. I feel it would have given me a perspective that I don't have only knowing myself with George. If you want her, you have to at least try."

"I'm glad you're going back to school."

"Are you going to tell her?"

"I don't know, but you've given me something to think about."

The bell rang. Before Kendra could get to the door, Mary Jane and Fred entered the kitchen, both wearing red. "The door was open, so we let ourselves in." Mary Jane kissed Kendra's cheek and handed her a large bottle of red sangria.

Mary Jane kissed Jude's cheek, then asked, "Where's Alex?"

"She's not feeling well."

Mary Jane pursed her lips. "No doubt it's because of the roller coaster she's been riding with Will. They're on, they're off. I don't know if you know this or not, but he has *really* hurt her. You should talk to him. I don't think Alex has expressed this to him in a way that he understands, 'cause he just keeps coming back. And every time he leaves, he rips more of her heart out. I had a relationship like that once. It took me years to get over it. You should tell him that if he doesn't love her or if he can't be there for her consistently, he should man up and leave her the hell alone."

Jude shifted on his feet. "I did tell him."

Jude

When Jude thought about what Mary Jane just said, it made him wonder if Will was lying to Alex, telling her that he loved her, so he could have another chance only to abandon her again. Maybe he needed to ask Will what he was doing going back to Alex after he had said it was over.

It was too tricky, though. If Will said he didn't really love Alex and was "just hanging out with her," then what would Jude do with that information? Would he tell Will the truth, that he loved her?

No, Alex loved Will.

You're an idiot, man. Stay out of it.

Mary Jane looked at Jude, inspecting his face with wandering eyes. "What were you thinking?"

"Nothing. Just that maybe I should talk to Will again."

"You should. Definitely."

"Who else is coming?" Mary Jane turned to Kendra.

"A few of my friends from the hospital and maybe Michael. It was last minute."

"Well, I brought my swimsuit this time. Fred insisted." She gave him a coy glance and he released a hearty laugh, wrapping his thick arm around her.

The party was enjoyable. Some of Kendra's friends came. Michael showed up for a drink. He asked Jude where Alex was.

"She's not feeling well."

Michael squinted his eyes and ran his hands down his chin. He parted his lips like he was about to say something, but just nodded and turned away.

Jude was distracted all night by Kendra and Mary Jane's words. On top of that, Will had texted about playing basketball tomorrow and asked him to stay for dinner with

Alex and him. He had agreed, even though he felt awkward with the two of them together. As he texted back, that same question bothered the shit out of him. Why had Will said he wasn't interested in Alex? *"It's not going anywhere,"* he had said. *"I don't love her."*

When Will had said that, Jude had thought: *Why not?* How could he possibly *not* love her?

Loving her was easy. Like the sun, Alex emanated warmth wherever she went. You couldn't help but look at her glow.

Maybe he did need to ask Will again. Simply a *"Man, what happened? I thought it wasn't going anywhere."*

He'd go tomorrow and see how it went. He would decide then if he wanted to say anything after he hung out with them.

He left the party around eleven. Kendra walked him out. "You sure you're OK?"

"Yeah. I just need some quiet time."

"I understand." She touched his forearm. "She's a nice girl. I don't think she would ever make you regret telling her how you feel. Think about it. Hard. And Jude, thanks for the talk."

"You really ought to think about leaving him."

"It's never that simple in a marriage. Years of life together. You try your best to hold onto what's good. I keep thinking if I have sex with another man, George and I are back on an even keel. Believe it or not, this is how many of my friends reconcile staying with a cheating husband." She shrugged her shoulders. "It's a skewed world."

"That *is* skewed. I'm not that cynical. I believe that if two people want to work things out, they need to communicate and compromise. But I've never been married."

She squeezed his hand. "You're a good friend."

"You too. I'll talk to you later." He kissed her cheek and left.

Communicate. He had told Kendra to communicate. Maybe he needed to take his own advice.

Chapter 32

Alex

I groaned, placing the back of my hand along my forehead. "What hurts? What can I get you?" Will asked.

I laid sprawled out on the sofa in my living room with the air conditioning blasting. "Nothing. I just need to rest."

"Is it your head?" He sat down and placed my head on his lap, then massaged my temples with his fingers. "How's that?"

"It's nice."

"When did you start feeling sick?"

"It came on slowly after I got home from school. I didn't even swim. I've been laying here. I think I'm just exhausted. Why don't you go to Kendra's without me?"

"I'm not going to leave you when you're sick." He ran his fingers through my hair. "I want to take care of you."

"I'm probably only going to watch TV and sleep. I want you to go to the party. Have some fun."

Where You'll Land

I needed to be alone. I wasn't even sure if I was sick or not as I lay there. It started with a dull stress headache, then moved to stomach cramps, becoming overall weakness, or perhaps weariness. Maybe I was getting my period. "Ugh, can you get me some Gatorade?"

He nodded, kissing my forehead before he got up.

My life was a mess. A convoluted mess of emotions and secrets. I had called Carter at work and asked him to spend time with me that night. I needed to talk to him, to someone who was not connected to Will or Jude, or to anyone from school. I had assumed Will would go to the party without me. But now Carter would be home soon, and Will wasn't leaving.

Funny how I had so wished that all his locked-in emotions would be unleashed and laid bare for me. Now that they were, I hadn't a clue what to do with them. As I lay there with my head in his lap, his fingers delicately grazing through my hair, I thought of Zach and how when he finally decided I was *the girl* he wanted, it was too late.

Love can be like a seesaw. When one person is up the other is down. And I realized as I thought it through that it was something I didn't want anymore. Maybe that's what made Jude appealing. He seemed like someone who could keep the relationship balanced even.

"Maybe we should go to Key West next weekend like we had talked about. You need to take a break, and I know you will never rest if you stay in your routine," Will said, in his slow, easy voice. I felt close to him right then, the way he knew me. We met eyes and he leaned down, kissing my lips.

"We're in the middle of the semester. We can't go away until break."

"Aren't you going to go to your family in New Jersey for the school break?"

"Maybe. Let's talk about this another time. My head hurts."

I heard the jiggle of keys, as Carter came in the front door.

He looked at me on the couch, Will with my head in his lap. "You alright?"

"Yeah. Just tired. Achy."

Carter tried to conceal his aversion for Will, but I read it in his countenance when he said, "Hello, *Will*."

"Hey, Carter. What's up?"

"Nothing much." Then to me: "Are you well enough to have dinner? I wanted to get your advice about that *thing* we discussed earlier."

At first, I looked puzzled.

"You know, that *thing*. That problem I'm having."

I nodded, slowly catching on.

Carter looked at Will. "Man troubles. Alex gives good advice. Mind if I borrow her for a few hours?"

"She's not a possession."

"Uh, for the love of God, lighten up. It's a figure of speech."

I sat up. "Go to Kendra's. I'll be fine. I promised Carter I'd lend him an ear."

"I'm not going to go to Kendra's. I'll go to Thelma's to eat and come right back. If you need me, call me." He kissed me as he got up.

"'Kay." I smiled with my lips, too widely, trying to act loving. Meanwhile, all I felt was a knot of anxious anticipation waiting for his departure.

Carter and I sat in suspended animation, watching Will as he walked toward the door. "I'll be back soon," he said as he opened it.

I smiled again, nodding, hoping he didn't feel my eagerness for him to leave.

As soon as the door closed behind him, I released a huge sigh of relief.

Carter gave me a shrewd look. "What's going on?"

"Aye-aye-aye." I put my hands against the sides of my head and shook. "Is it that obvious that I'm having an issue?"

"Please, girl. When Will's about, an issue isn't far behind. Besides, your face had a look."

"What kind of look?"

Carter smirked at me. "A *help me* kinda look."

I took a heavy breath. "Have you ever thought about how every choice we make is related to every choice before and the decisions of people around us? Like we are all interconnected."

Carter put on a sympathetic smile and sat on the sofa, lifting my feet and putting them on his lap in the process. "Girl, we *are* all interconnected. We aren't fucking islands in an ocean with no one else on the horizon. Now what the fuck did you go and do?"

I squeezed my head, trying to shrink my headache. "One mistake after another."

"We all make mistakes. When I think about mistakes I've made, I'm sure I'd make different choices now."

"This is deeper. It's like when you watch a biopic and you can see looking back, how the person's life unfolded one choice at a time and the influences of other's choices on theirs. Maybe we miss the interconnection while it's happening because we don't know yet where they will lead."

He tilted his head. "I know you love these big philosophical questions. And as much as I normally enjoy the intellectual stimulation… spill it. What's this *really* about?"

I looked him in the eyes as he waited with anticipation. I hesitated, because once the words were out there, I couldn't take them back. I inhaled and then blurted, closing my eyes for a second as the words flew out. "I slept with Jude."

Carter got a gleam in his eyes. "Well, well, well. Do tell."

"Don't get all Jude-is-hot on me. This is serious. Please."

"Fine, Jude is a total, grotesque ogre. But I still like him more than that juvenile Will."

I nudged his leg with my heel. "C'mon, Carter."

"Fine. What happened?"

So, I told him everything: Will's whole family trauma. The tragedy of Bethany's death. All the things Will said to me when he finally opened up to me. Then what happened between me and Jude. And my feelings about him. "I don't know what to do. Do you think I can really be in love with Will and want Jude at the same time?" I asked.

"Hmm." He leaned back, contemplating. "I do, yes." He nodded slowly. "I think we want to be with different people for different reasons. And I think those reasons change and evolve. It sounds like you want them both, but for different reasons."

"I'm starting to think that I fell in love with Will's brokenness. I connected with that. It made me feel close to him. If I could heal him, then maybe my own wounds would heal. Maybe I felt his need for me, and I needed that. But after he kept hurting me, I stopped wanting to be close to him. The hurt created a resentment that I just can't shake. And I think I became attracted to Jude because I needed him. See, he's strong in a different way than I am. His confidence and certainty about me gave me, *gives me*, something I think I've needed since my ex, especially after Will kept rejecting me. And he makes me feel sexy in a way I have never felt before."

"OK." He gave me a steely look. "I was going to ask you who you really wanted, but maybe the question is: Do you want either of them for the right reason?"

"I don't know. I've asked myself the same thing. But now I can't think beyond the things Will has shared with me and how much I love him for trusting me. I'm the only person outside his hometown that he's shared all of that with. I feel responsible."

"But you're not. Regardless of the reason, he's hurt you over and over. He was hanging around with another woman here in our building. He never considered your feelings. What happened to him is terrible, but it's not your responsibility."

"Why do I feel I betrayed him then?"

"Because he trusted you with something personal without knowing you were involved with his friend, a friend you have feelings for. But his behavior is not rational. He treated you like shit. And girl, that shit ain't right."

"Yeah." I contemplated. "Maybe. But I did tell him that I loved him, and he trusted me. And then I slept with another man."

"Because it was *over*. Remember? You keep leaving out the part where *he* left *you*. No explanation. You were trying to move on, and Jude just happened."

"What if it was Jude that I wanted from the beginning, but I was too afraid to admit it."

"Why would you do that?"

"I don't know. Maybe because I felt I would grow from being with him and I was afraid of that. I dunno. I'm not sure that's true. It's just something I've tossed around."

"You didn't even know Jude when you first started hanging around Will. You know it's OK to change your mind about who you want to be with. You must live your own life. Are you going to tell Will the truth?"

"Noooo. He can never know the truth. I've thought about this. It would hurt him too much."

"My experience is that a secret like this builds momentum."

"I can't. I just can't."

"Then what, my little drama queen, are you gonna do?"

"I'm not a drama queen, am I?"

"Of course not. Well… maybe a teensy bit. But, you know, in an entertaining way." He patted my legs. "So, what's the decision, darlin'?"

"Break it off with Will. And see what happens. Maybe I'm not supposed to be with either of them."

"Maybe you're afraid of what you really need."

"And what's that?"

"To be alone."

"I wanted to be alone, yet I wound up with Will, and then Jude." I placed my hand on my forehead and shook my head. "Wanting to be alone led me here."

"If you say so. I mean, you *are* the therapist in training. I'm just the insightful gay roommate who is never wrong. About anything. Ever." He raised his eyebrows at me. "OK, maybe there was that one time."

We broke into laughter.

"Listen, if you want the answer, maybe you need to retrace your steps. Go back to the beginning."

I contemplated, then nodded slowly. "You're probably right."

"I know."

I thought of that August morning in Michael's bed, when I was horrified for a moment thinking that I had slept with him after I had promised myself that there would be no emotional entanglements in Miami, and then that night I met Will at the pool and felt drawn to him despite my commitment of no commitments, the first kiss with Jude at Mary Jane's party. *Where was the beginning?* I wondered.

I thought of what Michael had said about needing to play out this thing with Will until it was done, even if it was painful.

Carter got up. "How 'bout I order a pizza? You know cheese always makes you feel better. And it's been so long since I've had carbs, I'm teetering on the brink of a homicidal fit."

I chuckled. "Sure." As we waited for the pizza, my mind drifted to the night I saw Zach at The Battered Drum with the yellow-haired girl and realized what I had known deep in my bones but was afraid to admit to myself: Zach was lying. We were never getting back together, but he wanted to keep me around to fulfill his sexual and emotional needs until he found someone else. Seeing him with that woman broke me, but it pushed me to end it. *I* was done. That was *playing it out*. I did not want a repeat of that, playing it out to the point where I crumbled into so many pieces that I no longer recognized myself.

I was more than the person who had loved Zach, who loved Will. But maybe in the process of putting myself back together, I became lost among the pieces.

"Just what the doctor ordered." Carter returned with wine for each of us. As he handed me a glass, "Oh, and girl, at some point you'll have to spill the beans about the sex with Jude. We're roommates. It's an unspoken pact."

I blushed. My body got goosebumps at the thought of Jude touching me. "We'll see."

§

Will came back about an hour later. When he said, "Jude's coming over tomorrow. I'm going to play basketball with him in the afternoon, then we can grab dinner and study together," the headache the wine had chased away quickly returned.

"We'll see how I'm feeling but keep the plans with him either way."

"You want to watch a movie?"

"Yeah. Sounds good. Something light."

Will scrolled through comedies on Netflix. "Bridget Jones? That always makes you laugh."

"OK."

Will and I laid on my bed watching the movie, and it was nice. I tried not to think about what Carter had said, but it lingered in the periphery of consciousness.

"Go back to the beginning."

§

The next day I watched Will and Jude pound the basketball along the court from my balcony. I still felt sick. Achy. The confusion in my heart seeped into my bones. How could I have loved Will, yet not know what I wanted now?

Maybe love changed as people grew. Whatever it was that I had wanted when I met Will was changed by the experience of loving him and losing him. And now, I wanted something different. Or needed something different. A man who would challenge me to grow, a man who demanded that I become the free, courageous woman I was capable of being.

Even if Jude was more of an infatuation or simply an unfinished possibility, the experience of being with him pulled something out of me, a part of myself that hadn't developed yet. I was evolving. I realized that I wanted someone who was certain of me from the beginning. Maybe that's what going back to the beginning meant. Starting with someone who was ready to be with me right out of the gate.

I sipped iced tea, the echo of the basketball reverberating. My book sat on my lap, but I kept reading the same line over and over without absorbing the content. Then my phone rang.

"Hey, Kendra." I picked up.

"Alex, honey. Jude said you were unwell last night. I wanted to see if you were feeling better."

"Aww. Thanks. Yeah. Just exhausted from everything I've been doing I think. How was your party last night?"

"Nothing too crazy. We missed you. And Will. Glad to hear you're alright though."

I took a heavy breath. "Yeah, I'm alright."

"You still sound tired."

"It'll pass."

"George is still away, I thought maybe we could get together for lunch or dinner. If you're up to it. I could come to South Beach."

"Is Mary Jane coming?"

"Oh, I hadn't thought to ask her. I can call her and ask her."

Kendra had never invited me out alone before. I wondered if Kendra needed a friend to talk to, maybe about marital problems. Regardless, having her come to dinner with the three of us would reduce the tension.

"I'm supposed to have dinner with Will and Jude. Why don't you come with us?"

"I'd love to. So, things with Will, they're better?"

"You could say that." I heard the flimsiness in my voice. "I mean, yes. Things are great, actually."

"That's good news. Be careful though. A man who wavers back and forth the way Will does is bound to pull back again."

"I hear what you're saying, but we have talked. Things are different now."

"Really? It's been my experience that people don't change. At least not so easily. I just hate seeing you so upset."

"What is the purpose of studying to be a psychologist if you don't think people are capable of change?"

"With therapy and time, change is possible."

"Don't you think people can have a corrective emotional experience outside of therapy? I do. I think when we love people, we offer them the opportunity to break the barriers that prevent them from finding the love they deserve." I had shared too much. "I appreciate your concern. And you're right, he could pull back again. But what is love if there is no risk. Love by its definition implies risk, because you are giving a piece of yourself to someone else."

As the sentences rolled off my tongue, I realized that I couldn't protect Will's heart. He had touched me, and me, him. It was his choice to open up. We came together and broke apart and came together again, each of us changed from every break. Even if we weren't going to be together, at least we had both grown from knowing each other. Kendra seemed cynical, and I wondered if Jude was right about her husband having an affair.

"I'm glad you have everything under control," Kendra said. "I'm not sure I believe patterns can be corrected within a romantic relationship, though. But I'm glad you think so."

"Do you want to come tonight?"

"What time and where?"

"I'll text the info in a bit. I'm guessing around seven, not sure where yet."

"Sounds good. See you tonight."

§

We went to *The Galleria* on Lincoln Road, a fancy pizza place. The walk over was better than I had thought it would be. As long as I didn't stand too close to Jude or hold his eye contact, I could pretend that everything was the way it had always been. I was with Will, and Jude was our friend. Granted, an inconveniently handsome and charming friend, but a friend nonetheless. We strolled west on Lincoln toward the restaurant. Will weaved his fingers through my hand. He had never done this before. Irritation coursed through me. I looked down at our joined hands, my jaw tightening.

Why didn't he do things like this before? Before everything changed? Before it was too late.

The irritation simmered, causing sweat to accumulate along my neck. I noticed Jude looking at our joined hands. My annoyance graduated to anger.

I wiggled out of his grasp, pulling my hair off my neck. "It's warm."

"It's not *that* hot," he said, looking disappointed.

Kendra was already seated when we arrived. She wore a low-cut dress, sky blue. I felt awkward for a moment in my cutoff shorts and T-shirt but shook the discomfort. Jude kissed Kendra's cheek and gave her that "Heeey." It gave me a shiver. The way he drew out the E's was sexy. Then, to make matters worse, I could almost feel the brush of Jude's leg to my right where he sat next to me.

Will's leg lay beside mine, touching me on the left.

Aye. Yi. Yi.

Kendra sat across from me, ruby red lipstick enhancing her full lips. She placed her hand on and off Jude's hand as she talked.

The conversation stayed surface: the weather, some of the galleries on Lincoln road, class assignments. We ordered a bottle of wine and a large pizza. The sensation of Jude's leg against mine on one side and Will's on the other kept my stomach twisted into a ball. When the wine came, I guzzled the first glass like my life depended on it.

Will squeezed my leg. I felt Jude's eyes observing us. Tiny drops of perspiration crept along my hairline. I guzzled more wine.

"Take it easy. You were sick yesterday." Will put his hand on mine.

I pursued my lips and took my hand back. "I'm feeling better."

Actually I felt worse.

The ball in my stomach grew, a knot mixed with anger, guilt, sadness. The wine went straight to my head and I felt queasy, then nauseous. "Excuse me." I got up, hurrying to the bathroom, trying to walk a straight line. Beads of sweat along my neck dripped down my back and torso, causing moisture to dampen my shirt. I pulled it away from my chest and fanned it. I picked up my pace, covering my mouth and trying to swallow down the gags emerging into my throat. I flung the door open, ran into a stall and bent down. Kneeling in front of the bowl, I heaved and heaved, trying to will the contents of my stomach to toss into the water. I felt it coming, and I kept gagging, my stomach acidic and gurgling. I was hot. I briefly debated taking my T-shirt off and lying on the dirty, tiled bathroom floor, letting the coolness soothe my skin.

I needed to get home and lay down.

I drank the wine too fast to try to drown the messy emotions that gnawed at me, eating at my insides like an infection.

The door opened into the bathroom. I heard Kendra's mild voice, "Alex? Are you OK?"

"Yeah," I said weakly.

"You've been in here for a while."

"I know. I feel like I'm going to throw up. It must be the wine and the heat."

"Can I come in?"

She opened the stall door.

"You don't look well."

"I think I need to go home. I must have pushed myself too hard before I felt better."

"We'll get you an Uber."

I stood, and I felt wobbly. Kendra wrapped her arm around me, and we ambled back to the table.

"Alex isn't feeling well," she announced to the men.

"I need to go home."

"I'll take you," Will and Jude said in synchrony.

Will looked at Jude, "I'll take her, you stay with Kendra and enjoy."

"No. Let me go myself. You stay," I beseeched him.

"I can't let you go home by yourself when you're not feeling well." Will stood.

"No," I said. "*Please*. I'm not an invalid. I simply don't feel well and want to be alone."

Will took my arm. "You're being silly. I want to help you."

Fury coursed through me. *Give me some fucking space*, I thought, but swallowed the words. Though I managed to maintain a measured tone, I felt my eyes pierce him. "I want to be alone. When you needed space, you always took it. You never gave me a choice. And I'm telling you, I need to be alone."

Will winced.

"I just need to be alone. Please respect that."

"Fine." He sat back down, a glower spread across his face.

Jude gave me a look.

"Sorry guys. Have fun." To Will: "Call me later."

"Yeah," he responded through twisted lips.

I walked east on Lincoln, my right hand resting on my abdomen. Instead of calling an Uber, I ambled home, stopping at the pharmacy on my way to get an antacid and sucking candy, even though I knew what I needed wasn't in the pharmacy.

What I needed was a temporary break from Will and Jude in order to get my head straight.

Chapter 33

Jude

Jude observed the interaction between Will and Alex, and he knew something was up. She never spoke like that, especially not to Will. Jude had always admired her gentleness and consideration toward him. It took a strong woman to be that patient and kind.

He thought Will's mistake with Alex was that he underestimated her strength. A mistake he had made himself when he was younger. A woman like Alex loved unconditionally, allowing the person she loved to be completely himself, giving a lot of latitude. A freedom. It was the freedom she felt about herself, deep inside, even if she didn't quite know it. She didn't follow what she didn't agree with, unabashedly herself, free despite the insecurities it created living in a world where people were judged because of individuality.

He found her self-consciousness irresistible because he knew it was a sign of her freedom. Being able to stand alone — being a maverick — looked easy from the outside, but often underneath the subversion was a sensitive soul. Someone who felt the ills of the world. That type of perceptiveness made people like Alex self-conscious. But there was nothing like being loved by a free woman. They could never be held onto for too long, but they loved fiercely, the same way they lived: with searing passion.

It took a strong man to be with a woman like that. And he realized as he observed them that night that that was why Will had kept saying he wasn't that into her. He felt it too, and it terrified him.

He felt like an evil excuse for a human being because he saw the hurt in Will's eyes, yet all he could think was that there was *hope*. Hope for Alex and him to be together.

Will sat with his arms crossed, clearly upset. As a friend, he knew he should ask if he wanted to talk about it. In student-shrink-land, no one lets a friend sit with their arms crossed, clearly distressed, without bringing it up. But he felt like it was an added betrayal to pry open his emotions.

Kendra said, "She's sick. People are not at their best when they are under the weather." She placed her hand on Will's shoulder.

"It's not a big deal."

"You look upset." She tilted her head at him.

"I was only trying to help."

"Of course, you were. She knows that. Young women can be capricious with their needs. It takes years for women to be firm in what they want."

"It's not an age-thing," Jude chimed in. "People's needs change. Sometimes by the hour. Human emotions are never static."

"True," Will said. "I'd like to believe that I know Alex pretty well, and that was out of character for her. It's fine though. I'm not upset."

Jude thought: *You don't know her the way you think you do. You're missing all the magnificent hidden parts of her. The ones I've seen.*

He couldn't get the image of her lying on her back naked from the waist down with her legs spread wide open the other night. He had licked her insides deliberately, using his tongue to find all the places that aroused her. When he took her shirt off so she would be totally exposed, he saw her nipples harden. Lust coated her eyes. Between heavy breaths she had said, "Keep going. No one has ever touched me like this."

That was the only evening Alex and he had spent the whole night together. She had slept naked in his arms, and in the morning, she opened herself up for him again. This time she screamed his name. Afterward, she had said that she had never let herself go like that. He knew how to touch her physically, because he understood her emotionally. He wanted to guide her toward finding that wild, sexy and strong free woman he knew she was.

He swirled the wine in his glass, then took a long sip, trying to drink away the desire he felt thinking about that night. *Those* few nights with her.

Kendra asked Will what he was really doing with Alex. Jude swallowed hard. He trusted Kendra, but still, having another person there that knew the truth made the secret sitting at the table rest more heavily on him.

"What do you want from her?" Kendra shot Will a pointed look. "You've hurt her. She talks to me. And as her friend, I feel I should tell you that you have hurt her."

"I know I've hurt her. I'm trying to make it right. Honestly, though, I wish she wouldn't have talked to you. It's between her and me, and we're working it out. Not to sound rude, but it's *none of your business*."

"You're right." Kendra smoothed her dress at the waist and adjusted the napkin on her lap. "I just know what it's like to be with a man who doesn't really love you. Or says he loves you but doesn't act like it. Never mind."

"Is there something about *your* life that you want to talk about, Kendra?" He turned his body toward her.

She took a frustrated breath. "Jude knows. My husband is having an affair." She sipped her wine. "It's really left me bitter. I used to be a warm person. A hopeful person. But this — it's broken me. George has broken me. The lies upon lies. And the fact that I have only known myself as a woman with him makes me feel… lost, I guess. Angry. And lost."

Will's eyes filled with pain as he absorbed what she shared. "I'm so sorry to hear this, Kendra. I really understand how painful it is to find out that your life has been based on the lies of others. The best way to find yourself is to recreate your life with your own narrative. Take control. Don't let George define you."

Jude watched as the two shared a moment, their eyes trapped in a gaze. Kendra placed her hand on his lap, and to Jude's surprise Will didn't move it.

Interesting. He sipped his wine, his eyes squinted in contemplation.

"Did something like this happen to you too? Have people's lies hurt you?"

Jude shifted in his chair. He had thought the same thing as Kendra. Will's understanding of what she went through seemed personal. Or maybe he was so empathic, that he conveyed his understanding as if he knew it personally. Either way, Kendra's question felt like a bright light had been cast upon him, revealing the lie that now defined their friendship.

Will contemplated.

"Will?" Kendra placed her hand on his shoulder.

"Do you think we should call Alex and see if she got home alright?" he asked, seeming faraway.

"I think she asked to be alone. Perhaps send a text in a little while." Kendra's eyes wandered across his face, the question still hanging.

"No. Nothing like that happened to me. But I know some people who were betrayed by the people closest to them. And from watching them go through it, I know that the only way to change is to rewrite your story without them."

"I told her to communicate with George," Jude chimed in. "He doesn't even know that she knows. To Kendra: "After twenty-five years of marriage, don't you at least want to try to work it out?"

"I'm so angry, I don't know if I can. Sometimes the negative emotions build and build in a relationship, so even if you want to work it out, you can't go back. There's too much damage between you, too many broken pieces. I've seen a therapist and I've talked a lot about this. George has made me a bitter, resentful person. And I don't want to live like this anymore. I thought maybe if I found myself another man, somehow it would make the pieces fit. But that's not right. That's not who I am. That would make me like him."

"Right," Will said. "So, make your own decision. Find a way to glue the pieces back together without him. Your pieces. Alone. A new you."

"You're awfully wise for such a young man."

"Age is a number, right? Life should be measured in terms of experience."

"I'll drink to that." Jude raised his glass. Will and Kendra raised theirs.

Chapter 34

Alex

I laid on my couch staring at the blaring white ceiling with an ice pack across my forehead. My head throbbed at my temples, making the light glaring off the ceiling painful. I kept my eyes squinted.

My phone buzzed with a text, sending a piercing sensation right through my skull. I twisted my neck to check who it was, assuming it was Will. I wasn't going to pick up. I needed space. When I turned my head, a wave of nausea coursed through me. I put my hand over my mouth and turned my head straight again. I wouldn't abandon him, like he did to me, without explaining my need for space. I would explain it calmly and diplomatically once my headache passed.

Then my phone rang. The *briiiing* felt like someone shoved a piece of metal right through my head. *Ugh.* I groaned into the empty apartment. I reached my hand over to the coffee table without moving my head and grabbed the phone.

Through squinted eyes, I looked at the screen and saw Will's number. I hit "decline call."

His text said: *How're you feeling?*

I figured if I didn't write back or answer his call, he'd assume I was sleeping and leave me alone.

A half hour later, he knocked at my door. "Alex?" I heard his voice.

I remained glued to the sofa, my hand spread across my brow, wishing he would just go away.

His knocking turned to banging and his voice became louder, "*Alex?* Are you there?" Bang. Bang. Bang. I heard him huffing and the swoosh of his feet going back and forth on the hallway rug.

I sat up on the sofa, rolling my eyes. I was so fucking annoyed, but I sighed and said, "Will. Give me a sec."

I rushed into the bathroom, threw cold water over my face. Staring at my reflection, I asked myself, "What are you going to do? What are you going to say?" My gaze became more penetrating as I looked directly into my own eyes. It was strange to look at myself so purposefully. For a moment, I felt as though I had never seen myself before. "Who am I? Has everything I've been through in the last thirty years, led me here? Involved with two men? Afraid to know myself? So afraid of what I want that I don't even know what that is?"

When it comes to love, confusion isn't a state of not knowing what you want. It's being afraid of the truth of what you do, I thought.

"Alex." He knocked, more mildly. I heard the affectation in his voice and felt horrible for what I was about to do. I pulled my hair back into a ponytail, tied the drawstring of my sweat shorts tighter and went to the door.

Will stood in front of the door, his eyes severe, his mouth tight.

"Come in," I said, feeling his intensity.

He rushed into the living room, went toward the patio door, looked out through the blinds. His mannerisms were sharp and abrupt. He turned back toward me and asked, "What is it? What?"

My heart raced. What was he talking about? And given his intense manner, I wondered if he knew something. "Wh— what is what? Wh— what's wrong?"

"You tell me." His eyes pricked mine.

Heat coursed through me. Jude must have told him, or he figured it out. Here we go. His eyes looked pained and desperate.

"I don't know what you're talking about."

"You've been acting weird ever since I shared the truth about my life. What is it? Talk to me." The worry in his eyes made my heart bleed. How could I hurt him?

"What do you mean? I'm the same as I've always been."

"NO!" he shouted. Then in a measured tone, "You've been distant."

"No. I haven't."

"I'm sensitive to these things. I can feel it."

The irritation surged through me again. I was distant. *I* was distant. After the way he pushed me back and forth, he had the audacity to accuse me of being distant. God forbid,

I took a little emotional space from him. "*I'm* distant? What about all of the times you were distant."

He plopped onto the couch, buried his head in his hands. "I wish I could take it back."

I looked at him and felt twisted in a knot. I was furious at him, but looking at him sitting there, I also knew he was right. I had been acting distant.

I didn't want to do to him what he had done to me.

He looked deep into my eyes. I saw his pain. Not only pain of the moment, but the immeasurable pain only seen in the eyes of someone who had buried years of hurt, disappointment, betrayal. Someone whose pain remained trapped inside. It broke my heart. He broke my heart. I broke my own heart. I wanted to tell him the truth but felt stymied.

Instead, I took his face gently in my hands and kissed his cheeks, his nose, his lips. A tear dripped down my cheek when I finally looked at him and said, "You're right. I'm sorry. I didn't mean to be distant. The truth is, I'm feeling uncertain about what I want. And I need space to figure it out."

"Because of what I told you. It's too much?"

"No. Of course not. I love that you shared that with me. It makes me feel good to know that you trusted me enough to tell me. But, it doesn't erase the back and forth that happened before that. You broke my heart, and even though I now know you didn't mean it, I don't know if I can move past it. I need time to figure it out. This isn't about you, it's about me."

"It *is* about me. I fucked up. We wouldn't be here if it weren't for me."

I looked at him, with pure honesty. "I don't want to hurt you."

He took my hand. "Say we can work this out, together."

I averted his gaze and shook my head. "I wish I could say yes. I want to say yes, because I really do love you, but I— I just can't. I don't even know how to explain it or how to undo it. It's how I feel. OK?" I looked up at him, my eyes softened. "Please don't make this about what you shared. No matter what, those things that happened aren't your fault. They don't make you anything less than what you are, which is a warm, kind, intelligent man."

He took the few wayward strands of my hair that hung out of my ponytail and wrapped them around my ear. He smiled through his pain. I got lost in his gaze. Was I making a mistake? Maybe I was afraid of how much he loved me, the need I felt in his love. Maybe Jude was a distraction, an obstacle I created to protect myself from falling into something too intense with Will. Maybe I was the one who was afraid of love.

Our lips met. And we kissed. Hungry kisses, desperate kisses, two broken people trying to fill the emptiness within each other. He pulled my shirt off and pulled me close to him, running his fingers down my back, his fingertips wispy along my skin. I melted against him, enveloped in this moment of pure abandon. I ran my fingers through his hair, smelling the robust scent of his shampoo. My heart felt full and heavy at the same time.

Something deep inside stirred. Not about him, about me. Something had changed, healed, grown, something I couldn't quite make sense of, but I knew then that this would be the last time we would be intimate. Without words, I took his hand and walked with him into my bedroom.

Within minutes we were making love.

Chapter 35

Jude

After Will went home, Kendra and Jude walked along the beach.

"I've never seen Will so intense before. I could always feel his intensity, but I've never seen it quite so obvious. I see why you want to back away. He loves her."

"Yup."

"The thing is, I'm not so sure she feels the same about him. Something's going on with her. And if I didn't know what happened between the two of you, I might not have picked up on it. But I saw her looking at you, trying to be inconspicuous."

"Maybe because she felt me looking at her. You know how it is, feeling someone looking at you makes you look at them."

"I don't think so. I saw the pain in her eyes in the bathroom. I know that look, not physical illness, but emotional distress. When you've raised two children you learn to read the nuances in the expression of pain. I still think there's a chance for you two."

"You said yourself you understood why I backed away."

"Just because I understand it, doesn't mean I don't think you should follow your heart. Talk to her. At least find out how she really feels."

Jude took a sharp breath. "Maybe. There's something with Will. The way he talked to you about George, like he had had something similar happen."

"No, he's sensitive. Empathic. I think Will is like a turtle, soft and vulnerable on the inside, wearing a shell that's hard to penetrate on the outside. People like that are naturals at understanding other people's pain because they feel everything."

"I don't think that's all it is." He looked at her, his brow raised. "You like him?"

"He's handsome. You brushed me off so, I've got to focus my attention on someone." She laughed.

"C'mon, you know I respect you and your marriage too much to be messing around like that."

She stopped walking and faced him. "You did me a huge favor. You held a mirror up and made me look at what I had become: a woman who would violate her own values, compromise her own integrity just to make her marriage make sense. I don't know if I can leave George right now, but I need to work on it. I need to figure out who I am now that the kids are independent, and I can see all of the problems between us." She released a cynical laugh. "I was going to go after Will after you rejected me. I told myself that the reason it didn't happen with you was because it was meant to be him. How stupid of me. Like an adolescent. George has reduced me to this, a woman without pride."

"You're not giving yourself any credit. Using the experience as a time of self-reflection and growth means you're strong, Kendra. My opinion is that George can't see your strength. Maybe because you can't see it in yourself. Maybe you lost it along the way. Or maybe he needed to keep you down, so he would feel up."

"You don't know George. He's strong and powerful."

"Sometimes people who seem the most powerful or crave the power, are the weak ones. The ones who feel internally powerless. I don't know George, but I feel I know you a little. I think you are a strong woman, someone who will be just fine on her own."

"You're a good man." She smiled, warmly. "I promise to think about everything you're saying. You must promise to think about what I'm saying. If you love her, you have to tell her. If nothing else, she has a right to know."

He nodded. They continued their walk in a comfortable silence, each in their own private reverie.

Jude wondered if Kendra was right. Was it possible that Alex didn't love Will? Should he at least tell Alex how he felt? He imagined her face when he told her that he loved her, big eyes, jaw dropped. No, that image wasn't her. He reimagined it, this time her eyes squinted, creases around the sides, lips pursed. She would contemplate what he shared, then he imagined her wrapping her arms around his neck, standing on her tippy toes, whispering "me too" into his ear, acting restrained, the way she often did. He would kiss her lips, and that wild, fiery side that she had would unleash and they would kiss fiercely and helplessly, consummating their love with an evening of passion.

Is that really how it would go down, though? It was just as likely that she would smile warmly, regretfully, and let him down easy with "Jude, you know I enjoyed our time together, but I love Will."

He didn't want to hear that, but he could take it if that's how it went down. He needed to tell her, he needed to know what she wanted. If she did want him, how would they ever tell Will? Jude would forever be *that guy*, the dude who fucked over a friend. He didn't like that idea at all, but what was he supposed to do? Step aside in an act of self-sacrifice, like some hero? And was not telling Alex how he felt about her really gallant? No. Telling her the truth took more courage.

He looked out at the ocean, the water rising and falling, the sound of the waves crashing and washing up the sand. He used to go to the beach at night in Los Angeles when he needed inspiration for his music. It felt a lifetime ago, even though it hadn't even been a year since he had left. He had promised himself that if he found another woman who he loved as much as he had loved Suzanna, he would not let anything mess it up.

He reached for his phone in his pocket. He would send a text, asking if Alex felt better, casually, friendly, in case Will was there. If he wasn't, Jude would go there and talk to her. He would lay his cards on the table and let her decide what was in her heart.

He felt a rush of adrenalin as he went to write the text, then hesitated.

"What's wrong?" Kendra gazed up at him.

"Nothing, why?"

"I heard your breath catch, and you stiffened up." She stopped walking and searched his face.

"I was about to text Alex and see if I could gauge if Will was there. I need to talk to her. But I chickened out."

Kendra pulled her phone out of her purse. "I'll call her and find out."

"I don't want to get you in the middle of this."

"I'm not in the middle. And you have been a good friend to me."

She put her ear up to the receiver. "It's ringing."

"Hi, sweetie. It's Kendra. I wanted to see if you're feeling any better."

"Oh, Will's there. *Was* there." She glanced at Jude. "Um, hm. Um, hm. Good that you were honest. I understand." She looked at Jude again, raised her brow. "Yes, I am with Jude. What? We are walking along the beach. OK." She turned to Jude. "She asked if you would call her."

"Now?"

"Now?" she asked Alex.

She nodded to Jude.

"OK. Sweetie. Feel better and call me if you want to talk."

"What happened?" Jude asked Kendra.

"She said she told Will she needed space. Even though she loves him, she's not sure she can get over all the times he hurt her. She sounded choked up. And she wants to talk to *you*." She smiled.

"Mind if I walk you to your car? I wanna go over there."

"I can walk myself to my car."

"I'm not letting you walk alone."

"Don't be silly. I'm fine. Once we're off the beach, there are people everywhere. Go."

They walked off the beach. Stepping onto the concrete, they heard the buzz of Collins Avenue, laughter, talking, cars. "My car's only a couple blocks down."

"Please text me when you get home."

She nodded. "I will."

He kissed her cheek and hurried toward Alex's.

Section IV
The Moment of Truth

"We are never so defenseless against suffering as when we love."
—Sigmund Freud

Chapter 36

Alex

After Will and I had made love, he turned to me and asked, "Does this mean you've changed your mind?" I knew we probably shouldn't have been intimate. Our sex wasn't unemotional and for a moment I felt confused again. While we made love, it was easy to forget the pain I still felt, and everything that happened between us. But I knew that pain was still there. It echoed my feelings those last months with Zach while I had desperately hung onto something that had been irreparably broken.

I needed not to fix it this time. Leaving the broken pieces broken wasn't easy. It was like leaving shards of the most beautiful glass scattered across your floor, wanting to try to put it back together and finding that the pieces were just too shattered. And now, you had to step cautiously around the fractured wreckage in order not to slice yourself from the remains.

I knew my uncertainty would resurface.

And I knew how hurtful it was to be pulled in close, to believe in the honesty of that type of intimacy only to be pushed away. That was less than a baseline of nothing. Having someone you love push you away without knowing why, that was less than zero. I couldn't do it to him.

I watched as he stormed out in a passionate fury. I sat alone in my living room, lights out, the glare of the moon shedding a dim light into the room, swirling my wine. Jude would call any minute.

What exactly do I plan to say to him? Who am I? was the real question. Bouncing back and forth between two guys who were friends. Fucking both of them. And not knowing what I wanted.

Or was I not allowing myself to know what I wanted. Was I afraid of what I wanted?

Will was a repeat of Zach, I thought to myself, as I tried to figure out the pieces of my life. Both were emotionally unavailable, coming on strong only to push me away and pull me back, an endless and painful cycle of emotional ping-pong.

Then came a thought that kept drifting uninvited into my consciousness, slipping in and out. I didn't like it, which made it seem all the more likely that it was the truth. Jude was a reaction to feeling broken by Will. Jude was the glue I used to try and seal myself back together, because Will had broken me over and over.

And before Will, I had already been broken.

And for the first time I allowed that thought to become fully formulated. Maybe I would never be whole unless I found a way to glue myself back together. I sat mulling over this, absorbing it for a moment, then I pushed the thought away. Something felt unfinished. I needed to see him.

I looked at my phone. Feeling impatient and on edge, I rang him.

I heard a phone ringing on the other side of my front door. The knock came.

I tiptoed to the door, looked out the peephole. Jude stood there.

I took my hair out of the ponytail, flipped my head over, shook my hair. I flipped my head back up, smoothed the sides of my hair and opened the door.

"Heeeey." His eyes twinkled under the hallway light.

"Hi."

We shared a long gaze.

No words, just a long pause.

"Can I come in?" he finally asked.

"Yeah." I backed up and I could smell his fresh, robust scent as he walked in.

He stood right in front of me, so close I could taste his aftershave. He grabbed my face and kissed me, kicking the door closed with his foot.

I wanted to talk to him about my feelings. I wanted to stop the kissing before it went any further. I had just slept with Will. I hadn't even taken a shower. And the sense that Jude was another attempt to heal something that only I could heal within myself was still there in my peripheral awareness.

But Jude had this way of taking over. He made me think that what he did was what I wanted, or it became what I wanted. When he stuck his hands into the sides of my shorts and rubbed my bare hips, I felt hot and tingly. I took my own shorts off, then my panties and my shirt. I stood naked before him. Jude unleashed something in me, something that had been caged there all along, a simmering, unquiet passion.

He smiled at me, his eyes filled with emotion. I felt it too, as I smiled back at him. Lust. Passion.

Love.

Or the feeling of love when you want someone to ravage you because the chemistry is so strong. You tell yourself that it's love. It must be love, the only kind of love you could ever want, because what else could it be.

Being caught up in passion was always good for disregarding any consequences. Lying with Jude afterward was also good for disregarding anything outside of our little shared world. I inhaled, taking a couple of seconds before I had to bring up the inevitable.

"Alex?" he whispered.

"Yeah?"

He shifted position. Resting his head on the same pillow, he faced me. The light was dim, but I recognized the emotion in his eyes, the blue swirled around, layers of thoughts woven deep into his irises. "I want," he touched my cheek, "to be with you."

"You are." I smiled, lost in those blue irises.

"I don't mean just right now…you know what I mean."

The way he said, '*you know what I mean*,' felt so intimate and it gave me a shiver deep in my bones. Maybe he's what I wanted, and I was just afraid of that.

"I do." I looked into his eyes, trying to find the right words. "I— I, um, I don't know what to do."

"About Will?"

"Yes. And about me. It's all complicated."

He stroked my hair, then said lovingly, "Because you're complicated."

I looked into those irises, searching for the words. There was so much going through my mind, and I didn't want to say the wrong thing.

"What is it?"

"There are things — things that he has shared with me. I can't tell you, but they make it very hard for me to make my feelings a priority. I know it probably sounds foolish to you. He's treated me poorly in the past. He has hurt me. But this is who I am, empathic, compassionate, forgiving. I don't want to hurt him. And this, me and you, would slice him to the core." I burrowed my head into his chest.

He rubbed my back with the tips of his fingers. "I know the compassionate, forgiving person you are. It's part of what makes you special. Never apologize for being yourself. Only a strong woman could be so compassionate. The question is do you want this?"

I searched his face. "Yes. And. No."

He questioned me with his eyes.

"I'm afraid. I'm just not sure what I am afraid of. I really like you. And this, what we have in here, is like nothing I have ever experienced before. Very passionate and freeing. But I need time to understand what exactly I'm feeling."

"Time alone?"

I nodded slowly, almost regretfully. "Maybe we try to go back to being friends and see what happens. I dunno."

Jude sat up.

I sat up next to him, our backs resting on the headboard.

"Alex. You and me. We can't be 'just friends.'"

Don't say it, I thought. *Don't tell me you love me*. I saw it in his eyes. I swallowed.

"Do you trust me?"

I nodded.

"You don't have to be afraid. I would never tie you down or expect you to be anyone other than who you are. I know you like your independence."

"How do you know that?"

"It pours out of you. How could I not know it?"

I touched his cheek. "I really think we have to stay away from each other for a little while. I mean, not be meeting like this."

"What did he tell you?"

"I can't tell you. He told me in confidence. It's bad enough that he trusted me with his feelings, and now I'm hurting him by not being with him. Worse if I would violate his trust."

He took a sharp breath. "I'm not going to say anything."

"I know, but I would know. And like I had said, I really do enjoy this," I motioned my hand around the bed, "but I don't know what I want. I don't know if I want something more than sex, or if this is right for me. I need time."

"I'm not an overly patient person."

My face grew long. "I don't know what else to say."

"I'm staying tonight. I'm not taking no for an answer." He wrapped his arms around my bare waist and pulled me close.

"You have to leave before the sun rises." I kissed his ear, then his cheek, then his lips.

When he slipped inside of me again, he whispered, "I love you, Alex," in my ear.

And despite my best effort to let the statement roll off me, unaffected by it, I said, "I love you too." Because right then I felt like I loved him. How could I not?

§

When he slipped out at around five a.m., my bed felt empty. I folded the pillow we had shared around my head, inhaling his lingering scent. Sexually, the guy had me spinning. I stayed in bed until eight that morning going over the details of the night: the way he felt, the way we talked, the way he just seemed to see me.

Jude was different from Zach and Will and all the boys I had dated before. He knew who he was, which made my problem glaring. I didn't know who I was. Maybe even more vexing, I was afraid of who I was. I needed to find a new therapist in Miami.

Nothing that week felt easy.

Will kept looking at me through pained eyes. He was polite, but not overly forthcoming. I had expected that, but it broke my heart that I broke his. Meanwhile, Jude and I spent every night talking on the phone for at least an hour, as *'friends.'* Every time we ran into each other at school, I felt weak in the knees. I was dying for him to touch me. A few times the eye contact between us was so intense, I thought for sure someone would pick up on the chemistry between us.

Toward the end of the week, I saw Jude and Will playing basketball. I watched from my balcony. It felt uncanny, like nothing had changed. Me, watching the two of them like an outsider when Will had shut me out. But everything was different. I didn't want to be with Will, and I might want to be with Jude. At the very least, I was bursting with the desire to have sex with him.

That night, Will banged on my door and made everything worse.

"Will. Hi." I was surprised to see him, and I felt sad and awkward and anxious all at once. I opened the door wide for him to come in. Carter scurried into his bedroom, but not before raising his eyebrows.

"What's up?" I tried to sound casual to diffuse his intensity.

"This is killing me." He paced in the living room. I watched him go back and forth, my heart beating so rapidly I could feel it in my throat. I did not want to have this conversation. He stopped pacing and held my shoulders. Looking deep into my eyes, he said, "I miss you."

"I— I, aye." I inched backward a few steps, my arms dropping to my sides. "I don't know what to say. I can't help how I feel. *I'm sorry*. I really am. Sometimes too much happens, and no matter how much you want to, you just can't go back."

"How can you act like there's nothing between us?"

I felt his need for me permeating off him almost like a physical hand gripping and holding me so tight I could barely breathe. It made me angry. Angry that he pushed me away, controlling the intimacy to suit his own comfort, hurting me over and over. Angry at myself for feeling guilt about Jude. It wasn't my fault, but I felt like it was. "Will. I'm not acting. It's how I feel. What do you want from me?"

"I want *you*."

"It's not possible. Not now."

"I don't believe you. I think you're afraid."

"What?" I tried to hide my growing exasperation. "I'm not afraid. I'm finally figuring out who I am and what I want. You hurt me. Understand? You hurt *me*. I have feelings too, and you disregarded them. You treated me irresponsibly. Sometimes we figure out what we want too late. I'm afraid that's what's happened here. I think it's too late." I didn't mean to say that last line. I hadn't even admitted the full truth of it until it flew out of my mouth.

I had to stop protecting his feelings. I had my own life to live. I had to stop living and making decisions for him or for anyone else. How was I ever going to figure out what I really wanted if I kept being pulled by others' needs.

I was furious looking at him and disgusted with myself for having chosen another man who couldn't give me what I wanted when I wanted it, and now having to deal with another roller coaster separation.

"I need you to go. I hope someday you will understand, and you will forgive me. I love you as a person. I want you to find the happiness you deserve, but it's not going to be with me."

I reached for his hands, but he pulled away and gave me a pained, furious glare. "You're making a mistake."

"Maybe. But if I am, at least it's my mistake. A mistake made through my own growth process and not a mistake of trying to get someone to love me who wasn't able to."

He pleaded. "I did love you. I *do* love you."

A tear dripped down my cheek as I looked up at him. Why couldn't he have said all of this when I needed to hear it, before our relationship cracked into pieces that couldn't be put back together. "I loved you too, but it's over now. Please, don't make this harder than it is."

We shared a heavy look. I had never felt stronger. I had always worried about the broken pieces that I felt in other people. I had always worried that I would say the wrong thing, do the wrong thing, act the wrong way, not be responsible, hurt someone's feelings. In that moment, I felt sure of myself in a way I never had before. "I think you should go. There's nothing else to say. If you ever need to talk as a friend, about your life, about the things from your past, I am here for you. But I don't believe we will ever be together again. I want you to know the truth, so you can move on."

He turned with his head bowed, and said without looking at me, "I still say this is a mistake."

"I don't think so."

Overcome by my own strength and conviction, I almost told him about Jude, because it would be a load off my mind. In the last second, the words hanging on my lips, I decided to hold my tongue. First, I would talk to Jude about it. Maybe I wanted to be with Jude and was afraid, or maybe he was the glue that sealed me back together while Will was busy breaking me apart. Whatever it was, I wanted to explore it.

Will walked out and slammed the door so loud it reverberated through the apartment for several moments, shaking the frames on the wall.

I cried alone in my room when he left. Carter knocked, asking me if I wanted to talk. I responded, "Thanks, hon. Not now. Maybe later," between sniffles.

Jude called a little while later, just when I had reached the point where I had cried myself into numbness. I sniffled. "Hey."

"Heeey," he responded. The E's sounded rickety.

"What's wrong?"

"Are you home?"

"Yeah."

"I know we said we wouldn't see each other, but I want to come over."

"What's wrong?"

"We need to talk."

I gulped. "About?"

"I'm at Thelma's. I'll be right over. This isn't something I want to talk about on the phone. *I want to be there with you.* It's important."

"OK. Come over."

Chapter 37

Alex

Jude arrived, his eyes bloodshot, his hair disheveled. His "Heeey" sounded feeble.

"What's wrong?" I asked. I had never seen him seem so deflated.

He opened his mouth to say something, then stopped. He squinted his eyes, contemplating.

"*Jude*. Tell me." I felt like I was about to burst. Whatever it was, I could feel him agonizing over how to say it.

He pulled me close and kissed me, a strong, lingering kiss, which seemed contradictory to the consternation splayed across his face. I wanted to pull away, but I couldn't bring myself to. After the kiss, he looked at me with an expression of longing mixed with agony.

"What?" I searched his face. He looked worried. Confused. Torn.

"It's Will." He exhaled a frustrated breath.

"Did he say something? He came over, but nothing happened. I told him it was totally over."

"He told me today what had happened to him. He told me everything. About his mother, about his girlfriend dying and about how he felt it all affected his ability to let you close. He cried, Alex. He cried to me about losing you. He admitted that he didn't tell me that he was in love with you because he was afraid to love you. When he had told me he wasn't into you, I believed him. But it wasn't the truth. He loved you all along. He loves you now. I felt like a total scumbag when he shared all his past with me. I don't know what to do with this information. I've been drinking and racking my brain for the last hour and a half since I left him." He paced the living room. "Now I know why it was so hard for you to let him go. To tell him the truth." He brushed the front of his hair off his forehead, then turned and took my hands. "I love you. I want you to know that. I want us to be together, but I don't know how to do this. I feel like I screwed him over and stole the woman he loved."

"You didn't. How were we supposed to know how he really felt? He spent days, weeks, distancing himself from me. How on earth would we ever know that it was fear? I know how you feel. I don't want to hurt him either, but what? We stop talking? I decided that I want to explore this, *us,* to see what's really there. I've been thinking. I think the lie would make him angrier than if we gently tried to explain the truth. He was hurt by a lie. If his family had told him the truth, I think he would have had an easier time. I don't want to repeat the pattern of his history."

"You can't try to think this through like he's your patient."

"I'm not. I'm just trying to use what I know about people, about Will, to figure out how to do this. I don't want to hurt him. I know what it's like to lose someone you love. But, I also realized that it's wrong to want to be with someone who isn't with you 100%. Someone who isn't brave enough to take that leap into the unknown." I looked at him, wondering if it was him.

He pulled me into an embrace.

"I think lying is more hurtful than the truth," I said into his chest, then looked up at him. "The truth will hurt, but he will heal. I want to see where this goes and so do you. How long do you really think we can hide the truth? And it would be worse if somehow he figures it out."

Jude paced. "I don't know. There is a covenant with guys that you don't mess around with someone your friend loves."

"Women have that too. *But you didn't know.*" I looked at him through sympathetic eyes.

"But I know now."

Desperation coursed through me. Was Jude pulling back from this, from me, after he had told me that he wanted to be with me. After he chased after me. I crossed my arms. I was not going to do another emotional roller coaster. "You told me that you loved me. You can't rewrite things. I always say, 'if I knew then what I know now, it wouldn't have been then. It would be now.' We did what we did with the information we had then. We didn't know how he really felt, because he didn't tell us. We're not wrong."

"You were the one who put the brakes on when you found out the truth."

"True. But I've thought about it, and I feel certain that telling him is the right thing. And there's something unfinished between us. I want to know what that is."

He shook his head. "I'm not ready. Maybe I'll come to where you are after some thought, but right now it feels like a total violation of his trust."

My eyes narrowed. I felt like a cat about to hiss and then attack. "What are you saying?"

He uncrossed my arms, and I let him take my hands in his. "We need to try and go back to being friends. At least for now."

"Are you fucking kidding me?! You chase after me. You tell me that you love me and that you want to be with me, and now you're playing the same bullshit games as Will. I let myself feel something for you, because you came on so strong. What bullshit." I pulled my hands out of his and turned away from him.

He put his hand on my shoulder.

"Get off of me." I wiggled away from his touch.

"Look at me. Please."

I turned with my arms crossed and my lips bunched up on one side. "What?"

"I'm not playing games. I want you. *All of you.* I just think we need to let some time pass to make this easier on Will. OK? You had said it yourself, we need to wait."

I looked up at him, and my heart ached. I felt ripped open, totally exposed and I knew he could see it. "You should go."

His eyes morphed from anguished into longing. I could see the love in them. "Wait." He pulled me close, kissed me, then said, "I don't want to leave you. Let's spend the night."

"What, so you can have sex with me, then leave in the morning? I don't think so. You need to go."

"No. I want *you*."

"You can't have me like this. Like a secret on the sidelines waiting for a friend to lick his wounds. How long do we have to hold off? A week? A month? Two, three months? No. Until we have everything, we have nothing. So, I can't do this with you. I'm already broken, and you're going to destroy me. You need to go." I pointed a determined finger at the door.

"I love you."

"Words mean nothing without actions." Tears licked the corners of my eyes.

"It's going to be OK. Alllexx. We will be together. Just give me a little time. OK? I promise."

I looked at him and nodded. I wanted to say, *Please, stay. If you leave, I don't think I will be able to open my heart to you again.*

But I couldn't speak. All I felt was a knot of tears, and inarticulate emotions rising into my throat about to release in a wail. I was not going to cry in front of him.

This was the final straw. I was too vulnerable for another dance of uncertainty. I needed to figure out how to put my own heart back together.

I watched him walk out the door, his shoulder slouched. Looking at the empty space where he had just been left me feeling so lonely, thinking of what could have been.

I cried myself to sleep that night.

I didn't go to school for the next two days. I could not deal with seeing either of them. I wanted to take the whole week off, but we were only allowed two absences per class, per semester, so I only had forty-eight hours to pull myself together. Jude sent a text on the second day: *Are you OK? Call me.*

I wrote back: *I'm fine.*

He tried to call. I didn't answer. Part of me was dying to talk to him, but I wasn't going to do the back-and-forth dance, the endless up-and-down of emotions, hoping he stayed and fearing always that he would leave.

He left a message. "Alllexx, call me. We will figure this out."

I didn't respond.

But I thought about him a lot. Too much. I thought about Will too. I felt sad about losing him, even though I knew it was the right thing. Intimate relationships were oddly precarious. You let someone get close, someone who knew your body, your private thoughts, and suddenly you didn't know them at all. And although they were gone, they remained a permanent part of you, having forever altered your life path.

The thought of sitting in classes with the two of them was unappealing. As irrational as a transfer seemed, to quell my angst, I went online and looked for graduate programs in psychology to transfer to. I had excellent grades and competitive GRE scores. I sent emails to a couple of programs in New Jersey and New York City, asking for information. Maybe I should go back home.

Until then, though, I had to maintain my current focus. I was in Miami for graduate school. I could not compromise my goals because of heartache and melodrama. Or because of a late-stage identity crisis. So, on the third day of my mission to avoid Will and Jude, I picked myself up and went to class. Dark sunglasses hung on my nose when I ran into Mary Jane in the parking lot.

"Chickee, where have you been?" she snapped her gum.

I tilted my head, allowing Mary Jane to catch a glimpse of the dark circles and swelling around my eyes, a casualty of forty-eight hours of nonstop crying.

"What happened to you? You look like you've been crying for days. Will again. Right? I'm going to fucking kick his ass."

"It's not that simple. Can we talk?"

"Of course."

"We need to go somewhere very private. This is a big secret."

"C'mon. We don't have class," she looked at her watch, "for over an hour. Let's get in my car and go somewhere quiet."

I nodded, following Mary Jane to her car. I saw Jude out of my periphery but ignored him. Mary Jane noticed him and waved.

She raised her brow. "Did you just ignore Jude?"

"Hurry," I whispered in a pressured voice. "Let's get in your car. I'll tell you everything. But not here."

We slipped into the car, my heart raced wildly. As Mary Jane pulled away, I looked back and saw Jude watching the car. Our eyes met. I turned forward and sat with my hands in my lap, fidgeting with my fingers, willing the tears away.

Mary Jane glanced at me from behind the wheel. "What happened?"

I sighed. "I don't even know where to start."

Mary Jane pulled the car into a parking lot of a small park. She turned toward me and said, "Whatever it is, you can tell me."

"Everything I say has to stay between us. No one. Not even Fred can know." I gave her a steely look.

"Absolutely."

"I have been with Jude and— "

Mary Jane was about to say something.

"Let me tell you everything before you jump in." I was tired of everyone talking about how hot Jude was. Like that's all he was. All people saw. It was what I had seen when we first met him. But now that I knew him and we had been intimate, this fixation on his looks annoyed me.

"I've spent time with Jude, and he told me he loved me. I said it back. I'm not sure that I meant it, though. We experienced a passionate connection, which has felt like love in moments, but it's not the same way I had felt about Will."

Mary Jane's eyes shot open. "Wow."

"This all happened under the assumption that Will wanted nothing from me, but it turns out that wasn't the truth. The truth was that Will was afraid of trusting a relationship because of some things from his past, which I can't and won't say, so please don't ask. So now, Jude and I have basically betrayed Will without meaning to. Jude had wanted us to be together. But now he feels like he needs time. I think it's really to give Will time to heal. So, I'm stuck with emotions for yet another guy who won't go all in. And I'm sick of it."

"Wait. Slow down for a minute. What did Jude say? He told you he loved you, then pulled back?"

I explained the exact chain of events between Will and me and Jude, including the last time Jude was over and I had asked him to leave. "Jude seemed to really know what he wanted and after Will's ambivalence and distance, I found it… attractive, freeing. He made me feel sexy and desired. But, now I can't be anywhere near him. I'm sick of being the one always fighting for the relationship. I've sent away for graduate schools up north. I may transfer if this gets to be too much. Don't shit where you eat, right? I should've known better."

Mary Jane shook her head. "You can't run away from this. You underestimate your strength. Shrinking from something uncomfortable isn't who you are. You, who will dive into turbulent water and swim for miles through exhaustion and hunger. You, who moved here without knowing a soul. You, who was brave enough to open your heart to two men, even though you were hurt by that guy you left in New Jersey. You're training to be a psychologist. How are you going to help people confront challenges if you aren't confronting your own? Screw Will. And if Jude can't be the man he said he was, then screw him too. You don't need either of them."

"I didn't really think I would transfer. I guess I needed to feel there was a way out if I needed one."

"It sounds like Jude just needs some time to figure out how to handle this with grace."

"I'm sick of waiting around for guys to figure it all out."

"He's not figuring out how he feels about you though. This is different than Will."

"I feel… lost in a way, because I spent almost all of my free time with the two of them. In another way, I feel found. I feel strong in a way I have never felt before. I've settled for less than I deserve. I've made excuses for men who didn't deserve them. I'm not doing that anymore."

"See. You are strong. I think society makes women like us — strong women — feel afraid to find and express our own strengths. We are not the dainty, feminine, polished types."

"Times are changing."

"Some things change, but I think some things stay the same. I like you with Jude."

"Don't even start with his looks. This has nothing to do with how he looks." I rolled my eyes on purpose.

"I get that. No one is just how they look. Keep yourself busy and give it a week or two."

"I think you gave me the same advice about Will."

"At least I'm consistent." She smiled. "I like Will. He's nice, and he can be warm. But he's also standoffish. I never thought he was strong enough for you. Jude, on the other hand, is a man. I think it could be good. And if it doesn't work out, you will be alright. Why don't you come stay with me for a night over the weekend? Maybe we could have an intimate gathering on Saturday."

"It would be good to get away from the building. I'm skulking around the halls trying to avoid running into Will. I feel like a stalker without being an actual stalker."

§

Telling Mary Jane helped to make the next two days of school easier. I had someone who knew what I was going through nearby. It also felt good just to share what was going on with someone who knew the people involved.

Will gave me polite acknowledgements in class; other than that, he ignored me. It hurt. The space between us, the emptiness of the ending of something that had been ripe with possibility, hurt. But it was better that we didn't talk. There was nothing to say anyway, unless he needed to talk as a friend about his past.

It was over.

Jude was another story.

He tried to talk with me in the hallway. He snuck up behind me. I felt him even before he said, "Heeeey," making my knees wobbly and my heart race.

When I looked at him, I thought I could melt just from the intensity of his gaze. Our eyes gripped each other's, and he took my hand. Desire swelled between us. "Can we talk later?"

"About what?" I shook the sensation of wanting him to pull me close and kiss me.

"Alllexx, this is hard for me too." I wiggled my hand out of his.

"I'm not falling for the charm, Jude. Until you've got something to say, there's nothing to talk about."

He looked hurt. "I do have something to say."

"Oh?"

"Not here."

"This something you have to say, is it a friend-talking thing?"

"Aren't we friends?"

I gave him a sharp look. "Are you kidding me? We are *not* friends. I told you that."

"Wait. I didn't mean it like that. I meant that we are friends too. We will always be friends too."

"You sound cryptic. Are you ready to tell Will the truth?"

"I dunno. Maybe we can see each other without telling him for a while."

"That's worse than being a secret in waiting. I'm not sneaking around anymore. It will hurt him more in the end. And honestly, it will hurt me too. It makes me question your integrity." I said, piercing him with the last line. I noticed him wince. "I gotta go." I rushed away from him and into the ladies' bathroom. Sitting alone in a stall, I tried to get my heart to stop racing.

I had to stay away from him. I was so weary of this nonsense. I thought I sensed my feelings for Jude beginning to wane.

When I finally exited the bathroom, I saw Michael walking past. "Hey, stranger," I said.

He stopped. "Stranger is right. What's up?" He put his arm around me and squeezed. I leaned into the embrace.

"Nothing much. How's Julianne? Figured you were hot and heavy, because I haven't heard from you."

"We broke up. It was never serious enough to be a *real* breakup. But it was fun, and now it's over."

"You're a commitment phobe," I teased him.

"No, I am not, really. You always say that, but it's just… well, I don't make compromises unless I'm certain about someone, because I don't do small relationships. She was nice, but she wasn't at my level in terms of wanting something more serious. Sure, her modeling kept her busy, but sometimes it felt like excuses. I wasn't going to compromise or let myself get that involved with someone who seemed, I don't know— " he looked at me, "ambivalent. I'm done with those games."

I studied his face. "Are you making an innuendo about me and Will?"

"No, of course not. Interesting, that you would hear it that way, though." He raised his eyebrows, "Are you alright? You look tired? Will's on the off side, again?"

As I looked at Michael, I thought that actually I was alright. "I'm good. It's over with Will. I ended it, which was one of the hardest things I have ever done. I feel strong. And, so, I'm done with those games too." I squared my shoulders and stood tall, striking a purposely proud demeanor.

"Hmm." He eyed me curiously.

"You don't believe me?"

"I dunno. Maybe. You do seem a little different. Why haven't you come by the bar?"

I was with Jude, I thought, but there was no way I was saying that. "I'll come this weekend or maybe we could do something the night you're off."

"I'll text you." He kissed my cheek.

"'Kay."

Jude

He had to tell Will. He was losing his mind. As terrible as he felt about this whole thing, he had to come clean. He had to be with her. She was right, too, sneaking around was the act of a weak person. They both needed to face up to the truth, tell Will, and deal with their guilt.

Besides, he loved her. Watching her, talking with her, knowing she was physically close without being emotionally close, made him want her even more. Whatever he had kept in abeyance when he had thought she was with Will became a burning passion. He would do whatever she needed in order to be with her.

He called Will and asked him to hang out later. He would tell him tonight. It was a Friday. It would give Will the weekend to deal with the information without having to see Alex or him in school.

He called Alex to tell her, but of course she didn't pick up the phone. He left her a voicemail saying that he was going to tell Will tonight and that he wanted to stop by her place and talk with her about it first.

Alex

Jude called. I didn't pick up. I didn't listen to his message, because I already felt like I was going to give in to him. I was done with his dance of ambivalence.

I hurried to put my bathing suit on to go for a swim. I had begun using the pool at the apartment complex down the street. At least for now, I didn't want to run into Will in our pool. He seemed to be avoiding it too. A couple of times, I had watched him come up from the ocean in his swim trunks after an open-water swim.

I could not find my goggles. Huffing, I searched all around my room and in the bathroom, mumbling under my breath. "What is wrong with you? Stop. Focus."

Maybe I should just listen to the voicemail.

"Ah, there they are." I found them under my desk. How they got there, I hadn't a clue.

I threw a towel around me and was about to head out, when I heard a knock at my door. My heart jumped, thinking it was Jude. I opened the door. Standing before me was Will, a furious, pained look on his face.

He rushed in. "How could you?"

Chapter 38

Kendra

George came home. When he kissed Kendra on the cheek — the same perfunctory exchange they had whenever George came home — she could smell Adeline's perfume. It wasn't the first time, but it would be the last. He didn't even try to cover it anymore.

George was a cold man, careless with others' emotions. Jude's warmth and empathic nature made her take a cold, hard look at George, her marriage and, most important, who she had become.

Marriage was a beast of its own. The union with George insidiously usurped her sense of self, her independent spirit. She became who he needed her to be, but when he didn't want who she was anymore, he found a younger version, a youthful, naive, malleable girl: Adeline Cook.

She laughed in her head as she felt George's hand resting on the small of her back after he released that perfunctory kiss, Adeline's perfume violating her nose just like George violated their commitment.

She had been a young, idealistic girl when she met George. Now she was an angry, desperate woman. The only way to glue the pieces of her broken self back together was to break away from George and this farce of a marriage she was surviving.

Of course, a man like George wouldn't go down without trying to shame her. She was prepared for it. "I know about Adeline Cook," she said flatly. She had given the man enough of her life. She was not going to give him any emotion.

Inside she fumed.

He turned, mechanically, said in an even voice, "Who?"

"Oh, George," she smoothed her hair with her hands, pursed her lips. "Don't try to act innocent. I know everything. And I'm leaving." She pointed to two suitcases next to the sofa.

George glanced at the suitcases, opened his necktie and began to unbutton his shirt. "Where are you going?" he asked without looking at her.

"To my sister's."

"You don't even like your sister."

"That's not the point. I'm sick of pretending. Aren't you? You can't even look at me. In fact, I don't think you've seen me in years." As the words came out, she felt more and more certain that the ending of this relationship was a new beginning. He stopped seeing her, and when that happened, it was like she disappeared. And to think she nearly reduced herself to sleeping with Jude or Will out of desperation. "Do you love her?"

"Who?"

"George, I have been with you since I was a young woman. Have enough respect to tell me the truth. Do you love her?"

"I don't know what or who you're talking about." He loosened the knot of his tie and shook his neck. "What are we having for dinner?"

"George." She placed her hands on her hips. "Look at me."

He turned.

"Tell me the truth."

"I never stopped looking at you. It's you."

"*Me*. How dare you blame your affair on me."

"You hate what you have become, and you blame me. My choices. The politics. But it's not me. I never asked you to give up anything."

"How was I to raise our family without sacrifice?"

"You are a great mother." He turned away from her, took off his button-down shirt and threw a T-shirt on. "What's for dinner?"

"Stop, avoiding this. We need to talk. Now tell me the truth."

"Talk? We don't talk. We have never talked."

"Maybe that's the problem. We used to talk all the time, now I feel like we barely say anything that matters to each other."

His expression softened. "You stopped talking to me about things that mattered to you. You used to have so many of your own interests and ideas."

She sat on the bed, placing her hands between her knees. "It's what you demanded of me. To fit in to this world that you wanted. The politics. The fancy parties. The image. I did it for you."

"That's not what I wanted. I wanted the woman I had married."

"That's not true, George. I felt your need for me to become the woman you needed in that role. But I guess Adeline fulfills that better."

He looked down.

"Do not ignore me. I know the truth."

He sat beside her and took a sharp breath. "Not better, different. It's more about need, than love. Let's be honest, you and I haven't been what we were for a long time."

She put her hand on his thigh. "Having an affair is not an admirable way to deal with what is missing between us."

"You're right."

She was angry, but she understood. She had tried to fill the gaps with another body too. "I feel it too. We, as a couple, are broken." She looked at him, perhaps seeing the man she had once loved for a moment. "I don't think those needs can be fulfilled by another person, though. I think we need to fill our own gaps." She got up. "I appreciate you telling me the truth. Finally. We can't live like this anymore. We need to be separated."

George nodded, then sighed. "I don't want a media scandal. Please, let's do this as quietly and gracefully as possible. For the kids too."

"Is that all you care about? Your public image."

"I don't know what to say. It's not all I care about, but I am in politics." He gave her a hard look.

"I don't want a media scandal, either. You should know that. I need you to see who I am. I need you to respect me the way you used to."

"I do respect you." He placed his hand on her arm.

"Then act like it. We need to both be there for the kids."

"I know. I will. And, I am sorry."

"I appreciate that."

He looked at her with a sincere gaze. "This has been the most open we have been in years."

"It's a start."

Chapter 39

Alex

Will looked incensed.
"What are you talking about?" I tried to remain calm, but his agitation was contagious.

"You told Mary Jane our personal business."

"No. I told her *my* business. Calm down. I didn't tell her anything you shared with me. I wouldn't tell anyone that. I promise. What did she say to you anyway?"

"She told me to leave you alone, that I have hurt you one too many times. But I already know that I hurt you. I don't need your friends making me feel worse about this. Never mind that she knows my business."

"I told her that I was hurt. That's my business. Not yours. I have a right to talk with my friends."

"This is driving me crazy. I don't know what to do to undo the hurt I've caused you."

"There's nothing you can do. In time, it will heal. I forgive you."

"If you forgave me, we would be together the way we had been."

"We can't go back. I wish we could. Too much happened. And I've changed. I'm not the same now as I was when we first got together."

"It wasn't that long ago."

"True. But I'm stronger. Or maybe I was always strong, but I was afraid to assert my strength. Either way, I have grown from being with you. The hurt forced me to grow. To look inside and see who I was. What I wanted has changed."

"This kills me. You have grown from being with me to the point that we can't be together? Really?"

"Maybe you have grown from me too. You shared your story with me. That's a big deal."

"And look what happened."

"I've told you over and over. It has nothing to do with your story. It has to do with you pushing me away time and again because you were running from who you are. But you stopped running, and you told me. I'm grateful that you told me. Maybe it will be easier for you next time."

"Next time?" His eyes looked pained, and my heart bled for him.

"Come here." I pulled him in for a hug.

I felt a tear fall onto my bare shoulder, and I squeezed him tight. God, I hope he never found out that I had slept with Jude, and I hoped Jude just left me alone.

A knock at the door broke the moment. "Alllexx? You there? Open up. It's me."

Will swung his gaze between me and the door.

I froze.

"What's he doing here?" he asked me, while observing my obvious discomfort. He opened the door.

Jude's eyes widened. "Heeeey," he tried to sound casual, but I saw the severity in his gaze when he glanced at me. He was furious. He must have thought that I was with Will behind *his* back.

"What are you doing here? I thought you were running late." Will's eyes narrowed.

"Um… I stopped by to see if Alex needed help with her statistics. We had spoken about it in class."

"You didn't mention that."

Jude looked at me. Will observed the exchanged eye contact between us.

"What's going on?"

Jude looked at me, then said to Will, "I didn't want it to be this way."

"What?"

"*I love her*. I love her, and I want to be with her," he gushed. "It's killing me. I've been trying to fight this from the very beginning, because of you and how I thought you felt. But then you said it was over, that you didn't want her. I believed you, and Alex and me started something. Now that I know the truth, I feel terrible, but I can't fight how I feel. I want to be with her."

Will looked stunned, then his expression morphed into fury, as he turned to me. "What the fuck, Alex? Is this why you can't be with me?"

"Let's sit down and talk about this." Tears brimmed my eyes.

"No. I don't want to sit. I want you to answer me. How long have you been fucking Jude behind my back?"

"No." Tears streamed down my face. "It wasn't like that. It *isn't* like that. Let's sit. I'll explain everything."

"There's nothing to explain. Your facial expression told me everything I need to know. You have been lying to me. After I trusted you." He glared at Jude. "Both of you."

He glared at both of us, his face bright red.

"Will," I pleaded. "Please. Let's talk."

He gave me another long glower, turned and ran out.

"Will!" I hollered after him. I looked at Jude, my eyes overflowing with tears. "I've got to talk to him."

"Let's go after him."

"No. Let me go. It should come from me."

"What was he doing here?"

"He was angry about something I said to Mary Jane."

"And he just showed up in your apartment?"

"*Jude*. Not now. He needs me. This isn't about me and you. It's about him." I gave him a hard look.

"I had planned to tell him tonight. Did you listen to my message?"

"No."

"Everything I said to him, I meant. You still love him?"

"I don't know what you want me to say. I had wanted to give it a shot with you."

"Wanted?"

"*Wanted. Want.* I dunno. This is messy, and I need to go to him. I can't even think straight right now. This has nothing to do with love, or maybe it does. Wait here. We can talk when I get back."

§

"Will. Stop. Wait for me," I shouted as loud as I could, when I finally spied him at the edge of the beach. The ocean breeze and the waves drowned out my voice as I hurried toward him. "Will." I hobbled through the unpacked sand with my shoes on, rushing to reach him before he hit the water.

I thought he was going to dive in and swim. That's how we both dealt with pain, drown it out and burn it off in the water. I worried about him diving into the ocean though. Night had settled in, and the waves were big. He was upset, and I felt a responsibility to get to him.

I ran, tripping a couple of times before I got close to the ocean where the sand was packed from the water. I screamed his name once more, nearly behind him. The waves breaking on the beach sucked at our feet. "Please." I touched his back.

He turned toward me, tears covered his face. "No." He walked into the water, waves crashing over his body before he dove in. I threw my shoes off and went in after him. The undertow was strong. I struggled to get out beyond where the waves were breaking. I was near him when I called his name again, my voice only an echo above the roar of the turbulent waves.

He turned right as a huge wave swallowed me. The water was fierce, and it tossed me around. I knew not to panic as the ocean shoved me onto the sand floor, shells piercing my legs and arms, the water pushing from different directions. Salt water entered my nose and mouth, burning my eyes as I swam against the pull of the sea. I lost my direction, no longer being able to sense which way was up. I felt the water entering my lungs as I struggled to get my face into the air. A severe panic coursed through me. *Stay calm*, I told myself as I pumped my arms furiously. My knees scraped the sand and I pushed off the ocean floor toward the air.

Right as my head peeked out of the water, I saw Will near me through blurry eyes. I was trying to catch my breath when I felt the rise of the next wave scoop me up, then push me under. A rush of salt water went into my throat, choking me. My chest felt heavy. I struggled under the water, breathless, my arms and legs feeling flaccid as I tried to rise above the sea again. My strength was waning. Unwittingly, I opened my eyes into the murky quiet. I moved my arms looking for the ocean floor, trying to stay calm while my heart was beating wildly, and my body felt heavy. Suddenly, I felt him around me, pulling me above the water, carrying me.

He cradled me. I burrowed my head into his chest, shivering as the air hit my body. Will took huge steps to get out of the deeper water, his soft huffing the only evidence of the strength he was exerting to carry me to the shore.

Panting and squinting, I looked up at him as he held me, feeling his body against mine.

"Please be OK," he said between heavy breaths.

"I'm OK," I said, through pants and a weary smile.

When he walked out of the water, he laid me onto the sand, then sat next to me.

He looked deep into my eyes. His pain was exquisite. It made him real, strong, sensitive. I saw how much he was touched by the world. It's what I had fallen for when we first met. He was touched by all that hurt him, all the ills of the world, all the mistakes and lies of his childhood. He was touched by all that was beautiful too. And I had wanted to be part of what touched him. I rubbed my hands along my shoulders and down my arms. I felt chilled even though the humid air warmed my skin.

"I'm sorry," I said, breaking into the stillness. "The last thing I wanted was to hurt you, especially with a secret." I swallowed.

"I love you," he whispered. "If you would have drowned, I never would have forgiven myself. I can't believe I ran away and almost— almost caused— "

"You didn't." I put my hand on his arm. "I'm OK. It was my choice to run after you."

His expression turned pensive. "We repeat the things we are most afraid of."

I nodded slowly, searching for the right words. "It's uncanny, isn't it? It can look totally different in the beginning and somehow turn out the same in the end. Until we realize what we're doing, and we can start the beginning with different emotions."

He tilted head.

"We have to face our fears first, and only then can we start over. We can't come into a new beginning running from fear or trying to control the outcome because of past mistakes or hurts. That's starting over. I was running away from my pain too. But I believe we have both grown from each other. Maybe we won't repeat our fears again. Hopefully."

I recognized the affection in his eyes and smiled.

He sat up. "I know I have hurt you. But, Jude?"

I sat up beside him and put my hand on his back. "I'd like to explain."

"I don't want to know the details. All I want to know is what you want. Would you ever give this, us, another chance? Can we try a new beginning, together?"

Looking at him, I felt like saying: *Yes. I want you. It's always been you. I love you and you have changed my life.* But I didn't think I could ever be with Will. I was caught up in the moment and feeling the closeness we shared. Maybe I would always love him, but as I looked into his eyes, I knew what I had to do.

I touched his arm. "You will always be important to me. You have taught me so much about myself, but I need to be alone to figure myself out."

He winced.

"I'm sorry."

"So, not Jude either?"

I shook my head. "Alone."

"And then what?"

"I dunno."

"I'm not sure I can let this go."

"You have grown from this too. Maybe you can't see it yet, because you feel regret, but once the regret dissipates, I think you'll see what I mean."

His eyes looked pensive and pained as he stared into mine.

"It's going to be OK. You'll see," I said.

He heaved a shaky sigh, then kissed my cheek. He rubbed the sand off his legs, got up and walked away.

Will

He walked toward the building thinking about how he almost recreated his worst fear: destroying someone else he loved. Thank God, he got a hold of himself, and there was time to rescue her. Never again would he run from fear or pain or humiliation. This whole thing with Alex was his fault. His distance. His fears. His issues.

Mixed in with his regret and deflation and rejection, he felt a sense of pride wash over him. He felt himself standing straighter and his head higher, and not in an attempt to seem stronger, but really feeling strong. He could love. And he could set aside his own needs for another. Something had healed inside. Alex was right. Something within him had grown from being with her. From loving her. She had said she needed to be alone right now. *Right now*. Maybe someday they'd have another chance.

When he reached the pool area, Jude stood there. Will felt the fury course through him. He wanted to punch Jude in the face, but he did not want to be that guy. So, he gave Jude a steely look and said, "She's down there."

"Will."

"Man, there is nothing to say."

"You said you weren't into her. I never would have made a move if you had been."

"I think you would have. You certainly didn't give it any time."

"I thought you were dating, Lilane."

"It doesn't matter. Does it? Because in the end, it's what *she* wants."

"Are we, you and me, going to be able to get past this?"

"Maybe. But I don't think so."

Alex

I watched him walk up toward the apartment building, his body diminishing in size the further the distance. The breeze blew through my hair and kissed my cheeks. I still had chills from the intensity of everything that had just happened.

I had wanted both of them. Each one for a different reason. Jude because he made me feel like a woman, sexy and strong and feminine. Sexually, he was experienced and passionate. But perhaps the biggest reason was that he filled the spaces that Will had left empty when he distanced. It was unfair to Jude, but I let myself fully know what I had always known on some level: Will broke me and Jude was the glue that resealed me. But it was a flimsy seal. It could easily be broken again and again.

I didn't love Jude, not in the way that I loved Will. I had made myself vulnerable to Will, and for better or worse, our connection felt complete. I didn't think I could be with Will, though. I was pulled into his brokenness, because I, too, was broken. The only real way to fill those cracks was on my own. Even as I thought it through, I felt strength seeping into the spaces of my broken sense of self. Somehow, I knew everything would be OK.

I walked back toward the apartment building, wiping the sand off my thighs and arms. I saw Jude coming toward me. I sighed. This was not going to be easy.

"Heeey," he said, as he reached me. I heard the uncertainty in his tone.

Perhaps he already knew.

I looked up at him, so handsome, so charismatic, so easy to be with.

"You're soaked," he touched my shirt.

I smiled at him. He was Jude after all.

"What happened?"

"Nothing."

"Not nothing?"

"We talked a little on the beach."

"Good." He tilted his head. "And?"

"He's going to be OK."

He wrapped his arms around me and kissed my lips. "That's good. Right? We're free now."

The kiss was awkward. "What?" He looked at me hard. "It's him. You still love him."

"Yes," I whispered. "I care for you very much." I searched his face. "But I'm afraid I dragged you into the situation. I was broken, and you fulfilled something I needed. I don't like to need things. I don't like to feel dependent. I think I grew dependent on Will. For the first time since the long breakup with my ex, I let myself need someone. I let myself be vulnerable to someone. When he kept leaving and when he told you that our relationship didn't mean anything when I had thought it did, that need I had for him became a need I had for you. This was all my fault. What I really needed was to find the strength within myself."

"You used me."

"No. Not in the way you mean, anyway. Maybe we all use each other along the way as we try to discover who we are. You taught me a lot about myself. Who I am, who I am afraid of being. The way you saw me helped me see those things in myself. If you call that using, then yes, I did and I'm sorry. I can't be with you, though. I need to be by myself."

"So, you're not going back with him."

"No." I shook my head.

Jude raised his arms, then slapped his thighs. "I cannot believe that you are doing this. I know how you felt when we were together. You couldn't fake that. It was real."

"I wasn't faking, and it was real."

"And now it's done. Well, fuck you, then."

My eyes widened as I watched him storm off. "I'm sorry," I said to the air, putting my hand across my forehead.

Chapter 40

Three Months Later
Alex

I left Dr. Appel's office on a Friday afternoon. The sun shone bright and I looked up with my eyes squinted, letting the warmth kiss my face. Whenever I left her office, my face felt tight and contorted, squeezed from the intense concentration and twinges of discomfort that came from honest introspection.

I had entered therapy immediately following that night on the beach. I knew I needed to figure out how to fill my own heart. And as much as a big part of me wanted to go back to Will, my gut instinct was that it wasn't right. Too much had happened between us. The relationship had run its course. I entered therapy to keep from going back to Will just because I longed to feel that closeness with him — or with somebody.

It hurt. It hurt to see Will at school. Or swimming. The distance, as always, with Will, hurt. But the truth was, Will was the wall I broke myself against. As I tried to tear down his walls, I was freed from my own. In many ways, I had never felt better, freer. I was finally, at thirty-one-years-old, finding out who I was. Will had played an integral role in that. I hoped that one day, maybe, we would be friends.

Two weeks after that night on the beach, he had come to my apartment and asked me what I wanted. We had stood in the living room, and I could feel the intensity between us when he had said, "Alex, I know it won't be easy to get past everything that happened, but I'd like to try."

My eyes had wandered across his face and along his shoulders, then back up along his face, finally meeting his eyes. "I can't. At least not right now. I need to figure myself out."

He parted his lips as if to say more, but stopped and nodded, then he pulled me in for a hug, turned and at the door he said, "I don't think we should talk for a while."

I looked at him and I felt a stab to my heart. "I agree."

A few times when I was at the pool, he came down, but as soon as he noticed me, he left. He also left the coffee shop, the library and the computer lab. The only time we were together was in the classes we had, and he sat with other people, across the room. And so did I.

It was over.

I heard from Mary Jane a few weeks ago that he had started dating another woman from school, Cecilia. It hurt a little. I wish I could tell you that it hadn't, but the truth is, I still loved him. Maybe I always would. I was proud of myself for finally understanding that love wasn't enough and though some people came into our lives and would remain important in our hearts, they needed to be released. In order to free ourselves, we have to free others.

Jude recovered from the situation more quickly than Will. Maybe it was his age, or perhaps because he didn't have the trauma that Will had. Maybe he was more resilient or maybe he didn't feel as much for me as Will. Like Will had been for me, I think I helped Jude break through some of his own barriers.

He had said to me about a month after that night, "You will always be the most beautiful girl in school." He had bestowed that smile on me, and I blushed.

"Really, Jude?" I teased back. And that easy banter we had returned, almost like nothing had ever happened between us. Honestly, the guy still made my knees weak, but I knew I didn't want to be with him. I wanted something steady, less complicated. I didn't want to fall in love. I wanted to *be* in love.

The connection between Will and Jude and me was the opposite of steady. Through my therapy, the repetition became abundantly clear. I chose someone to fall for who couldn't give me everything I wanted. Someone who gave me just enough to keep me there, but not enough to fulfill me, to make me feel safe, to add to my life. I went for men who were turbulent oceans, and I kept expecting and hoping for a placid lake. The whole time, it was my own tsunami I needed to settle.

As much as I hated doing it, it needed to be done. I called Zach. Dr. Appel helped me understand that I needed to forgive him. *That* was going back to the beginning. It only cost me about ten thousand dollars in therapy to get back to where it all started. And that was early-in-the-relationship Zach, way before the infamous hope-string-year that had nearly broken me.

I fell for Zach when I was young, innocent. I didn't see that, although we loved each other, we had nothing in common. Our values were different. Our ideas of fun were different. He wasn't a thinker, and I needed someone more curious. He couldn't give me what I wanted, because he didn't have it to give. I saw an ideal of him and kept trying to get him to fit that mold because I didn't want to let go of the illusion of who he was.

When Dr. Appel had said that, it resonated and I felt my heart lighten. Who knew he was a burden that I carried everywhere and that letting go would make me physically lighter.

When I had called him, he picked up immediately, and for the first time hearing his voice had little effect. "Alex. It's— I'm glad you finally decided to call me back. It's all my fault," he gushed. "I was an *asshole*." I thought, *yeah you were*, but said, "Listen. I just wanted to tell you that I understand why you needed space. We weren't right for each other. It should have ended after the first year."

"We loved each other."

"Yeah, we did. I'll always be grateful for that, but love doesn't mean two people should be together."

"I thought you called to say you wanted to come back."

"I'm never coming back. You don't really want me back, Zach. You think you do because you're so used to having control over me. I was young, idealistic and in love for the first time. You want back how I made *you* feel, the adoration. But I'm not that person anymore. I've changed. This call isn't about you, it's about me and my growth process."

His tone turned sharp. "So, all this time that I've been calling you for another chance, you *finally* call me only for your own interests. And you called *me* selfish. *You're* selfish."

I was irritated, but I wasn't going to feed into the old dynamic. "I'm not selfish. I'm just learning to take care of me. Anyway, I forgive you for everything, and I wish you the best."

"Yeah. Same to you," he said, flatly, then hung up.

I sighed, thinking that the call hadn't gone how I had hoped, but it was done. The door was closed on that chapter. Finally, I could start a new one.

§

When I arrived back on South Beach, I parked and walked toward Lincoln Road. As I turned the corner, Michael stood waiting. He smiled as I went toward him. "Hey," I said.

"Hey, how was session?"

"You know, not easy, in a good way."

"You want to go to the gallery first or eat first?"

I shrugged my shoulders, moving closer toward him so I could feel the brush of his arm.

"You have the 'I wanna eat' face on." He elbowed me.

I smiled and nodded. "Let's eat."

Michael and I had been hanging out as friends, but I felt something burgeoning between us. It was a quieter kind of feeling. At first, I didn't quite recognize it as romantic because of the subtly. He took my hand and wove his fingers through mine, and I thought of what my therapist had said about him during our session.

He was the calm after the storm.

Note to Readers

Thank you for reading *Where You'll Land*. I am always grateful to those who take the time to read my work. I hope you enjoyed your experience. If you follow my writing, you know that I am always looking to understand more about the human experience through my characters' journeys.

I usually write from multiple points of view, because I'm very interested in the way each character's decisions and motivations influence the others. In *Where You'll Land,* I explored the interrelationships between people; how our choices affect not only us, but those around us, and then how those choices affect their lives and so on. I also wanted to show how we come together in relationships and then break against each other, revealing how even painful relationships may be part of a larger growth process.

As you've read in the story, the tendency for us to repeat what we are most afraid of is something that seems uncanny, but is a dynamic that we all encounter. We all have narratives that shape our sense of self, our purpose, our understanding of who we are in the world with others. We interact within our world anticipating confirmation of these narratives and sometimes they are painful and false; for example, "I am not loveable," may be one. Although incorrect (because we all deserve love), confirming this narrative becomes an unconscious quest that we often recreate over and over, until we realize what we're doing and can change the emotions and concomitant false narrative. Someone with that mindset will push people away to confirm that they aren't loveable. I tried to show how insidiously this happens; meaning, it happens without us even realizing it and even when the beginning seems different, we often find ourselves at the same end.

I don't think psychology should be exclusive to those of us who study it and are familiar with the theories and jargon. My hope is that this book was not only entertaining, but also provided some deeper understanding of relationships and the various dimensions and complexities that arise as we come together, for better or worse.

Where You'll Land is the first in a series of books that will continue with these characters' stories, added new ones, all with the intention of exploring various dynamics that arise within our relationships.

I am currently working on two books. One is a spin-off of *Forever and One Day*, called *The Crooked Path*. Please check my blog at jsgunn.com/blog/ for more information. I have started a nostalgia column through the blog which ties into the plot of *The Crooked Path*. This is a place for people to write in to others, words that have remained unsaid, words you may have only understood you wanted to say in retrospect. If you are interested in submitting a piece, please write to me through my blog, my Facebook page, Jacqueline Simon Gunn, or Instagram page @jacquelinesimongunn. You don't need to be a writer to submit. This is place for anyone to share messages, those words we've carried for too long that beg to be written.

I have also started the second book in this series, and already I can see new and interesting relationship themes emerging. I will be posting more about the book and my writing journey through my blog and Instagram and Facebook pages if you're interested in following the progress of the book.

Reviews on Amazon and/or Goodreads are greatly appreciated. Reader reviews are very important. Your opinions matter. A lot. Also, please feel free to contact me through my blog or social media pages if you have any thoughts or questions. I always enjoy hearing from readers. And thank you, again, for your interest in my work.

Acknowledgements

Thank you to my editor and forever friend, Carlo DeCarlo, for once again working magic with his brilliant edits, content suggestions and feedback. As always you have provided endless support along every step of this process, making this book possible. Thank you for all of the brainstorming. You have the extraordinary ability to help me consolidate the ideas swarming through my mind – like 50 tabs open at once – into the story that I want to tell. You have been the most influential person in my evolution as a writer, both through your teaching and your support. I am so grateful for you.

To Elizabeth Bonaiuto, I don't know where this book would have 'landed' without your help. Thank you for reading and rereading and talking me through the many questions about the plot and characters. I am so grateful for your creativity, for contributing the title, *Where You'll Land*, which just seemed perfect as soon as you said it, and for contributing your beautiful poetic words for the pieces opening the sections in the characters' voices. You know that I love quotes and/or poems at the start of my books. I am so grateful to you for contributing pieces exclusively for this book, making it extra special.

To my husband, Joseph Gunn, for his constant support and love, and for creating another brilliant book cover, I love you and thank you. To my father, Philip Simon, thank you for always believing in me and supporting me. I am so lucky to have you. I love you.

To Heather Ricco, Gina Fowler Spiers, Lanna Lebet, Lisa Vainieri Marshall, Mike Alonzo, Ross Kenyata Marshall, Jess Faulkingham and Paula Sadlon-Pascual for reading drafts, proofreading, listening to the story as I was writing it, and providing thoughtful feedback and creative inspirations throughout the process. I am so grateful to have your help and support.

About the Author

Jacqueline Simon Gunn is a Manhattan-based clinical psychologist and writer. She has authored two non-fiction books, and co-authored two others. She has published many articles, both scholarly and mainstream, and currently works as a freelance writer. With her academic and clinical experience in psychology, Gunn is now writing psychological fiction. Always in search of truth, fiction writing, like psychology, is a way for her to explore human nature – motivation, emotions, relationships.

In addition to her clinical work and writing, Gunn is an avid runner and reader. She is currently working on multiple writing projects, including two romance novels.

Other Books by Jacqueline Simon Gunn

Non-Fiction

Bare: Psychotherapy Stripped
(co-authored with Carlo DeCarlo)

*Borderline Personality Disorder:
New Perspectives on a Stigmatizing and Overused Diagnosis*
(co-authored with Brent Potter)

In the Long Run: Reflections from the Road

In the Therapist's Chair

Fiction

Circle of Betrayal
(*Close Enough to Kill* series – Book 1)

Circle of Trust
(*Close Enough to Kill* series – Book 2)

Circle of Truth
(*Close Enough to Kill* series – Book 3)

What He Didn't See
(*Close Enough to Kill* series – Novella)

Noah's Story
(*Close Enough to Kill* series – Novella)

Forever and One Day

Made in the USA
Middletown, DE
16 January 2019